Find the author:
E-mail: troy@chaoswords.com
Twitter: @Chaoswords
Facebook: Chaoswords
Website: www.Chaoswords.com

Library of Congress Control Number: 2017910899

ISBN 0-9835184-1-6

ISBN 978-0-9835184-1-9

Printed in The United States of America

This book is dedicated to the memory of my grandmother, Birdie Johnson (1924-2014).

A true believer who championed my every cause, no matter how insane it was. There is absolutely no way in hell that she would have read this book, but she would have supported me all of the same and would have absolutely defended me to the core.

"Ish!"

1

His recovery felt alone, isolating.

Lance Caron's fingers clutched a 3-month coin with a triangle in the center, a promise he held to.

Ignoring the decades of respect from his peers that may have vanished overnight. Respect that could never be bought back, but had been sold cheaply. Lance didn't want to think of the journey to get to this point. Feels like re-entry into a world I remember, but has moved on a little without me.

Lance was no longer the kingmaker, but a lackey, a stooge. His blackness didn't bother him as it once had either. Nor did his whiteness. His entire life, he had sat on the fence of never being accepted by either community. Always a little less than. Today though, he felt none of it, and walked into a land where everyone had always been treated like shit. It reminded him of a certainty; no one cares how long your ancestors lived in a place. They only care who bought it last. Because that's who runs the joint, at all times.

Lance Caron entered The Rivers End Resort & Casino with caution. The new promotion to assistant general manager appeared ceremonial, and felt it. He had no idea whether he belonged there anymore. *Where do I belong, in general?*

Thirty-nine days ago, he was made a fool. Sitting before a tribal intervention, in front of the Chief, Richard Yazzie. There were a lot of folks he could fool, but not a group of natives. Yazzie gave the ultimatum. Either he was fired, or he cleaned up his act and dried out somewhere else. They knew the signs, had seen it in their own children, listened to all of the lies, believed all of the bullshit. No one, especially not Lance, had the ability to keep himself from being naked with the truth.

The Rivers End was looking massive now with the new construction complete. But that didn't mean it carried less incidents because of its expansion. Lance had been made aware of several issues that occurred during his absence. All of them made him wish that he had fought Yazzie to stay longer on the job. *How's Scott Tsosie going to react when he sees me?* There was the issue of an uneasy reunion. Scott had stayed away during Lance's treatment. Never once visiting, even when Lance was at his worst.

The casino offered fresh cons to separate people from their money each time Lance watched the floor. The casino's newest con Diamond Club Cards traced customer activities, altering odds per bet. Only Oklahoma and California licensed more tribal casinos than the thirty-two in Washington State. The Rivers End was the largest in five hundred square miles. The sad reality of casinos was that amid the neon lights, plasma TVs and slot machines, people's addictions were abused to pay for the excess.

We are all addicts of some kind or another.

The Yamenhi tribe had offered gaming for locals since the first shovel went into the ground fifteen years ago. The Rivers End was south of Spokane, off Highway Nine, running down the far end of the state. It sat on a purchased parcel of land over a hundred miles from the Yamenhi reservation which was devoid of potable water. Its city center location created a massive customer base forcing local card rooms to go dark four nights per week. The Diamond Club Cards had caused the largest lure to draw guests through its doors.

Five thousand guests filtered through the casino each day believing when they gambled, they would win. Few understood that the casino's odds improved as a customer's play increased. The Diamond Club cards formulated odds providing initial bets of a ninety-two percent win rate for the customer. Those odds lowered as a customer progressively gambled, dropping to a thirteen percent win rate by the tenth bet per day. The calculation altered how customers perceived their visit. The majority played long after they had little chance of winning. And the tribal gaming commission green-lighted the odds differential because the initial bet offered was heavy in the customer's favor.

Number psychology rests in calculation as space and time are measured between each number as long as it is larger than the one previous. A person's psychology changes with it. A gambling payout divides in similar fashion. A person's first bet winning allows them happiness. But they risk less and quit because there is no need to raise the stakes. If they lost the first bet, they would risk less to avoid being cheated. But the art of payouts in the gaming world is similar to con artist. The winnings need to force the gambler to increase their bets so they sit longer and risk more while attempting to achieve the happiness in the beginning. *Reminds me of when I drank. Everything after that first drink had been trying to get back to the original feeling.*

Lance moved away from the slot machines and to the degenerate side of the casino floor; the off-track betting center. Old men with three dollar-exacta bets on horse seven in the third puffing cheap cigars, wearing crooked hair pieces. *It's a ritual to boast to their friends about the success of their bets and to show off their Bermuda shorts.* The center offered old men with silly stories about what they saw on the telecasts. Local retirees let their wives play on the penny slots while cursing out some trainers or jockey they didn't know for having a horse pull up limp on a dirt track during a light rain.

Lance entered the off-track bar, eyes locked on the Bacardi on a glass shelf. *You aren't that person anymore, are you?* He waved at the bartender to serve him but had Holly Murphy twist her way behind the bar. She batted long eyelashes at him offering a smile that meant more than anything she could have said. The woman was known as a frequent mattress-flier at the Rivers End, a twenty-three-year-old who giggled and dated the right people. Murphy had moved up the corporate ladder from slot machine hostess to food and beverage assistant manager since his absence. *Everyone gets promoted while I'm gone, don't they?* Murphy was a bottle-blonde wearing tight blue skirt, who smiled as she was reluctant to pour him a diet soda.

"I could fix you something stronger," Murphy said, suggestive.

Lance: "I'm on the clock."

"Maybe later then," she said.

"I'm a workaholic."

Murphy shrugged. "Too bad."

Murphy caused havoc to the men who dated her. Brad Riggs overseeing slot machines and Gary Templeton who was the casino's head chef. A fling with Murphy meant she was promoted and they were fired. A lot of men and women offered up the same story at the Rivers End. *It's only a matter of time before she sets her sights on me or Scott Tsosie.* Lance figured Murphy's climb might be hindered by the new tribal policy which prevented non-Yamenhi tribal members from holding executive positions within the operation. *I am one of the last exceptions to the rule.*

Racism held different forms at the Rivers End. Native sons would speak to Lance because his skin was dark. His mother white, his father black. White people the Yamenhi excluded, but Lance shrugged it off. He knew Scott Tsosie's feelings on the matter. *It's not as if the great white majority don't have their own clubs they exclude us from.* Lance shook that feeling off. *I'm starting to sound like Scott.* Sometimes his boss was not the most cordial person around white people that Lance knew.

The Rivers End general manager was in the casino's night club which never filled and offered overbearing music with little green laser lights from the ceiling cutting through fog onto an empty dance floor. Tsosie sat in a far corner table wearing a black sports jacket, pants and an open collar red dress shirt. A woman at each side, Tsosie offered a taste of the city's local elite. Millionaires were never strong-suited for the city, but being a Yamenhi native was now a birthright to wealth.

Tsosie two-fisted double-whiskeys every time the bartender came around. Lance eyed Tsosie's drink, resisting. One month, nine days and thirty-five minutes since his last drink. *Come on, you can do this.* Lance's focus turned toward the plasma screen showing highlights of the Boston Celtics basketball game. Lance chuckled, eying the bartender who nodded to him. *We both know the final score on that one too, don't we?*

"Lance, welcome back," Tsosie said. The Yamenhi native raised his glass in a toast, then dropped his face when he realized his mistake. "Oh, sorry, man."

Lance waved it off, eyes at Tsosie's abdomen. *I missed stopping that from happening, too.* "How are you doing?"

Tsosie grinned, gesturing to his abdomen. "It's fine. Man sliced me and I got a badass scar to show the ladies."

"I'm sorry," Lance said, placing his hand on Tsosie's shoulder. "I should have been there."

Tsosie shrugged, taking a sip of his drink. "Life is random. Working here, you know that."

"Yeah," Lance said. "I'm just passing through before going home."

"Oh, bullshit," Tsosie said. "Keisha can wait. Enjoy the good life."

Tsosie stoned, wrapped his arms around Lance, spilling his drink on Lance's jacket. The charcoal smell soaked into the fabric. *I want it more than anything else.* Lance shook off the temptation. *One month, nine days, thirty-seven minutes.* Lance eyed the two girls that were with Tsosie. Both turned their attention elsewhere when they saw he was not native. *They know I am not important in the Yamenhi world.* Lance looked at Tsosie.

"Heard you have a meeting with the Caha tribe," he said.

Tsosie released Lance, took a sip, smiled. "I'm taking care of it."

Lance: "Can't believe the state would let them put a casino that close to us."

"The government loves it when we fight with each other," Tsosie said. "After our meeting, they will see the light."

"Hope so." Lance worried about Tsosie's interaction with the Caha. *He can go into any room and make friends, but he finds more time to make them enemies.*

Tsosie collapsed into his seat, a hand on each woman's thigh, rubbing soft. Both jockeyed closer. Tsosie kept his gaze on Lance, winked. "Good to be the king, ain't it?"

The woman to his right slapped his stomach, frustrated. Tsosie grunted, his focus shifting from Lance to the woman. He slapped her on the face light, holding his stomach, fighting tears. The two women moved from Tsosie, up past Lance, exiting the club. Tsosie hurt and confused, grabbed his whiskey glass, downing the rest as his pain subsided. *He's changed after the attack.* Tsosie hurled the glass against the bar, smashing above the bartender's head, breaking three bottles.

The bartender ducked, saying nothing. When a Yamenhi native wanted something at the Rivers End, they got it. *The place is their castle.* Lance signaled for the bartender to perform last call. The music turned off, the lights up. Tsosie looked around, confused.

"Party's over?"

Lance: "Yep."

Tsosie exited the nightclub with Lance as a stone-cold sober executive despite his intake. Mouth spray covered fumes as he spoke, offering Lance a smirk while plucking a toothpick from a coffee stand which got jammed into the corner of his mouth. The casino floor was full of old ladies playing Diamond Club Cards at the slots, straddling oxygen tanks between their knees. *Someone has to pay for the bottles that Tsosie broke.* The pair passed the cashier cage, up the ramp leading to the hotel section of the casino.

A large embankment of slot machines sat next to the ramp, with an escalator toward the hotel. Tsosie turned to the other side of the ramp toward the sports bar which housed three massive high definition screens. Lance joined him, witnessing as the screens all automatically switched from a local game to the Boston Celtics basketball highlights. The sports bar crowd groaned in mass, but Tsosie showed no sign of noticing. He eyed Lance, his attention away from the bar as all three screens returned to the local game which ignited the crowd's applause.

"Damn, Boston is going good this year," Tsosie said.

"I would not bet against them."

Tsosie's gesture to the escalator drew Lance's attention to the Yamenhi tribal leader Brian Locklear, who rode down from the hotel toward them. "He never goes home, does he?"

Lance: "Let me do the talking."

"Good idea."

Lance offered Locklear his hand, then patted him on the shoulder. The Yamenhi tribal leader wore a Hawaiian shirt, denim jeans and short hair. "Floor is packed. We need to get those slot machines from the Samias in Clearwater to avoid complaints."

Locklear nodded at Lance, said to Tsosie, "Do you agree?"

Tsosie did not speak, nodding with a smile, hands in pockets. Locklear did not appear to notice the intoxication or said nothing about it. Tsosie refrained from movement to avoid stumbling. Locklear turned his attention to Lance.

"Getting more machines is not easy, but we can have them at a good price," Locklear said. "TGA will have to be a part of the discussions."

Slot machines at tribal casinos was not as easy as buying more. State and federal laws distributed specific license numbers, allowing less than two hundred thousand in Washington State spread out between all of the tribes. The set-up was done through the Tribal Gaming Commission known as TGA. *But I call it "The End."* The TGA representative for the Rivers End was a Yamenhi elder named Richard Yazzie. If TGA did not like an employee or sought to decertify someone, it happened. TGA was the end of the conversation, invoking the anti-money laundering Title 31 of the IRS code as a blunt instrument. Neither Locklear nor Tsosie could save an employee that TGA did not like. That person was banned from the casino or the operation was shut down.

Locklear put his hand on Tsosie's shoulder, eying him. "You get some rest, Scott. We got the Caha to deal with. They will think I'm working you too hard."

Tsosie nodded, Locklear shook Lance's hand before departing then Tsosie smirked at Lance. "Man can't even tell the difference between exhaustion and being half in the bag."

They went toward the hotel together with a pit stop at the lobby bar where Tsosie cut between customers to get to a bartender. He tapped his fingers on the counter, received three double-whiskeys before anyone else got their order. No Rivers End employee challenged Tsosie's actions. Either they served a Yamenhi tribal member the drink or they got a pink slip. Lance noticed Tsosie wincing again, still affected by the woman's slap to his stomach. *He feels it even if the doctors say he can't.*

Tsosie drank indifferent to patrons waiting in line behind him while the bar's television switched to the Boston Celtics highlights. It was no secret Tsosie was a Celtic's fan. He once had a Celtic preseason game pre-empt the World Series in the sports bar. *We oblige him to keep our jobs because the odds are stacked against us.*

Tsosie showed the effects of drinking once the elevator doors sealed and they were alone, the lift heading to his private suite. Standing for Tsosie became difficult, he leaned against Lance, stumbling from the elevator into the hallway once they had reached the top floor alone. Even VIP guests were below Tsosie at the Rivers End. Lance helped Tsosie inside, then to a large white sofa. Tsosie sprawled across the sofa, gestured to the far end of the suite where a large black piano sat. Lance raised an eyebrow. Tsosie clapped, laughing.

"Surprise," Tsosie said, happy. "Had five people get it up here without you noticing."

"I'm tired, Scott."

Tsosie, scolding: "No, you're trying to get out of playing."

Lance shook off the request, saying some excuse he knew wouldn't work.

Tsosie's face dropped his smile, offering a stern look. "Fix me a drink, then play something. Remember, I'm your boss now."

Lance focused on the suite's bar which he had noticed upon entering. *One month, nine days, one hour, fifteen minutes.* New bottles of Jack, Bacardi, and Smirnov with fridge housing ice and juice underneath. *Make the drink for him and leave.* Lance mixed a drink for Tsosie while resisting his urges. *One month, nine days, one hour, sixteen minutes.* Tsosie drank from the glass that Lance offered, then gave him a confused look.

"Who the hell drinks a rum and orange?"

Lance eyed the glass, stupid. Made his favorite drink for Tsosie. *An ass kicker.* He played cool. "Thought it was what you wanted."

Tsosie gestured with the glass. "Sounds like it was what you wanted."

"You want something else?" Lance reached for the glass, but Tsosie refused.

"No, it's fine," Tsosie said. "You know, you were a lot of fun to drink with."

"Sorry," Lance said.

Tsosie: "At least you didn't get religion over quitting."

"Tolerance is the new religion," Lance said. "Unless you believe in God, then there is no tolerance for your beliefs."

Tsosie winked at him. "Cute. You come up with that one on your own?"

"Had a lot of time to think about it," Lance said, checking his watch. "I should go."

"Keisha worried?"

Lance: "I don't think Keisha and I are anything, anymore.

Haven't been for a while."

Tsosie offered sympathy, "sorry, man."

"It is what it is."

Tsosie changed his demeanor, offering a stern look. "Play me something and stop worrying."

Lance headed to the piano, sat and let his fingers glide the keys. He thought of the days where he dreamt of being a professional musician. Before Keisha had convinced him there was no money in it. *Said be practical, live in the real world.* His fingers tapped Bach by muscle memory. *Almost two months since you played, you know that?*

"You gonna play the damn thing or what?" Tsosie said.

Lance touched the keys, lids closed. The first sound came and he continued to play. The music was rough at first, but he doubted Tsosie noticed. The flow came back as the first notes went without interruption. Lance kept his lids shut, imagining huge notes floating by with each key. A smile formed on his lips as the music reminded him of the summer months he used to spend playing as a child. *Wanting it more than anything.* He marveled at how beautiful his music sounded while sober. *I haven't played without a drink since my wedding night.*

Lance arrived home after midnight. Car into the drive, he noticed that the lights were on in the living room. He left the car, cautious. *Keisha waiting for me.* Lance walked slow, a light rain fall slapping his clothes. The front door opened as he touched it, sliding back. *Waiting to see blood again. To see that this time, she has hurt herself to punish me.*

Instead, Keisha sat on the living room couch, with an electric fireplace warming her feet. The surround sound offered classical music. It took Lance a moment to realize it was his piano, her violin from their time at Julliard that was playing.

Keisha looked at him, quiet. She held a glass of red between her fingers at the stem. Lance's eyes focused on the divorce papers he had left for her that morning. They sat undisturbed on the coffee table. Lance was unhappy to see the papers unsigned. Next to the papers was a small revolver and a box full of bullets. *What's she going to do with the gun?* Lance stayed in the foyer, feeling the soak of the gentle rain from outside.

Keisha took a last sip of her wine, keeping the glass on her lap. "Do you remember when we made this?"

"About ten years ago," Lance said. "I don't have any regrets."

Keisha gestured to the papers on the coffee table. "Are you sure about that?"

"We're not happy," Lance said, eyes trained on her hands, making sure she didn't pick up the revolver. *Does this have to end with one of us dead?*

The recording of their music together ended. Keisha got up from the couch, grinning as she wrapped her arms around him. "You can't leave me, Lance. I won't let that happen."

She held him, his body limp as his eyes stayed on the revolver. He glanced over, seeing a bottle of pills spilled out on one of the sofa cushions. *Oh, Jesus, how many did she take?*

Keisha pulled apart, smiling in a drug haze. "I can't let you go. I won't."

"What did you do, baby?"

"I made the pain go away," Keisha said. "Your love hurts so much."

She collapsed into his arms, the weight enough for Lance to hold her up with a grunt. He laid her down onto the carpet and pulled out his cell, dialing 9-1-1. Foam came out of her mouth as she lay, dying. *I shouldn't have given her the papers. Look what I've done.*

2 The civilized ended differences over alcohol or tribute. The Serg finished feuds with bullets. Few angered the old Russian and lived. Peter Volov witnessed no sign of The Serg slowing with age. The Serg held his vodka and territory with ferocity. *I can testify to that.* Peter was helping deliver The Serg's message in a beat-up cream-colored van sitting on East Sprague.

The Serg's top lieutenant, Oleg, sat behind the wheel with a cargo of two muscle boys tough, big and mean. *And they got that pink shit in them too.* The muscle boys hammered syringes full of Pink Cadillac into their arms. The needle heads snapped against the pressure laid on as the plunger went down. The boys tossed damaged stems to the front of the van, drawing up a fresh needle for a new hit.

Oleg grinned at Peter. "They do not get enough."

"That's Brother Zachariah's problem," Peter said. "Boss ain't sucking wind. He means what he says."

"True."

Peter shook his head, knowing the muscle boys were dope fiends with pecs but not strung-out, slimy characters from the boardwalk. Prime specimens of bulk mass. *I would not want to mess with them, that's for sure.* The two were large enough to take up the entire cargo hold of the van. The blonde was Chase, veins popping out of his red neck while babbling up to his partner, Wright.

Both out of a Coeur d'Alene gym on vacation from The Sides after two-year stints for extortion on first offenses. The Serg contracted out his enforcement, guys with nothing to lose. Guys who got big. The Pink Cadillac made Chase and Wright huge. It created a harder, stronger, faster man. *That's why we are here, isn't it?* Peter eyed the mosque across the street. The muscle boys were supposed to send a message, pay a visit, target Brother Zachariah.

Zachariah Terrell had been a hardcore from Pocatello Penitentiary. A five-to-ten thug for robbery, at Pocatello, Zachariah had been a victim of a shakedown artist, a three-time lifer con named Lewis Jackson, who threw lighter fluid in Zachariah's face, lit the match. Upon his conversion to Islam thereafter, Zachariah came to the conclusion that it was the white man's incarceration of Jackson which led to the Brother's burns. His Islamic teachings brought him to the belief that the only way to cure a person's infection of whiteness was by death. Jackson was stabbed to death two months later in the prison shower.

Brother Zachariah founded the East Sprague mosque after his release. One of his devout followers, Renard Jeffs, had instructions to take on the scourge of drug dealers around the former discount grocery store turned religious center. Zachariah was not a man of mercy to a drug dealer. He sent Jeffs on a jihad. Man rammed his truck into a nearby stash house filled with The Serg's Pink Cadillac vials. Jeffs' truck ripped out a quarter of the house, hit the gas line, exploding the house, Jeffs burning up with it. And The Serg was pissed.

Irish Pete had held down the territories with his enforcers. The Irishman had burned alive in his own home, causing land grabs to occur a few months later. Gangs battled with rightful force. Some had indignant motives such as morals. Others used negotiation. The Serg had the muscle boys doped up on Pink Cadillac to send his message about territories. The boys got MP5 carbines to bring the mountain to Zachariah. More syringes with bent needles flew near Peter's feet on the van floor. He eyed the rearview, seeing the boys hitting every dose they could, chasing one stem after another.

Oleg said, "Are you ready, Pete?"

"As ready as I will ever be," Peter said, allowing Oleg to call him "Pete" because the Russian had trouble with words ending with the letter "R." Anyone else would have had a baseball bat across their back for cutting his name short.

Remember, Peter, you gotta be the good guy in this. He could hear Anthony Batellini's voice in his thoughts. Man turned him from being a crook to an informant. *Now I'm his only salvation.* Peter was trying to find a way to get out of The Serg's operation without getting killed. *If Anthony is able to survive, that is.* Peter ventured into the Exit One gentleman's club basement during every fight, witnessing his D.E.A. handler doped up on Pink Cadillac, fighting other men to the death. *They broke him, but he is alive. There is a chance to get him out.*

Batellini was a Drug Enforcement Agent who approached Peter while he was operating meth labs for some Russian gangsters out of Oregon. Peter spoke Russian well but received it less when it was not spoken directly at him. *Anthony got me out of doing seventy-five years in a Supermax with the bosses, as long as I introduced Batellini into The Serg's operation.* The Serg trusted no one from the streets so Peter's introduction was crucial. Only bad part was that The Serg wanted Peter to join his crew as well. *Lucky me.*

Batellini had been found out as a D.E.A. agent, The Serg ordered all of his goons watched. That meant Peter had no way to walk. Nor could he approach his D.E.A. contact. They wanted Batellini back, weren't trusting Peter otherwise. *I'm a lone wolf out in the wilderness.* Peter existed under the radar of suspicion. The Serg never questioned his loyalty but always made sure he went with Oleg everywhere. Peter eyed Oleg's .45 in his holster, wondering if he would use it on Peter. *I gotta get Anthony and get my life back.*

The muscle twins dropped their last vial of Pink Cadillac, dressing up their bruised veins with a shared shot. The syringe joined the twisted pile mess. Wright laced his boots, Chase his Kevlar vest. Peter watched them silent as they prepped. *Twin bulls breathing, nostrils flaring in and out.* The breathing noisy, intense. Peter listened to the pair do long, hard snorts, their faces beat red. Each placed their head in their hands, between their knees.

Peter popped open a can of warm beer, offered it to Oleg who waved him off, still on the wagon for no good reason. Peter shrugged, foam bubbled out the can's mouth. He poured a slug of it on the alleyway, making an early morning boilermaker with a whiskey flask. *Need to take my mind from this reckoning.* He remembered his stint over at Coyote Farms for operating a meth lab, the minimum security prison about a hundred miles north of the city. He sat for three years, drinking toilet hooch, permanent vision dimmed. The rancid taste attacked his lips and he checked his watch, showing Oleg.

"Magic hour," he said.

Oleg nodded, said to the muscle boys, "Time for work."

Chase offered a tough man stare that made Peter's skin crawl, appearing to look *through* them. Gooseflesh riddled the nape of Peter's neck. Chase turned to Wright, sharing a *San Quentin Stare*. Chase unleashed a bellow at his partner, piercing Peter's ears. Wright returned it with a vocal volley of high decibel. Both spat rage intensity, forming fists, taking turns pounding the other on the shoulders.

Each slammed harder as the screaming became louder, the hits against their shoulders from the other's fists deeper, causing the van to rock. Peter and Oleg braced against the dashboard and doors, the broken syringes bouncing on the floor. Chase kicked free the van's back doors, spilling into the parking lot, Wright following. The shocks buckled from a sudden loss of weight. Both men grabbed their M5 carbines, left their ski masks behind. *They don't care who sees them.* Chase slammed the back doors shut as the muscle boys went to work.

Oleg said gibberish in Russian. He turned on his iPod which played *Tchaikovsky*, because it had always pleased his grandmother, helped the Russian goon feel closer to a country he had never stepped foot in.

"Understatement of the year," Peter said, without understanding what Oleg had said.

Peter finished his boilermaker, worried. *What the hell are you doing here? Walk away from this van before they realize you were in with Anthony.* He knew that play would not work, resisting the urge. The Serg had men to hunt, murder him in the street. No way the D.E.A. protected him without bringing Batellini in alive. *But how in the hell are you going to do that when he is hopped up on that Pink Cadillac shit? The stuff cracked his mind.*

His thoughts ended with the eruption of gunfire. A fireball belched from the mosque's doors into the streets. The muscle boys stood in the middle of the road, executing the occupants fleeing the mosque. Women, children and the old were gunned down. Peter noted the muscle boys' expressions as the M5 carbines emptied into the crowd. They smiled, enjoying the work. *It's not them, it's the Pink Cadillac. It has done the same with Anthony.* Oleg sat behind the wheel, said nothing, content. Peter's eyes dropped to the spent needles on the floor around his feet. *What the hell is in this shit?*

He would have shaved five years off his life to secure his father's love. Winning the body building competition that afternoon would do that. Dean Shockley wanted his father to hug him. Dean closed his lids, erasing sound. *Concentrate. Think like a winner. Be a winner*. His heart thump in his chest, praying. *Please let me win this. I need it more than anything else in my life. Don't let me lose in front of my father.*

Dean opened his lids, light attacked his pupils. His rival Ulysses Turner waiting off-stage, a black titan of ripped flesh with little blue trunks. Ulysses had a myriad of admirers, including the man who Dean had always called "Daddy." His father had posed with Ulysses for photographs, asked for personal autographs, and was proud of the builder. Dean noticed the happiness his father showed standing with his gray crew cut, his skinny arms and legs. Dean's eyes went to the ground. *Daddy should be no one else's fan but mine.*

His nostrils caught the manufactured atmosphere, crisp waves of air conditioning kissing his skin. He stood mindless while looking away. Daddy arrived with oil in his palms and took to massaging his son's right bicep in quiet motion. Dean felt rhythm from his father's touch. *I wish I could save this feeling forever.* Daddy was in his corner now. *He's all mine.* Most trainers refrained from speaking before a competitor's stage time. Daddy talked until Dean was called to the stage.

"Ulysses is a beast, isn't he?"

Dean hoped Daddy would stop. Sometimes his father received the message. Other times, he talked. *The last thing I want is to hear how large Ulysses Turner is.* No competitor wanted to hear how much good weight a rival had added. But Daddy kept talking. *He thinks it helps get my head right.* And his father always knew best. *Even if other builders mock me for using him as a trainer.* One of the builders in Dean's gym called Daddy a "hanger-on." *They don't understand how much I need him, though. How the training has brought us together.*

"Ulysses gave me his autograph," Daddy said. "Smiled, grabbed a sharpie, and did it without any fight. That's a real champ there, boy."

Dean let Daddy's voice drone out as he closed his lids to focus. *Don't let anything distract you.* He stood in his red trunks and prepped for the final pose down on stage. *This is that money shot for all of the judges. To make them love you. One final pose before you win this damn thing.* His heart thumped in his chest. Daddy's voice broke through his concentration.

"He's taller than you. Gonna hurt you with the judges, being so short," Daddy said. "That's from your mother's side, I'm sure of it."

His lids opened for a moment, then shut tight. Dean focused harder to instill quiet. He went over the prejudging portion of the competition. *I took the front lat spread, probably aced that side chest and side triceps.* Dean smirked but dropped it. *I turned my thigh in that one way which made a difference with the judges.* He assessed the portions that Ulysses had won. *He took the rear lat spread. I could tell from the judges' faces. He got the front double, maybe the back double biceps too.* Ulysses had done well in those categories.

"He's got that championship *feel*, you know?" Daddy said. "You can't teach it, you got it or you don't and he's got it."

Daddy never understood the brotherhood between builders. Ulysses posed for photographs with Daddy because the builder respected Dean. Aside from that verbal nonsense Shay Roberts pulled at one competition, no builder disrespected a rival. *That's why Shay got his ass banned from competing.* No pushing or shoving happened because of the respect. *We all know about the long, intense workout sessions in each gym.* Everyone knew what the other guy did to get on stage. *The rebels get washed out quick in this community.*

"I should ask Ulysses if he will let me train him," Daddy said.

"I've built you up, could do the same for him."

Daddy doesn't know the truth. But robbing his father of pride was not an option. The other builders mocked Dean for his father's counter-productive instructions. *I do it to keep him coming back each morning.* Before Daddy had decided to train him in the gym, Dean went through two years of hell, putting a lot of weight on each off-season. *Tossing two-to-three hundred pound weights each rep.* Cutting his caloric intake to less than nine hundred daily, trying hard not to think of a cheeseburger.

Daddy gave up his mornings for two hour sessions with Dean, then left to enjoy the day. Dean had nosebleeds because of low iron in his system but that's when the real workouts began. Two other competitors, Kyle and Stew, spotted for Dean to help him with those little things Daddy never cared about. *If I tell him the truth, our relationship ends.* Daddy would do another walk-out, ignore Dean again. *Before I got my photo in the newspaper he had no time for me. I gave him a son he could be proud of.* Daddy became Dean's trainer to prove it. *Stew calls Daddy a glorified oil boy, but he's near me.*

When Daddy trained him, everyone gave them distance. Kyle and Stew hung back. *Daddy says he does not like the looks of them.* Kyle and Stew had served two years each together in an Idaho prison. Sculpting their bodies was salvation inside. Dean almost threw the pair out when they entered his gym, *Shockley's Body Shop*, a year ago. *Thought they were casing the joint to rob.* But Dean listened to their goals to perform. Said they needed help. *I know about second chances because of my relationship with Daddy.*

Bodybuilding required isolation. For the first year that Dean ran his gym, no one but Blye was around to train him. And Blye was less reliable. Dean pushed deeper into the challenge of lifting. *More reps, drinking the right stuff.* No one was there to tell him how good he was, pushing him further. The gym changed with Kyle and Stew around. All three of them felt the same way before a competition. *We're all a little light-headed during the week before getting on stage.*

To a laymen, body builders pumped iron, oiled up and posed on stage. *It takes more than that. You have to be all-in.* They cut water and sodium from their bodies to alter how it was retained in their systems. Cut the carbohydrates to reduce muscle glycogen. *Pushed out every last carbohydrate until I've thought I'm gonna die.* Each dropped *X-Lax* during the last three days to rid themselves of every last drop.

Twelve hours prior to stage-time they dumped carbohydrates back into their system to fuel the glycogen. Dean, Kyle and Stew headed to a 24-hour donut shop on Francis. Put down five Ben

Franklins, ate five dozen donuts without a drop of any liquid to wash it down. *We freaked out the girl behind the counter who watched us gorge.* The sugar rush through his system made Dean feel as if he were a junkie. Sculpting a body took hard commitments. *Some guys have it, most don't.*

His father snapped his fingers to bring Dean back to reality. He focused on Daddy, receiving a stern look from his father. *I've always been a disappointment to you, haven't I?* Dean shook off the negative feeling. *I am going to make him so proud of me.*

"They're calling for you."

Dean moved to the stage amid lights beaming down white madness. Joe Maxon stood in his stage spot. *Joe finishes third, everyone mocks him.* Dean felt his weight as it pushed on each stage step, focusing his thoughts. *You can do this. Make Daddy proud of you.* The crowd erupted as the final pose down began. He smelled the heat of their excitement and let it ripple across his skin. *This is where you finally do it. Make the old man proud of you.* His eyes went over the large crowd. Faces hidden in the dark as the stage light masked their features. *I can see Daddy out there, watching me.*

Ulysses Turner entered the stage from the left as the announcer called his name. It was the crowd reaction which made Dean's heart drop. The crowd's collective gasp flew toward the competitor. *Daddy's right, he's a beast.* Ulysses' growth from the off-season shocked everyone. *They pissed him out several times in the bathroom to prove he's clean.* After Barry Gavin retired last season, Dean had been the front-runner to replace him as champion. *But Ulysses has it now. He stands out on stage, lets those eyeballs soak him in. He's got them now.*

This is supposed to be my season. Dean sized Ulysses up; a hulk with a wide smile showcasing a ripped chest of muscular perfection. *This can't be happening.* Ulysses had been a step behind in training to every other builder, but not this season. *He towers on stage.* His definition, dimensions expanded as Ulysses formed his pose. *Daddy was right; Ulysses has that championship feel to him.* Dean fought off negative feelings.

He tried to match Ulysses in his first pose but failed with the judges. *They're gawking at Ulysses' form.* The five judges offered Dean and Maxon less than a glance. Ulysses' form, definition begged for the judges' attention. Ulysses transformed his pose, arching his chest, smothering Dean's definition. *There's something to that mass that I can't bear to look at.*

His eyes shied away from Ulysses but he caught himself, mid-pose, sneaking glances back at his rival. *I can't stop looking at him. I'm a member of the crowd. He's dominating this stage.* Ulysses' size allured Dean's attention as it had the crowd. *It's so damn beautiful that you respect it.* He was lost in a champion's shadow. *Don't do this. You have to win this thing. Look into the crowd, get your confidence back and ride it home to victory.*

During tough competitions, Dean relied on the crowd. The audience could turn a competition for anyone who had their support. *Give me that confidence to pull this off.* His sight wandered through the crowd to Daddy. *Help me win, Daddy. Clap your hands, cheer me on, help me do this.* But Daddy's seat was empty. Dean faltered in his pose for a second, but recovered with another flex and hold. The judges had caught his error. Each marked their forms. Dean's focus returned to Daddy's vacant seat; then over to the room's entrance as his father exited. *Don't leave me, Daddy. Don't leave again.*

The competition was lost. *Daddy can't stand my weakness. I'm embarrassing him.* Dean held his pose for the remainder, fruitless. He finished his poses, then exited the stage when instructed. The judges would say their peace. *Ulysses has that championship feel to him. It's second place for me tonight.* He dropped his head beyond the sight of the judges. *I've failed you, Daddy. I'm sorry.*

At his locker, he caught his mirrored reflection. Dean let his eyes move along the tough ridges of his form. *No matter what I do, I'm never good enough.* He had disappointed his father several times in his life. *Why am I even doing this?* The season was finished after the Rivers End Casino competition in three months. *Is it worth the training? The exercise? All to finish in second place?* Dean wasn't sure.

He questioned accepting the second place trophy as a sign of personal failure. *What's the point if I can't win? In the end, if it's not first, it's not winning.* Daddy spoke in those terms about Gonzaga's basketball team. *Getting to the Sweet Sixteen isn't winning, is it?* Dean felt himself agreeing with his father's thinking. *I should get out of this. Stop wasting my time.* Kyle came to Dean, the naïve kid placed his hand on Dean's shoulder, supportive.

"You did great out there. Nothing to be ashamed of," Kyle said.

Dean glared. "Are you sure about that?"

Dean regretted his stare, knowing the kid was impressionable. Kyle couldn't be discouraged from training. *For Stew and him, this is all they got.* Dean developed personal schedules to prep them for the Rivers End casino competition. *Maybe they'll succeed where I can't.* Dean softened his manner to Kyle.

"It's a rollercoaster, kid," Dean said. "You sit there and wait for the ride to end, thankful when it finally is."

Kyle: "Your old man don't help things."

Dean eyed Kyle, rage brewing. *No one speaks that way about Daddy.* "He's a good man."

Kyle shook his head. "We all say that shit about our dads, but truth is none of them measure up. You want him to see you, I mean *really* see you. That ain't going to happen, bro. You just gotta move on."

"Move on to what?"

Kyle shrugged. "My sister pulled the same shit on me when I went in for a stretch. Whatever it is, you gotta move onto that."

Kyle left Dean with hands in the air, backed away, going to Stew. The pair exchanged words, agreeing. *Kyle got pushed into saying something.* Dean shook his head. *How many other people saw the way Daddy treated me today?* Dean eyed the edge of the stage where Ulysses waited to collect his championship trophy. He received people, got handshakes, greetings of congratulations from fellow builders. *That should be me.*

He hung his head, ready to accept second place. *It's still a good finish.* He noticed Joe Maxon, feeling pity for the builder. *I couldn't finish third like Joe.* Dean visualized the second place trophy, planning to hide it in his gym office. *Shows I have commitment to the sport. Second place isn't that bad.*

He noticed Maxon's position behind Ulysses, confused. *That's my spot, second place.* Dean froze, unsure. The competition producer waved behind Maxon. The perpetual third place finisher grinned sheepish at Dean.

"Guess we switched this time, huh?" Maxon said.

The producer instructed the three men onto the stage. Each builder positioned their pose behind their trophy, showing placement. Dean eyed the trophy in front of Maxon. *It's twice as big as mine.* Ulysses' trophy dwarfed the hardware of the other two. All three posed for the crowd, their names announced over the public address system. He smiled with a sickness building in his bowels, holding his smile until he left the stage carrying his trophy. He dressed, witnessing Maxon the recipient of family hugs.

Dean exited the locker room, attacked by the ninety-seven moisture-less air of summer. He donned sunglasses, stalked to his truck in the parking lot. His ritual was to park his truck at the end. *So I remember how many people came to watch me win. To show me how good I have to be for the fans.* Rows of cars greeted him in the boiling heat, followed by sections of vacant stalls while listening to traffic whip by on the lone highway beyond the lot. His 1993 F-150 sat alone by the lot's edge. Dean hung his head, shamed.

His attention was taken by Interstate 90 where a semi hauled a large, round red concrete tube past the lot. Police lights flashed providing escort, news helicopters hovered overhead with live broadcasts. The news headlines had alerted the public to Westin

Oil's movement of eight mega-loads through the I-90 corridor from the Port of Seattle to their oil-sands refinery in Alberta. Westin had plans to move thirty mega-load hauls throughout the summer. His gaze caught the 300-ton oil drum for the Canadian refinery. *Go big or go home.*

Area citizens along the I-90 corridor complained about the mega-loads, but states attorneys moved forward, in the name of capitalism. Five class-action lawsuits filed, claims that loads violated state laws to be traveling a twenty-five miles-per-hour maximum twenty-five. Dean guessed the load he watched was cruising at forty-five or fifty. *Imagine if he loses control of that thing.* The drum was three stories tall, a caravan of state patrol escorting. When the mega-load rolled through, the turnouts and ramps were barricaded in order to avoid traffic and protestors. *The world keeps moving, no matter where I finish in competition.*

"Hold up, man."

Ulysses Turner came from behind, stretched-out in a XXXXL t-shirt, sleeves ripped to fit his arms. Ulysses was a god to most. *Daddy wants him as a son.* Ulysses carried his duffle bag and trophy in his left hand. *He wants me to congratulate him. To show I'm still a good sport after where I finished.* Dean shook off resentment, ashamed he hadn't paid courtesy to the winner. *That's what we do in this sport, you know that.* Dean offered his hand to Ulysses as he stopped in front of him.

"Congrats, you deserve it," Dean said.

Ulysses released the bag, which hit the asphalt lot with a soft thud. The big man took Dean's hand, held it tight, pulling Dean close. "I was you about eighteen, maybe nineteen months back. You remember?"

Dean nodded. "Yeah, but you got bigger."

The black giant grinned. "I had no edge back then. You can admit it, I was lost. But now I got an edge."

"You beat the shit out of me up there," Dean said. "But Maxon's thrilled with his place."

"No, man, I ain't talking shrink bullshit. I'm saying something real," Ulysses said. "You want the edge I got? I'll give it to you. Nothing like having a guy like you, create some competitive fire that lasts a while, helps the sport grow."

"You want to train together? Stop by my gym, we'll do up a plan."

Ulysses shook his head. "Dean, you ain't listening to me talk sense to you right now, man. I'm offering a real edge. No bullshit. You gotta know where to look to get it."

"What are you getting at?"

Ulysses said, "Fireball."

"Fireball?" Dean said. "Nothing I ever heard of comes good from anything called '*Fireball*.'"

"Started three weeks back, now I'm ripped as shit doing forty milligrams a day," Ulysses said. "You go to Exit One, talk to The Serg. Ask for a taste. See what happens."

Dean leaned in, suspicious. "Why are you doing this for me?"

Ulysses said, "Because no one needs an old man acting like yours did today. Whether you ever understand it or not, I know how you feel. Take that edge, get it real good, and make your dad proud."

Dean nodded, grinned. "I like the sound of that."

"I thought you would."

Chase Bannister sat in the Spokane Valley police station's small interrogation room. He figured the sun had risen since his arrest. His reflection covered the mirrored glass on the wall across from him while examining seams of imperfection in the pane's mounting. *Seen enough cop shows to know what's behind it.* Chase went over his hulked mass reflection, proud of the beast. *Built myself from that puny kid who got kicked around.* Now, women ran to him. *They see my arms, that build, and they can't get enough.*

His reflection smirked back. *Wonder if any women are behind there, thinking of talking to me after this is over.* Maybe one would slip him her number after the show ended. *I've seen all kinds of women act frightened, then soften when I flex.* He thought of those nights at the Coeur d'Alene gym with Darren Wright. *When we picked up two or three women, showed them our power.* The time with three women offering fake chests, false minds while complaining that Chase and Wright lasted long after they finished. *We're warriors, meant to take the land, conquer the women.*

Chase tried to brush his hair that fell over his face. Handcuffs bound his wrists to a metal table at the center of the room, thwarting movement. His bonds were three interlocking cuffs to wrap around his thick wrists. *When I was a punk, one set of cuffs would have been enough.* As a warrior, extra effort held him prisoner. He felt weak as the Pink Cadillac from flushed his system. *Cops caught me as the lightning drained. Once I have another hit, they get to see my power.*

His massive arms draped his pecs. Chase wore his workout t-shirt and trunks, feeling the chair ready to give underneath his weight. He refrained from movement to keep from spilling on the floor. Chase focused on the door to his left, waiting for interrogation. *The hours without another hit has flushed the juice from my system.* His energy waned, his chin rested on his chest as the last of his fuel burnt out.

Chase's Samurai master, Shiba Yoshimasa, stood in the right corner. The Japanese emperor silent, watching his pupil. *He's fought by my side during rages, monitored lifts during those long nights with Wright in the gym.* Chase followed *The Code of the Samurai* during his fights, honoring his master. Weakness approached, causing Chase to tear. *If I stay here, I will betray The Code.* His hunger for Pink Cadillac grew.

One must die for honor, Shiba said to Chase.

"Death before dishonor," Chase said to his master.

Shiba told Chase to live *The Code.*

"I swear."

A slim young man in a suit entered throughout the door. *A clean-cut asshole to break me.* The man carried a dossier, angering Chase with his pompous demeanor. *The rage isn't carrying through my system.* It worried Chase. The fuel had evaporated. Chase summoned dank Pink Cadillac residue in his veins to function, stay alert. *Got to keep my head up, eyes open to keep from betraying The Code.* The man flashed his laminate.

"Sam Brown, FBI," he said. "You've been bad, Mr. Bannister."

"You don't know the half of it."

"Perhaps I do."

Brown sat across the table from Chase as his shoulders slumped. *The weakness attacks me inside.* He fought it, shook off the feeling as Brown opened the dossier, laying the contents on the table, tapping his finger at the photographs. Bodies of women, children lying dead. *The East Sprague mosque we did two nights ago for The Serg.* Chase eyed Shiba in the corner. The Japanese warrior was indifferent. *I followed The Code. That's what matters.*

"Don't seem to concerned," Brown said.

"Glad we understand each other."

Brown: "And the bar brawl?"

I honored The Code, I fear nothing. Chase and Wright had celebrated after the mosque hit. They were in a Spokane

Valley dive, juiced up on Pink Cadillac, fuel in their veins, hot. *Had assholes who thought they could take us.* The fight spilled into the parking lot where one of the punks swung a tire iron upside Wright's skull, knocked him dead. *I avenged my friend.* Chase grabbed the asshole, squeezing his head until it cracked, a squelched melon. *Took his buddy, tossed him through a windshield.* Chase grinned, remembering the night. *We're warriors in a savage land. I should end Brown as a matter of principle.*

"Why did you shoot up this mosque?"

Chase: "Some asshole killed my friend in a street fight."

Brown scratched his chin. "Darren Wright, declared DOA at the scene." Paused, then said, "Except he ain't."

"No shit?"

Brown shrugged. "Had his cheek bone shoved up into the left side of his brain but is still alive. Five hours of surgery for him." Paused, then said, "Once he's out, you're useless."

"He won't talk." Wright believed in *The Code* as much as Chase. Shiba solemn in the corner, unacknowledged by Brown, nodded. *Wright and I live by The Code. We ride for The Brand. Death before dishonor.*

Brown dug out a plastic bag holding an empty vial of Pink Cadillac and set it on the table. Chase eyed the label's Russian words half-torn, illegible. *I need it bad*. The chemical scent floated into his nostrils. *Reminds me of Wright and I hitting weights in the gym, nude, letting out screams cause nothing compared to doing a dose.* He fought the urge to attack the bag for whatever thin contents remained in the vial.

Brown gestured to the bag. "This the shit you're using? Got a crime lab back East doing tests on what we found in Wright's pad. Who makes it?"

His last hit of Pink Cadillac had been an hour before his arrest. That was how quick the fuel flushed his system. *Never paid mind to saving it or stretching out portions til I got more.* One hit melted into another. *Kept wanting one right after the other cause the shit rides fast.* He tapped his left foot, to make the need fade. *Be strong and followed The Code.* He eyed Shiba shaking his head, disappointed. *The hunger will break me and betray my master.*

Shiba reminded Chase that he was nothing without *The Code*.

Brown pointed at Chase. "You are in deep, asshole. Got a state hotshot, wants this off Federal's hands to prosecute before his run for Governor, promises you'll swing in Walla Walla in less than five years."

"Some things need doing."

Chase's heart thumped, his lids heavy, the rage subsiding. *No more nights where Wright and I scream while hitting five times our body weight.* The invincibility factor washed as Chase's arms weighed heavy. *I'm that eighty pound weakling my brothers picked on again.* The jerk never kissing a girl until he was twenty-two, watching women he loved flock to men with large muscles. *I hate that little asshole.*

Brown offered Chase a tissue. "You're drooling. This ain't good. Whatever you're on, it's bad news."

Chase jerked his head from Brown's gesture. "Get that out of my face."

The door opened, a tall older man entered. *The guy in charge.* Groomed gray hair, cold blue eyes, dark suit and a red tie. His stern demeanor glared at Chase, hovering over Brown, whose shoulders slumped. The man pointed at Chase. "Ten seconds to talk, asshole."

Brown appeared uncomfortable. To the man: "Weaver, I got this."

"Not from where I stand," Weaver said. "Stop dicking around with this punk."

Chase leaned in, sarcastic. "You two need a moment?"

"Weaver, I had him," Brown said, disappointed.

Weaver smirked. He offered a condescending pat on Brown's head. "Run along, Sammy. Let the big boys handle this perp."

Brown jerked away from Weaver. "Screw you."

The room crowded with Weaver, neither he nor Brown acknowledged Shiba's presence. *They don't respect The Code.* Shiba silent, held his sword tight, in a white tojo outfit, patient. *They disgrace him. But I serve him best.* Chase read *The Code* as a young man. The two FBI agents bickered in front of him about protocols and territory, Chase ignored them to eye his master. The Samurai warrior stood for honor, principle and never betrayed *The Code*.

Oily strands of blonde hair fell over Chase's eyes. He blew it away in puffs, eying Weaver. "You got anything on me? If not, let me go."

Weaver focused on him. "Whole new world we live in now. I can hold you forever if I want."

"Is that a fact?"

Weaver leaned forward, jammed his index finger hard into Chase's chest. "Yeah, that's a fact, asshole."

Chase's eyes focused on Weaver's finger burrowing deep and felt his pulse trigger. A bolt of lightning rode his system. He imagined his big toe hooked to an electrical socket, charging his feet, into his stomach, chest and arms. *The fuel's with me.* Chase's body pumped, veins belching fire. His pupils dilated as he focused on Weaver, grinning wide. *Now it's my turn, asshole.* Brown and Weaver appeared indifferent. Weaver turned to

Brown, Chase running his hands to the edges of the metal table, clutching it hard.

"You said he would talk," Weaver said. "He ain't said shit."

"You give him time, he talks," Brown said.

Weaver: "Time's up."

"Agreed," Chase said.

Chase yanked at the metal table, ripped the legs free from its concrete moorings. The bolts buckled, bent and freed from its foundation under the pressure. The force took Weaver and Brown by surprise. Chase screamed fire, positioning the metal table on its side, bottom facing the two men. He charged the table forward into them. Brown's head hit the side of the table, knocking him out on the floor. Weaver took a table leg into his chest and was thrown into the wall. Chase rammed into the concrete wall with the mounted mirrored glass, impaling Weaver with the table leg.

Weaver's back broke with a sickening *snap* upon impact with the concrete wall. Chase pushed hard, forcing the table leg *through* Weaver into the wall. The impact caused the mounted mirrored glass to shatter. A team of analysts on the other room screamed, escaping in panic. Chase laughed driving the table deeper into the wall. The leg embedded through Weaver, burrowing into the concrete mass behind him. Blood spilled from Weaver's mouth as he struggled to yank the table leg from his abdomen. Weaver passed out from the attack, head dropped, limp.

Chase released the table, but was bound by his handcuffed wrists. He yanked his wrists free of his bonds, letting it shred skin ribbons of flesh until the blood lubricated escape. Chase's wrists bled out while he pounded his fists against his chest, an animal rage overtaking him. *I feel alive again.* The rage powered his strength while splashing the room red.

I am Shiba's perfect warrior. I have honored The Code. Chase drew out his fat tongue, biting down hard until his teeth cut the surface. The taste of blood filled his mouth. He held his tongue firm, chewing until a hunk broke free, which he spat out onto the floor. Blood flowed quickly. He inhaled it until his head felt weak and dropped to his knees. Chase collapsed, lying on his side on the floor. He smiled bliss at Shiba who nodded, solemn, respectful at Chase's honorable death. He had respected *The Code. Death before dishonor.*

5 A tall glass of Jack Daniels with a pinch of cocaine served as breakfast for Rivers End Casino General Manager Scott Tsosie. The energy joint gave him importance. That *vibe* as when he walked into a room. *Everybody looking at me, knowing I'm strong.* People who saw him needed to form a solitary impression. *If you mess with me, it's your ass.* He wasn't going to be threatened by anyone again.

Today bore importance. He put on a fitted, hand-tailored suit from Italy worth five thousand. His eyes dropped to his mirror reflection with his shirt open. He focused on the nine-inch scar across his abdomen. Scott halted dressing, touched his old wound, reminding himself of his survival. *Get it together, Scott.* He refused to let the attack cloud his judgement, ruin the mood he was in. *Woke two hours early, got excited and did my presentation six times to get it down right.*

Scott had ventured out of his top floor suite down into the Rivers End spa. Had one of the ladies take extra time braiding his long hair until it sat as a black sword against his neck down to his shoulder blades. *Smile dressing my face to make sure they know my intentions.* Meeting with the Caha Tribe's leader would determine the Rivers End Casino's future, and that of the Yamenhi people. *Leaving nothing to chance.*

Scott had practiced his smile, got down his tone, for a week. Studied his manner, tried to find holes in his gestures. *Bringing my top game.* He rode the elevator down each flight of the hotel, occupied with the presentation. He walked with a sense of purpose and pride when he reached the casino floor. The sun caught a shine off the glass in the large main entrance of the Rivers End as the morning became late and afternoon edged near. Scott felt the warmth of sunlight, ready for the meeting with the Caha Tribe. Scott strode between rows of slot machines, layers of gaming tables, a crew of six security and executives tailing him. *I built this place with a vision. Another tribe won't take it from me.*

Flanked on his left side was his security team. The team leader, Colonel Civil-Fielder, a retired officer of the Royal Army, kept his men tailing Scott ten feet behind. *They don't want to scare the guests but they need to ensure my safety. If I go down, so does the Rivers End.* Scott eyed little old ladies playing their Diamond Club Cards affixed in slot machines. It caused him to chuckle when figuring the ladies' odds. The idea had been tribal gaming's Richard Yazzie's. He had given it to Scott to push forward and credit as his own. *They put in those cards and lower their chances to win.*

Scott knew the time by watching the casino floor. The

older crowd was a sign of morning. Midday held people from sixty-five to mid-fifties. By evening, the young adults in their early twenties came out. After midnight was reserved for the methamphetamine addicts who robbed the complimentary coffee carts of every sugar packet. *Amazing what people do to feed addiction.*

The early morning shifts changed the casino floor as diehard hotel guests played table games, awaiting payoffs. Staff vacuumed, buffed floors amid stale cigarette fumes in the rafters. *Can't do anything about the cigarette smoke, it's too dangerous.* The Rivers End Casino had hired a company to mount modules expending a chemical smell of roses to mask cigarette odor. Reports of eye infections came from casino staff. *I can only imagine what the guests suffered.* Scott had the million-dollar system dismantled, threatening the company with a lawsuit.

The interior designers hired to order carpet for the Rivers End had been bad vendors too. The carpet was jagged brown and gray lines, fused with streaks of yellow and blue. Scott sat in his office one afternoon, watching guest reactions on surveillance. *They gestured to how ugly the shit was.* The carpet was removed overnight, Scott made sure the other tribal casinos knew his interaction with the interior designers. *Screw with one of us, future work from any other tribe doesn't come.*

Scott passed by the main cashier cage, waving to Gloria as she counted cash standing in front of the vault. He exited through an employee corridor running next to the cage, cutting through to the other side of the casino. The corridor walls held plasma screens displaying visual histories of the Yamenhi tribe and its people. *We have to educate our existence. Too many people believe otherwise.* Rivers End Director of Hospitality Phil Quentin waited at the end of the corridor.

"You're late, Phil."

Quentin: "Eye-ninety was shut off for another one of those mega-load transports."

Scott paused, trying to detect a lie. Quentin apologetic, Scott didn't inquire further.

"Still haven't found our potted plant?" Scott said.

Quentin shook his head. "I reviewed the security tapes last night, nothing comes up."

A thief managed to steal a fifty-pound potted ficus bush from the corridor running from the casino to the hotel lobby. "Keep looking."

Quentin opened the exit to the other end of the casino, gesturing to the buffet. "We have a problem, sir."

The *King Neptune* buffet was all-you-could-eat for two-dollars-ninety-five-cents a person. An old food war tactic from the heyday of Vegas. One hundred feet beyond the buffet entrance stood elderly guests, gripping oxygen tanks and canes. More guests arrived behind them. Each had Diamond Club Cards, ready to use points built up from slot machine action. Scott gestured for Quentin.

"Get ten benches for the people in the next five minutes," Scott said. "Call our planning department, draw up ideas for a thousand foot expansion of the buffet to build in a month."

"Yes, sir," Quentin said.

Quentin removed his IPhone, jotted notes, fired off e-mails. Scott stood quiet for five minutes, watching. Within three minutes, twelve staffers arrived with benches. Each guest took a seat while waiting to enter the buffet. *If the Caha ran this, shit would not have been done.* Scott turned to Quentin, ready for his meeting with the rival tribe. *They better be ready for what I have to say.*

"Where is the meeting with the Caha?"

Quentin said, "*The Coho* room."

"Good," Scott said. "By the way, I want you to renovate *The Zone.*"

The Zone nightclub was Quentin's brainchild, it'd been running for six months. Prior to that, the area had been a successful dining area earning millions in revenue. Quentin presented the idea of redeveloping the space into a nightclub. It resulted in a multi-million dollar loss of revenue and a five hundred guest petition that found its way to Scott's desk. *It's time to give up your nightclub, Quentin.*

"What would we change it to?"

Scott shrugged. "Make it a family-style restaurant where seniors eat at half price, but double the menu prices for regular guests. The old people will drag families in there, we make money on each cover."

"But we need a nightclub for the casino," Quentin said.

"Do the nightclub thing starting at ten," Scott said. "I want the place driving revenue, not hemorrhaging it."

Quentin nodded in agreement. *That's right, Quentin, keep your job.* Scott did not want to fire anyone. *But they have to realize that the Rivers End is not on American soil. We're on Yamenhi land.* Several employees and guests made the same mistake. *No one can tell my people what to do at the Rivers End. We own the joint here.*

Quentin changed the subject. "How do we stop the Caha from their plans?"

"Think positive, Phil," Scott said. "After we talk, they'll think twice about doing this."

"You mean, think twice about messing with you."

Scott shrugged. "What's the difference?"

He moved toward *The Coho* room without Quentin. His security staff parceled off to monitor the casino, only Col. Civil-Fielder remained. The Englishman kept his silence and distance. Scott greeted resort guests without interference. *The colonel can stop anyone before they can attack.* He noted the Colonel's right hand on his sidearm when anyone ventured too close to Scott. *That is why he is here. To keep the Yamenhi people from losing the one who brought them the Rivers End.*

They both entered *The Coho Room* with confidence. The colonel stayed back, his hands against the wall, watching the door. Scott entered, displaying a smile with a grandiose gesture to suggest friendship with the Caha people. *Nothing is further from the truth.* He believed his body tone convinced his enemies of false welcomes. Scott eyed the Caha tribe's leader, Allen Nez, and wanted to deck him.

Nez wore a denim jacket with a long white mane that cascaded down his shoulders. The lenses of his glasses bore scratches. *Reminds me of a high school football player who never got in the game.* Nez had the size for the sport, but natives were enamored with the sport of basketball. Nez held memories in his fifty-seven years. Told stories of boarding school horrors that he and his brother were subjected to during their youth. *I cannot imagine what white people did to you.*

Yamenhi tribal leader Brian Locklear sat across the table from Nez. The two leaders held a long relationship. *They could be brothers.* Locklear had a buzz cut, dressed in Hawaiian shirts and faded jeans. *He looks ridiculous.* Both Locklear and Nez joined the U.S. Army together, served overseas. They held a bond that Scott doubted he would ever understand. *Does Locklear understand that the Caha tribe is trying to hurt our business?*

"The oil business must be good, I guess they've shut down all of the roads," Scott said.

"Yeah, gets the state to do whatever they damn well feel," Nez said.

Scott went to Nez, shook his warm hand with pride, widening his false smile. "Allen, thank you for meeting with us."

"Yeah, thank you, Allen," Locklear said. "You didn't have to do this."

Scott darted his eyes to Locklear. *What are you doing?* Locklear was letting Nez walk all over the Yamenhi people. *Of course he has to meet with us.* The Caha's plans for development could destroy the casino. Locklear appeared unconcerned. *He doesn't see what Nez is capable of. I have to show him.*

Nez to Locklear: "I do this as a favor to you, Brian. I'm not agreeing to anything."

Scott watched for Locklear's reaction but saw none. *See, the man doesn't get it, does he?* Locklear ruined putting Nez on the defensive. *The Caha feel entitled.* Scott felt heat crawl up his skin, loosened his collar, heading to the room's podium. The control panel made the screen drop on the wall, a projector turned on, the lights dimmed. Scott took a handheld remote, faced the screen. *Now, it's my turn, Allen.*

"I want to go over this with both of you," Scott said.

A map of the Inland Northwest showed on the screen with lines denoting rural and urban sections, population density. Scott's handheld offered a tiny red beam to point out specific map areas. He slid the beam east to west along I-90 from Coeur d'Alene to Spokane. The red beam was focused on the map where the Rivers End sat.

"Fifteen years of growth for the Rivers End as the Yamenhi hunt their own golden buffalo," he said. "The Caha fueling station is only three miles away, right where Nez's tribe wants to place a three hundred million dollar casino."

Nez shrugged. "We bought the parcel as you did with yours. We have the right to do what we see fit."

Scott clicked the handheld. The screen showed a diagram of numbers. "Our numbers show the Rivers End losing one-hundred-fifty-million in year one of your casino's opening. In two years, number climbs to three-hundred-fifty-million. If the Caha build so close to our operation, both casinos lose. I'm asking the Caha tribe to reconsider."

He touched the control panel. Lights turned up, projector off, the screen gone. Scott eyed Nez seeing the tribal leader offer an angry stare at Locklear. *Truth hurts, don't it?* Nez did not acknowledge Scott's presentation. Scott resisted his grin. *Wait for Nez to respond.*

"I've heard enough," Nez said, pointing at Locklear. "We can do whatever we want with our land."

Scott noticed Locklear about to say something. *Time to go with Plan B.* Scott moved to Nez, out-stretched his hand, offering it. "Well, then the Yamenhi welcome you to the casino business."

The old man shocked, took Scott's hand, shook it firm, rising from his seat, smiling. "I'm surprised, Scott. I thought you were talking tribal warfare, but this isn't. It's business."

"You're exactly right, it is business," Scott said.

Nez: "It's business."

"And we can't tell you not to get into the casino business."

"No, you can't," Nez said. "Glad you understand."

"And you can't tell us to stay out of the gas business."

That stopped Nez cold. He eyed Scott, frowning. "What the hell are you talking about?"

Scott smiled his teeth at the Caha leader. *Time to go for Nez's jugular.* The Caha tribe's main source of income was a large fueling station. It sold gas to the city population for fifty cents per gallon cheaper than other stations, because of paying no state taxes. The station's twelve pumps generated two hundred million in annual sales. That gave the Caha the competitive advantage needed to leverage the fueling station to any creditor for loan collateral in casino start-up costs.

"If the Yamenhi are losing one-hundred-fifty-million in the first year, three-hundred-fifty-million in the second, we might as well spend that money first," Scott said.

"You wouldn't dare," Nez said.

Scott: "This is Beirut with a different zip code, less gunfire. It's nothing but wheat fields and sand for miles. I can build anywhere. You want to build a casino next to us? Then I'm building the world's largest gas station."

Nez turned to Locklear: "Did you know about this?"

Scott snapped his fingers twice at Nez, gaining the old man's attention. "Don't look at him for help. Look at me. Know what I'm calling the gas station? Dollar gas. Sell every gallon for a buck. Be the Wal-Mart of gas stations. Hundred pumps built in six weeks. Build another hundred in by month two. Betcha I won't have to advertise, I'll have people driving from every state to buy from me. You think your station will survive? How much will it be worth in three months? Or even a month? Doubt any lender will let you borrow for a casino when your gas station goes belly up."

Nez hurt. "Why would you do this to us?"

Scott said, "Because I'm stupid, right? I want to get into the gas business same as you want in the casino business. You don't care if you destroy us, why should it bother me if we destroy you first?"

"That's tribal warfare."

"I thought you understood," Scott said, acting confused, hurt in his sarcasm. "It's business."

6

Brian Locklear watched the exit of Scott Tsosie from *The Coho* room. An emotional weight was placed on his shoulders. Allen Nez was angry. *I should have silenced Tsosie, ordered him from the room.* The Caha were different than the Yamenhi. *Allen would have done it to a member of his tribe.* Locklear realized Tsosie's worth to the Rivers End casino. *Tsosie may be a mutt, but he's my mutt.*

Nez drew close, using an older brother influence on Brian. *That's how our relationship has always been, hasn't it?* In the Caha tribe, native youth were punished or out-right banned for speaking disrespectful to an elder. *We Yamenhi are different.* The Yamenhi youth spoke their minds. *Tsosie may have gone a little too far, but he was playing the game Nez had started.*

Nez pointed at Brian, shaking. "This won't stand, Brian," Nez said. "We can have a casino same as you do."

Brian held up his hands, defensive. "I know Scott's methods are a little aggressive."

"A little aggressive?" Nez said. "He'll bankrupt our tribe. You need to stop this, Brian."

"His father was a brother to me," Brian said.

"I am a brother to you," Nez said. "Don't let some arrogant mutt come between us."

"He runs the casino operation, Allen. If he wants to start up a gas station, he will get the backing from the tribe."

Nez nodded. "I'm sorry to hear that. Really I am."

"It's business."

Nez held out his hand which Brian took, then exited, leaving Brian alone in the room. *What am I going to do with you, Scott?* Nez had a point. The Caha had the right to expand gaming operations. Scott was correct that another casino would destroy the Rivers End. Brian shook his head. Nothing decided today would change Scott Tsosie's tenure as general manager. *He built this place. He doesn't want to see the Caha ruin it.*

Brian exited to the casino floor where poker tables and slot machines were filled with guests. *This is a beautiful place that our people created.* Tsosie's vision of the Rivers End exceeded tribal expectations. *He came with a plan few believed in.* Brian remembered coming off his union job at the aluminum factory, wearing dirty coveralls to the tribal meeting about the Rivers End. *Told myself if this casino was a success, I was never wearing anything but Hawaiian shirts and jeans.* So far, Brian had kept that promise.

Brian passed the cashier cage, up the long ramp by the slot machines toward the sports bar and escalator. He rode the electric staircase, through the public corridor leading to the hotel. Video boards displayed Yamenhi history. He noted the photographs because they were from his family. His father and uncle fishing out of a canoe off Lake Riceno during an overcast morning. The little tobacco store where he sold cigarettes to men traveling up to save a little off of taxes. *We built something here to keep those memories away from being our children's future.*

In the lobby, Brian saw the bar in the middle which was getting set up. To his right was a Japanese restaurant that he had not eaten at yet. Beyond the lobby, the entrance to the atrium sat, the newest Rivers End attraction. By adding the atrium, The Rivers End's two-thousand room hotel tower allowed guests to look down through a glass structure housing exotic plants, wildlife. The atrium boasted pathways with glass ceiling, a large tunnel pane system where snakes and birds rested. Tourists ventured through the world without leaving the comforts of the casino. Tsosie was leaning against a wooden rail, monitoring the atrium's newest attraction, a Sumatran tiger.

The beast appeared ready to charge the bullet-proof glass. *He would kill any of us if he got the chance.* Brian did not care for the wild animals that Tsosie demanded be in the atrium. *You cannot trust wild things to be tamed or civilized. That's why we keep them in cages.* Tsosie insisted on the tiger. Thus far, it remained quiet, licking itself lying at the base of a waterfall cascading from the top of the atrium down four hundred feet.

Brian noted the security guards who stood near Tsosie as he approached. *Ready to jump if I make a false move.* Tsosie remained firm on having the security team despite Brian's discomfort. They were a separate team from standard casino security. *He worries someone else will attack him again.* Brian regretted thinking back to that day less than a month ago. *All of that blood.* Tsosie lying on the ground, holding his side, pale. *I thought he was going to die.*

Tsosie used to be approachable. *Now I feel his bodyguards bearing down me.* Tsosie was different prior to the attack, when the Rivers End was a small operation. A few slot machines, gaming tables and ten foot ceilings in a clap-trap operation people used to laugh at. *I miss his little boy smile.* The employment of Col. Civil-Fielder, head of Tsosie's security staff, was evidence that Tsosie's innocence was lost.

The Englishman radiated a sinister scowl. Thin gray hair, a trimmed mustache and cold eyes against a humorless face. Civil-Fielder's expensive suit had a right-side bulge of his firearm. *Scott's got a private army, thinks everyone is going to attack him.* Civil-Fielder glared but remained in position seven feet from Tsosie. Even security staff knew limits as Brian approached Tsosie.

"We need to talk," Brian said.

Tsosie shook his head. "Let's schedule something. I need to gather my thoughts before I say something we both don't like."

"No," Brian said, firm. "We talk now."

"I want us to succeed, not just survive," Tsosie said, complaining. "The Caha had their chance but waited. Now the Rivers End works, so they want in without the risk."

Brian's hand went to Tsosie's shoulder. "Treat other tribal elders with respect in what you say."

"We lose everything," Tsosie said. "The state will approve their casino because white men don't care what the natives do to each other. All they have to do is sit back, watch. We'll do it for them."

Brian shook his head. "Stop sounding like Richard Yazzie. His conspiracies poison your soul."

Tsosie opened his dress shirt, exposed his abdomen to Brian, who tried to look away. "White people haven't changed, Brian. I'm proof of that."

All of that blood. Tsosie was lying on his back, holding his side. *I held him until the ambulance came. Those guests standing around, staring at us.* Tsosie re-buttoned his shirt, fixing his suit. *He paid the price to have the Rivers End. That is why he is adamant about defending it.*

"Tribal relationships matter," Brian said. "That's all I want you to think about."

Tsosie hung his head. *I see his father in him, trying to do the right thing.* Tsosie's eyes raised to meet Brian's, nodding. The young man stepped into Brian's arms, hugging. *He needs a good teacher.* Brian held him, wishing Tsosie's father was alive. *You should have been part of his life, Russ. You were a better mentor than I.* Tsosie pulled away, his eyes glassy while aborting tears. Brian changed the subject, gesturing to the Sumatran tiger.

"He's a bit too much," Brian said.

Tsosie sniffling, pointed to the far end of the atrium. "Lion is over there. Feed it twenty pounds of meat to keep from killing the Silverback gorilla for dinner."

"When does the ape arrive?"

"Six weeks," Tsosie said.

The atrium tunnel drew tourists who stayed for the attractions at the Rivers End. *Keeps their entertainment dollar affordable instead of a stay-cation.* A flock of flamingos ran across the atrium's field to the excitement of young children watching. *Our operation grows by becoming a place that everyone wants to be a part of.*

Civil-Fielder edged close, glaring at Brian. *Makes my skin crawl. Need to do something about him.* Tsosie was never alone to have Brian perform an intervention on the excessive security. Civil-

Fielder was crass with a military background, lean and angry. *Probably needs twenty pounds of meat to keep from attacking people.* Brian watched Civil-Fielder stand nearby, uneasy. *He gives me the creeps.*

In the underworld a lot of people sucked wind.
Meaning they said things that never came to
fruition. Talked shit, letting their mouths write
check their asses couldn't cash. The Serg's
operation was different at the Exit One strip club. The Serg dealt
with matters head-on as they started to rise. Brother Zachariah
had issued orders for his boys to retaliate for the mosque shoot-
out. They raided one of the old Russian's meth labs west of
Spokane, three cooks executed. The Serg ordered a sit-down with
Brother Zachariah's representative, avoiding more trouble. Peter
Volov stood in the basement of Exit One, eying Darren Wright
who laid on his chest, sleeping in the fighting pit center.

Peter had Oleg wake him up at five in the morning, in the
apartment they shared. Walked right in, putting his foot on
Peter's mattress, rocking it until he stirred. Oleg saying that
Peter had to get up, ready, because Wright showed at Exit One,
unexpected.

"Came through the front in a dirty gown, tubes stuck in arms
and legs," Oleg said. "Freak show."

The Serg's concern about Wright changed into opportunity,
once news of the meth lab killings surfaced. Advantage was seen
with Wright's inclusion. *The old Russian needs leverage with
Brother Zachariah's group.* Wright was a mass of flesh in the pit,

a large forehead dent showing, right eye kicked beyond his brow. *That ain't never coming down.* Peter stood guard with a cattle prod in case Wright decided to go apeshit, as Oleg had instructed twelve hours before. Only taking short piss breaks, getting meals brought down by one of the girls, keeping himself ready for anything.

Wright laid weak, head turned sideways, eyes at the ceiling. *He's withdrawing.* Peter examined Wright's arms, covered in track marks where Wright loaded Pink Cadillac in a dope fiend haze. Other muscle boys pass through Exit One on the junk. The Serg had a stable for hardcore enforcement, guys ripped on Pink Cadillac. But Wright had hundreds of little needle marks, not ten or twenty.

Wright focused on Peter, drool foaming. "You got any, bro?"

Peter revealed a syringe gun in his right hand, loaded with a blue vial. "Stand up so it'll work faster."

Wright lifted himself off the ground, groaned as he towered over Peter by seven inches. Sounds from back of the room caught Peter's attention, getting him to eye the metal door. A pair of hands clutched open the slot to rip it open. Anthony Batellini acting like as a maniac, jealous another man was getting his junk. *How am I going to get you out of here, Anthony?* The junk had cracked Anthony's mind. *There is no telling how far gone he truly is.*

Wright lifted the back of his gown, offered his bare ass with three hundred old track marks covering his cheeks. *Did a lot of this shit, haven't you?* Peter squeezed the syringe gun barrel into Wright, emptying the vial. The big man dropped his gown and collapsed onto the pit floor. Peter eyed him, sure.

"Feel better?"

"Takes time," Wright said. "You get more, I want it."

Peter nodded, saying more juice was at the pad that Oleg was taking Wright to, so sit tight. *Keep him calm until Oleg arrives with the plan. No telling what The Serg wants to do.*

"What else am I gonna do?" Wright said.

An hour passed before Peter was pushing Wright up the staircase toward the Exit One parking lot. Telling the big man whatever it took to get Wright to move. *Man's a mountain going at his own speed.* Wright mumbled something about his mother but Peter didn't catch what.

Oleg stood near the idling cream colored van, opening the back doors. Tchaikovsky played lightly from an IPod in the van. He had a syringe gun, loaded with five blue vials and juiced Wright when the big man arrived. Squeezed off the vials, Wright thanking him, asking for more. Oleg shook his head, pointing to the van, Wright went in. He offered a tired, drained look back at Oleg and Peter, sitting on the bench, head between his knees, asking his mother if they were going shopping. *He's delirious from all the junk.*

Oleg slammed the back doors shut, got behind the wheel, Peter riding shotgun. The van moved onto the paved road running west next to the interstate, opposite direction was a large grouping of state patrol flashing lights with a semi running a large mega-load between the two states. Oleg calm, relaxed while checking the rearview mirror, eying his own cargo of Wright, asking Peter if the builder had been trouble.

Peter shook, saying no, man was a panda.

Oleg shrugged. "I expected sleep by now."

Peter asking why was that?

Oleg pointed to the vials in the syringe gun. Saying Xhang made it to block the pink stuff, was diluted so it doesn't stop the brain, heart. "It makes them weak, easy to move."

Peter played out mental scenarios. *I can free Anthony, get him out with that blue stuff.* Peter wondered how he would contact the DEA and get them involved. *None of them wanted to help me after Anthony went missing.* He was considered collateral damage to the agency. He eased forward, not wanting to seem too interested but needed more information. "You need a lot to make him go back to normal?"

Oleg nodded, saying Tony took blue vial injections when The Serg needed him to take a dive in fights.

"Glad I never bet on him," Peter said, gaining interest. *Where do I get those little blue vials? I could free Anthony and get out.*

The van's weight shifted when Wright collapsed off of the bench. Oleg slammed the brakes. They eyed the back, Wright face-planted on the van's floor, mumbling gibberish. *Man reminds me of a bear rug I saw in Oregon.* Wright sprawled, ass hanging out of a dirty hospital gown. Peter gestured to Wright, asking Oleg what they were going to do with him?

Oleg shook his head. "He makes amends. Rectify situation."

Peter saying it sounded serious.

Oleg: "Asshole and friend hit wrong side of mosque. Kill women, kids. Now, man they should have killed comes after Andrei's operation. It cannot happen."

Peter said, "It's business."

Oleg nodded, but saying that was not the first time this week. When Peter was gone on an errand, four hardcore brothers out on parole came through Exit One, packing shotguns. Smashed a little plastic number named Trinity in the face at the door. Oleg who'd had his pants around his ankles exiting the bathroom, put his .45 against the leader's head to get them to leave. Even a man with no pants can get his point across. The meth lab executions came after.

"Are we taking down the Brother's operation with Wright?"

Oleg saying no, Wright was a delivery so the brothers could show him the face of God. End the violence. "It helps he is white, too."

Oleg headed west down the main road until the asphalt turned to gravel. It kicked dust for several miles as the van went through potholes and jagged edges at fifty-miles-per. Oleg continued a couple of miles, parking at the drive that cut over a large drainage ditch. An old farmhouse and barn sat at the far end. The house windows lit, but the barn cold, empty with its doors open. The van idled at the end of the drive, then Oleg blinked the headlights in a short burst. A car next to the farmhouse offered a headlights blink in response.

Oleg gestured to the glove box, which Peter opened, finding Oleg's .45 that he handed to the Russian who sat it in his lap. Wright mumbled in the back, Peter unsure what was said but the big man was nervous. Oleg turned the van at twenty-five-miles-per down the drive. Peter eyed the area, a figure waiting at the end of the drive with an AK-47. The headlights touched the figure's features; a clean-cut black man wearing a suit and yellow bowtie, and horned-rimmed glasses. Oleg lowered the window slow, smiling.

The black Muslim asked Oleg about the package, speaking perfect English, impressing Peter.

"In back," Oleg said. "You take him out."

The Muslim nodded, motioning behind to three men wearing suits and bowties who exited the farmhouse and went to the van. They opened the back doors, gaping at Wright, who woke up, eying them, mumbling gibberish. The Muslim goons took his arms, forcing him out. The van rocked, its shocks buckling minus Wright's weight. Peter and Oleg sat quiet, ignoring the extraction. The three goons dropped Wright onto the dirt drive.

Oleg tried small talk with the brother holding the AK-47. Asked the brother if he wanted a cigarette. The man returned a cold look. Oleg's hand slid to his lap, clutching his .45, ready to go. Wright was escorted off the ground by the goons grappling his neck and arms, moving from the van to the barn's open doors. Wright no longer spoke, doomed with little choice. The group vanished into the barn, doors shut tight behind them.

Oleg grabbed the Muslim by the collar, jammed his .45 underneath the brother's chin, man stiffening, defiant while holding firm with a cold stare at Oleg. *He's waiting to die.* Oleg told him to drop the AK-47, which fell to the drive. A chainsaw started up inside the barn. Wright screamed as the saw hit bone. Oleg said to the brother, we want to get home without dying. He told Peter to put the van in reverse, steer while he worked the gas, keeping the brother in tow.

The van crept backward through the drive. Peter held the steering wheel, focused on the drive beyond the back windows. Oleg held tight to the Muslim goon, his .45 locked into place while the brother walked quickly. Wright's screams of forgiveness from a group that would show him none rose above the chainsaw sounds. The brother smiled as he walked, assured of righteousness. The van reached the end of the drive where Oleg released the man's collar, resting his .45 in his lap. The brother stood firm, eying Oleg, defiant. *He wants to be martyred.* They drove the van away, leaving the man in the darkness.

"What about this place?"

Stew referred to the Rivers End casino. Got Kyle Crowley thinking as the pair sat in the casino's sports bar. The mention surprised him. Both had been rolling along in the car, avoiding the highway shut down by a mega-load run, when Stew pointed out the place. Said let's go for a beer, you buy. When Stew suggested doing the casino, Kyle got the feeling that old Stew was making a comeback. The reckless type who thought every place was a five-and-dime, waiting to be taken down with a shotgun, ski-mask and a wheelman. *And I get to always be the wheelman.* Stew talked with Kyle that way before. *Back when we traded comic books, smoked weed; all kinds of shit.* Kyle dodged Stew's reckless attitude, remembering what had befallen them three-and-a-half-years before.

Kyle gave the place his attention, gaining a knack that Eugene Salters taught him at *The Sides. Momentarily glance, that makes you look like you ain't eying the camera next to the Ryne Sandberg jersey, or catching that manager flirting with the woman at the bar rather than checking IDs on people coming through.* Salters said to check how people act when they don't think anyone is watching. *Let your eyes roll around the room without moving your head. Be that quarterback who hits his receiver while looking the*

8

entire time at the tight end. He hit spots with his eyes without suggesting he was looking at anything at all.

Kyle shook his head. *Didn't we agree not to do this shit?* They didn't want to end up like other guys at *The Sides. Was there enough not to go back for seconds?* Money concerns hit Stew harder than Kyle. *I'm not worried about getting a new Xbox or other shit because other people have it too.* Stew wanted it all, calling rich people "lucky." He would point out rich guys at The Blacklight long before it stopped being a hang-out trend on the local club scene. Saying we should roll one of those cats. Get ourselves a gold chain and watch. Kyle realized half those guys worked with the blue. *You do up one of them, it wasn't the same as a punk.* Some city lawyer coming in with a plastic date on his arm also had the mayor's phone number on speed dial.

"Leave that shit behind," Kyle said. "Going back ain't an option. Free air is the good life."

Stew said, "Good life is on some porch, drinking Arnold Palmers while some bikini thing massages your temples, some asshole's kid mows your lawn. You can't be digging what we do now."

"Better than dealing with sugar fiends, GK assholes getting you to blood in, blood out," Kyle said.

Stew could not debate. *The Sides* was no life. A bad vibe structure every inmate conformed to, not the other way around.

Kyle remembered sleeping in that minimum security dormitory the first night, hearing whistles in the dark, finding out it wasn't for him but for a guy who pissed off a GK member. *The sleeping con got clubbed, woke up a permanent retard, bleeding on his pillow when morning call came.* For the rest of the time in, Kyle slept light. *I'm doing whatever it takes never to go back to that.*

"I ain't talking about going back," Stew said. "I'm just saying, you know?"

Kyle shrugged. "Long as you're just saying, not really thinking of taking this place; sure, I feel you."

"Course not."

They sat quiet in the Rivers End sports bar attended by men waiting while their wives got hotel spa pampering or spent some cookie jar money on the roulette wheel, betting black twenty-five. The gaming action had Greatest Generation veterans in wheelchairs lined up at the cashier cages with social security checks for a taste of winning big. Kyle eyed the crowd, casual interest on the Boston Celtics game displaying on three mega screens mounted above the bar. Kyle spotted the camera focused on the cash register to limit employee theft. Eyes went to casino security, seeing a black haired lady who had not missed a high-caloric meal in years. *She's got nothing but a walkie talkie to call for help, no weapons at all.* Kyle wondered why he was scoping the place. *Do I want to go back to The Sides?*

Maybe Stew misses eating that slop the trustees served us, but I don't. Kyle never wondered what the convicts of *The Sides* were up to. *Only good talk came from liars back from parole or who got diesel therapy from a facility down south.* Most of the stories were long on fiction, short on reality. *But that don't mean they weren't interesting.* Everything staled fast for Kyle. *Longest time was the last month there, waiting to see some gang member from La979 or the GK coming for me.* The main corrections officer, Steve Powers, had been always willing to show inmates how *The Sides* guards did things in the 208. *That's why I live in the 509.*

Stew eyed Kyle, smirking. "You scoped this place."

"Looked around," Kyle said, shrugged.

"Don't lie," Stew said. "You like it."

"I'm not going back," Kyle said. "I'm comfortable."

Stew: "Comfortable how? We ain't got shit between us."

"Got enough that holds me longer than it does you," Kyle said. "One tour of *The Sides* was enough for me."

"Who says we ever go back?"

Kyle: "You, from the sound of it."

He had learned to enjoy the world since his release. A lot of shit changing with cell phones, IPads. *Hell, you can read a good book if you want.* Kyle never said that to Stew because the man hated reading, saying it was a stupid waste. *He thinks reading is boring, wondering why they can't cut it out, make it a movie instead.* Man had a point with a lot of books. Kyle snagged paperbacks from the library, tossed them in the corner of his apartment to finish when Stew was off, doing something else. *Reminds me of those comic books Stew brought back when we weren't cons.* Back when we both were friends, Stew not acting all hardcore. *I miss those days.*

The Sides did not affect Kyle as much as the state of Idaho had. No absolution for his crimes. His sister, Tess, used to be his best friend. *She used to call me on my birthday, sit at holidays and catch-up.* Things were different since he became a crook. *When I call, she's got suspicion working in whatever I say. What was he doing calling so late at night?* She's really busy right now. None of that sibling stuff wondering how he's doing, what was going on?

Tess would hesitate or sit silent on the other end of the line. *Thought she felt guilty for not being there for me when I went to The Sides.* Then Kyle realized she was filling out minutes until she could hang up and be finished with him. Holidays were out because she was too busy. *Can't see my ten-year-old nephew and it's never a good time to call.* Kyle figured Tess didn't want her child picking up criminal skills from his uncle. Little things that Tess did bothered him. *She listens to what I say, then has a curt response. Let's me sit there, wondering if I can ever earn back her trust.*

Stew sipped his draft. "Hate this shit, not supposed to be this way for us, you know?"

Kyle patted his shorts, looked around, sarcastic. "Musta left that damn how-to manual back at my pad that says we were supposed to be guys who could play guitars with our teeth."

"You want this for yourself in five years?"

"Like being out, Stew," he said. "I never wanted to be a con in the first place."

Tension sat between them. *Did too much of what Stew wanted since I met him.* A sense of obligation remained. Outsides couldn't see when they didn't look deep enough, just assuming things. *Like the prison shrink thinking I was in love with Stew.* Kyle never felt that way toward his friend. *Too many people judge us without learning who we are.* The bond between them stayed at *The Sides. Stew grabbed the bottom dorm bunk while I laid on top. If heat was coming, Stew stepped in for me.* Kyle guessed Stew felt guilt over their incarceration. *His idea landed us at The Sides, so he dealt with the consequences.*

The Sides had an interesting set of sugar fiends stabbing people. Every time someone didn't like Kyle's looks and took issue, Stew stepped in, kicking the shit out of them. Kyle had a Copperhead attack him in the showers. *Grabbed me from behind, putting me on the ground, touching my junk and calling me his baby*. Stew pulled the man off, beat him with a shower spout pipe. *Crushed the man's throat, watched him die in front of us*. Stew never got time added because it was a Copperhead. *Not some real person.*

Kyle felt protected around Stew. *He's a brother to me. Man was there to point out things, show you what was what because he had gone through that experience. Giving me stuff that I needed to know, wondering how I made it this far without a man in my life.* No uncles cared, dad did two walk-outs on a chain-smoking wife before she got the message and moved as far as she could with two babies a year apart. *By the time I was twenty-two, I was doing nothing but thought I was living.* All of his high school friends had moved on. *Never smart enough for a four-year campus visit at the home of the blue football field.*

He worked at the Boise Airline Park & Jet after being done with kitchen deliveries at two fast food restaurants working dollar-over-minimum with kids flipping him shit about being a lifer. Parking job was easy. *Sit in your box, listen to your IPod, hand assholes a ticket when they roll up. Validate or take a wad of cash and change.* Gig was easy enough that Kyle became a fat belly with an eight-cell Maglite, double XL windbreaker. *Earning ten-fifty-one per hour watching cars while mister business man traveled this great land of ours.*

After a three-week training period with a guy named Homer drinking warm beer at five in the morning with a bad case of the farts, Kyle got scheduled for the graveyard shift. *Nothing to do once the airlines went to sleep.* He remembered scoping the area to ensure punks weren't keying cars or jumping concrete dividers with their skateboards to prevent the lot getting an insurance claim from a kid cracking his skull on the asphalt doing a 50-50 Casper with some weak plastic trucks on his board. Kyle sat restless on in cool nights when the temperature hit fifty-five, the buzzing insects staying out from ten-til-two in the A of the M. Times he forgot his IPod, he'd do regular radio, the DJs switching to national canned shit about three-thirty. *Enough with the Beatles, I heard their songs, danced their rhythms, they're great, let's move on.*

Night shift meant waking at 8 p.m., catching sleep while the world was awake. Everyone made noise, including the jackhammers and construction tearing up the streets while cars passed, honking. *Used to lay in bed with people fighting and screaming in the next apartment.* Turning on the tube meant seeing all of the baseball games finished by the time he woke up, the world moving without him. Time his shift ended at the lot, he was ready to go and do something, but it was 7 a.m. The mundane routine got him enough that he hoped something would happen on the job. *Hoped some asshole talked shit when he came for his car without a ticket.* Kyle had no cell phone to text anyone with, but no one he knew was in Boise anymore. If they were, they recognized him in passing, saying yeah, I think I took Bio-Chem at Timberline High with him. *Hard to admit, but I was damn lonely at that point of my life.*

Kyle started thinking about ending his career with as a parking lot attendant about six months into the job. *I wasn't earning shit, my belly fat on junk food, waiting for my shift to end.* He thought about video games, magazines and ignored the fact that girls ignored him. *I could have told you any movie title if you knew the actor and a little of the plot, but the inside of a girl's skirt was a mystery.* That was before his new parking lot supervisor named Stew Reading rolled up one summer night in a golf cart. *Showed me how he did jumps off the concrete ramps almost flipping the cart while slamming his foot on the gas to do thirty-five as he gained momentum.*

Makes me laugh of how Stew impressed me back then. Stew appeared lost in the shuffle now. *He's restless, crazy ideas about how to get rich.* Stew was never going to get to where Kyle was. *Realizing this is all there is, nothing better is coming. All I got is credit card bills and that call from the county sheriff asking if I've been a good boy and all.* Stew forgot he was a con, acting as if he didn't have a record holding him back. In the Rivers End sports bar, Stew gave Kyle a look which showed he was prepping for something.

"Sick of not doing more than getting by," Stew said. "You gotta be there with me, right?"

Kyle: "We can go legit. My cousin's got a record, and child support from a pair of twins, even though he can't remember the night he made them. He got on with a garbage crew, making good paper. Did it for eighteen years, ready to hit retirement so he can sit around and live that good life you talk so much about."

"I ain't up picking shit up to toss in a garbage truck, some kid's dirty diapers all over my hands," Stew said.

Stew saw certain tasks beneath him. If he didn't want to do it, shit didn't happen. He had been that way at the parking lot back in Boise. Boss would tell him to do shit, he would leave it for the morning crew, ordering them to do it because he was a supervisor. Then he took credit for it, long as his boss didn't find out, everyone was happy. Kyle noticed how Stew would hang around at night after he was due to go home. *He once told me there was nothing but sleep waiting at home for him.* Having someone to talk to made time go quick and Kyle developed his first friend in a while. *One of those guys you hang with and regret not having more time to talk to when the shift is over.*

One of Stew's high school buddies worked double-shifts at the Boise paper mill and got him stacks of comic books with the covers torn off. Everything from Marvel to DC to those graphic books they made movies straight out of. Stew brought stacks to work to share with Kyle. They would sit there in that little parking station box, look at the episodes of mutant adventure, not saying a word but enjoying each other's company. Stew hated reading so much he thought the little dialogue boxes were annoying. All of those superhero adventures coming into Kyle's hands for free.

Waking up each evening for his shift got easier. Except when he caught his reflection in the mirror, saw himself naked with large mounds of fat on his belly and hair in places that frightened him. *Had a paunch made of jelly donuts, sugar cola and a face of terminal acne reminding me of a horror movie skin disease.* He wondered why Stew even liked him. Stew had a build even back then, not as big as now, but still. Kyle could never figure why Stew would want to be seen with a loser.

Stew eyed Kyle now as they sat the sports bar, a little hurt. "You didn't have a life before you met me, don't forget that."

"I know, man."

Back then I was waiting to die of terminal virginity or a massive coronary. He tried to rationalize why his pants split in the crotch and butt or why the waist sizes expanded. Stew had lifted some, not as he did now, but had a decent chest, good arms. Kyle back then was in the opposite direction. Stew talked Kyle into joining a local gym for twenty-two-thirty-five a week, promising it would be fun. *Man kept his promise, got me a body that I always wanted.*

Kyle was amazed at what Stew had given him. The weight shed off, greasy skin going with it. *Stew went through my pad acting like an AA sponsor you see on TV, combing through my furniture and dumping all the junk food.* Whatever Kyle put in his system after that point was approved by Stew, including the wheat germ and ginkgo. The parking lot shifts became training sessions where they worked out with a chair and a towel. After shift, they headed to the gym for a two-hour session. *Stew was hard and unfair, but I needed that in my life.*

He remembered running around the lot at four in the morning. *Stew using a stopwatch and screaming for me to run faster, harder.* A year and a half later, that fat ass never showed in the mirror reflection when Kyle got out of the shower. He was lean, rock hard abs, toned and chiseled. Acne gone, confidence up. He and Stew started leaving the parking lot unattended for hours to head into the bars. Women fawned all over him. His first time was with two Cougars, one who kept pressuring the other to go forward because they had both talked about it for weeks before meeting Kyle. He slept with ten women in a the span of a week after that. He was thankful that Stew had saved him.

Kyle feeling guilt riding him now in the bar, said to Stew, "I paid you back in full, man."

"I know," Stew said. "But this is about getting what we deserve."

The two year anniversary of Kyle's parking lot tenure had Stew approaching him with ideas. *Took it as bullshit guys say when the conversation sucks. Saying stuff you would do to that girl, but not that one with the red hair. As if you had a chance to begin with.* After working out, Kyle started to feel things got easier. *I approached girls, get them into my car without trouble to catch some strange.* Things two years ago had been fiction to a fat ass with a chocolate milk buzz whose nightlife consisted of listening to sports radio.

Stew kept talking small, mentioning *Ringo's*, a bar with a lot of paper rolling in. *Said that bartender was weak, smash him in the grill with a forearm and he would do what he was told, Stew just knew it.* Kyle brushed the comments off, going to dance with a few chicks, getting a groove going with them later, letting them hop on him while he sat on some rundown toilet, eyes catching the walls of the stall decorated with graffiti written in sharpies and knife carvings. Stew talked about making real coin after money got tight. *Who wanted the night shift at the parking lot anyway?* Kyle nodded but forgot what was said quick after Stew stopped talking, the day shift about to roll in to relieve them from duty.

Stew pointed out the parking lot's cash slips from the weekend shifts. *Said look how much coin they got rolling? Talking about how we end up guarding the lot to take two in the chest from some Wet who wants a BMW.* Kyle would eye the slips, say yeah, but it was risky. Trying to make his friend stop talking but Stew had none of it. Stew mentioning how the bosses never collected money for weeks until after the Christmas season. *Said remember how hard the safe is to close with all that cash jamming the hinges?* Stew talking about how any asshole with a ski mask, shotgun could rob the weekend boys and no one would suspect the night shift staff of pulling the job.

Kyle relented and they formed a Saturday morning plan to go down at 11 a.m. where they would rob the weekend crew at the parking lot. Stew figured neither guy ever saw the night shift so there was no way to make any identification. Ski masks and shotguns came from Stew's second cousin. *Man would get a ten percent cut as long as the guns weren't fired, otherwise it was twenty-two.* They hit the parking lot on schedule, had the attendants handing the cash over in wads when Kyle wheeled the car through the booth, Stew aiming the shotgun at the attendant's chest. *Man pissed his drawers when he saw that barrel on him.* Excited, Kyle waited to slam on the gas, tear out of the lot in the car they lifted outside of town.

Problem with the plan had to do with the Idaho State patrol. They had started doing rounds in the lot because of suspicious packages left a few weekends before. Kyle and Stew had never had the I.S.P. guys come through during their weekday shifts and weren't told that it was a possibility. So when the I.S.P. came up behind the two as they robbed the weekend parking guards, flashing their patrol lights, the plan was doomed. Neither shotgun was loaded for fear of discharging, a fear of actually killing someone or paying Stew's cousin twelve percent more than they had to. The arrests went easy enough. Stew and Kyle got seven years, slapped down to five on appeal from the judge as first time offenders, then served out two for good time added up. They both wore orange jumpsuits on their diesel therapy up to Rathdrum, serving out their terms at *The Sides.*

They sat at the Rivers End sports bar as ex-convicts of the Idaho prison system and were supposed to be on the other side of the state line. But budget cuts saved them now that parole was an electronic monitoring system. They had a cell phone with a 208 Idaho area code, supposed to text their check-ins to the man.

The system was easy to manipulate if you know the right buttons to push. If they got called back to Boise, they had twelve hours to meet. Enough time to drive back before anyone recognized they were gone. Both men found work at the Blacklight club being paid under the table as bouncers so no I-9 forms could sell them out as a violation.

Kyle eyed Stew sulking at the bar, knowing he was letting his friend down. *I don't want to go back to The Sides, though.* Stew moved to Kyle, giving a clink of his beer glass against Kyle's. *Letting me know everything is okay while we drink our two-thirty-eight draft specials.* Stew gestured with his pint to the camera above the mega screens.

"Cameras are pulled back so they can't get a solid ID," Stew said.

"But who does a casino? Answer me that," Kyle said. "They got guys all over, in the rafters and the floor. Five times what a bank has."

Stew shook his head. "Assholes with tasers and walkie talkies who aren't more than mall cops don't make a security team. This place has illusion and some idiots taking self-defense classes down at the learning annex to know how to stop a drunk. None of that fire power that a bank has."

"You can't tell how they respond til they do," Kyle said.

Stew nodded. "You got a point."

"Salters used to say that until a place responds, you don't know how they react."

Stew: "Maybe we should rattle their cage, see what comes out."

The pair quieted which Kyle figured ended discussion as he drank his pint, letting the buzz stir his head. On the mega screens, the Celtics game showed them beating Charlotte and storming through a forty-two point margin after three quarters. *Raining down threes as if they're on sale or some shit.* Kyle sat waiting for Stew to talk. *That's when you know he's pissed cause he ain't talking.* Kyle watched the bartender named J.T. wander up the counter to check on them, wearing a referee's shirt and a casino name tag. Kyle asked for water while Stew went for another draft. Stew asked J.T. about the big screens.

"Why have the damn Celtics on every screen in the house?" Stew said to J.T.

J.T. grinned, pointed between Kyle and Stew. Path of his finger led to the back of the room where a native man stood watching the game, reacting to each basket. He wore a dark suit and blue shirt. "He decides what goes on the screen. When he walks in, Celtics go up no matter what."

"Who is he?" Stew said.

"General Manager of the place, Mister Tsosie," J.T. said. "That two dollar tip you're thinking of leaving ain't worth me pissing him off."

Stew set his glass on the counter, offering Kyle a wink. "Maybe Tsosie needs to hear from a customer."

Kyle latched onto Stew's wrist. "Don't start shit, man. I don't want to go back for a probation violation."

Stew pulled free of Kyle, heading over to Tsosie. Kyle eyed the native man, who smiled until he saw Stew coming. A huge man of mass weaving through customers had a way of giving anyone a fright. Kyle judged Stew was five inches taller, a foot wider than Tsosie. J.T. leaned toward Kyle, watching the scene with a smirk.

"He's one mean asshole when you piss him off," J.T. said.

"Tell me about it."

J.T. shook his head, laughing. "I wasn't talking about your friend."

Kyle offered J.T. a surprised glance at the statement. Stew could take care of himself. The talk was short and brief between Tsosie and Stew, who got animated as the native man stood there and ignored him while watching the Celtics play. Stew's voice got loud, other customers turned from the Celtics game to watch the scene. Stew pointed at the big screens, then jammed his finger into Tsosie's chest. The native man stumbled from the force, appearing to be frightened. Kyle moved to retrieve Stew, but J.T. grabbed his arm to hold him back.

"Too late for your friend," J.T. said. "The big boys are coming down now."

Three men in expensive suits moved through the entrance. They surrounded Stew, holding the lifter at the arms, one clutching the nape of his neck. He froze and stood straight, not struggling as a gray haired man with a mustache in an expensive suit entered the bar, coming between Stew and Tsosie, giving Stew a stern eye. Kyle broke free of J.T.'s grip, moving away from the bar to his friend's side. Kyle approached, seeing the three security men had sidearms jammed underneath Stew's arms. The weapons were hidden as the security and Stew pushed together. The gray haired man pointed to Kyle.

"Your friend has decided to depart and we agree with his assessment," he said, sporting an English accent and refinement of a lord. "My friends will escort you both to the parking area."

Tsosie edged around the gray haired man. Kyle caught booze fumes off the general manager's breath. Tsosie buried his finger in Stew's chest, hard. "A white man got me once when I wasn't looking. Now I got the Colonel here to stop it. Consider it payback for the reservations."

Stew smug, laughed: "You guys should have fought harder."

Tsosie's eyes ignited at the comment. He motioned at the entrance, telling his security: "Get him out."

The three security guards pushed Stew through the sports bar entrance toward a ramp leading through the casino floor. Kyle kept pace unmolested. The ramp came down by a large grouping of slot machines. Kyle's eyes hit the two cashiers in the cage managing a change cart with a ring of keys. No camera was on the main threshold, a security blind spot. They pushed Stew past the high dollar amount machines, then between the tables for poker, blackjack and roulette.

The camera lens were pulled back, not zooming in as Stew went past. Faces of cashier cage managers and playing dealers offered confused looks as security moved through. Kyle noted the regular casino security using their walkie talkies, trying to understand the situation. *There's a communication breakdown between the regular crew and Tsosie's men.* The group headed through the back of the casino past the auditorium that Kyle had visited last year when Dean Shockley was in the body building competition. The group pushed Stew forward, his chest and face crashing into the glass doors as they opened, leading to the parking lot.

The parking lot was empty as the group shuffled out of the casino. The cool air attacked Kyle as he kept pace. The security team released Stew, throwing him onto the asphalt in a heap. Stew went face-first into the ground, but bounced up to receive

a fist across the jaw by one of the security guards as he turned
to face them. Stew had a history with jaw injuries. *Spent three
months with his mouth wired shut after some asshole clocked him
with brass knuckles at The Blacklight last year.* The other security
members drew their sidearms, aiming at Stew's chest. Kyle
held up his hands, backed off. *Dear god, they're going to kill him
because of an insult.*

Tsosie emerged from the casino, moving behind his security.
The native man smug, winked at Kyle, then frowned at Stew and
offered a swift stomach kick. Stew grunted, collapsing. Tsosie
backed off, anticipating Stew to charge. *Stay down, man. Let it
go and stay down.* Stew remained on the ground as the security
members held their pistols, ready to fire. Tsosie leaning in on
Stew, eying him.

"My people fought hard for what we have here," Tsosie said.

Tsosie spat on Stew. Kyle watched the white blob remain
unharmed on Stew's face while Tsosie and his crew backed off
and returned to the casino. Kyle wiped the slop off of Stew's face
and offered a hand but the big man had none of it, fighting Kyle to
stand on his feet. Stew held his jaw, spitting a gob of blood onto
the ground, smiling.

"Cashier's cage on the main floor had the vault open," Stew
said. "Means the lady has the combo to get inside."

Kyle: "You jam a shotgun in there, between the bars, do the place in five."

"Try two," Stew said. "Tsosie's boys don't show unless he does."

"Yeah, they are private reserved. The regular staff didn't know what was going down."

Stew smiled. "Let's approach the other boys, see who wants in. Maybe get ourselves a little payback for tonight."

Kyle got a sinking feeling in his stomach. *I'm back in a game I don't want to play.* He was back to being that fat kid who had nothing and needed a friend. *How does Stew do that? Gets me to commit to shit I don't want to do.* He wondered if he would always owe Stew in some way. That he would always do what Stew wanted because of the alternative life he could have had. *Being some fat virgin handing out tickets in an airport parking lot ain't no life, man.* But Kyle wasn't sure holding up a casino was a life either.

FBI Field Agent Sam Brown was back on detail, sitting in a beat-up blue sedan with faded interior and a hole where the satellite radio used to be. Parked off the main strip in the low-end of the Spokane Valley, the sedan belched tan fumes from a broken muffler, idling. Back to days when his coffee was stale, the nights long. *When I had all those youthful expectations before I learned I didn't know anything.* He fought the numbness of staying in for the past five years when every lie by a suspect had been offered, every memo from the executive level counter-productive. The few days since Earl Weaver's death had been difficult but not as much as the bureaucratic nightmare which followed.

The situation with Chase Bannister should have been avoidable. *Right in front of me, I couldn't stop it from happening.* The images played in his head since, hindering sleep. *Saw his brown eyes become orbs with his face red, charging at us.* He questioned his interview skills, whether he had been too cocky. *Going in some room and talking smack to a juicer after a street fight. After what he did to that kid's skull, squeezing it like a melon?* The full-on craziness of the man's screams haunted Sam. It changed the entire case from a mosque attack, becoming an investigation into why Weaver was murdered.

Weaver was a dick who clashed with anyone while trying

to move up. Agents who did not steer clear of him, doubting Weaver's networking abilities, got washed out. Weaver was a head hunter no one tried to piss off. *He was one of the brass and things like murder don't happen to one of them.* Weaver moved through a few agencies trying to go higher without showing results. Those issues died with him, though. Once an agent went down in the line of duty, everyone treated Weaver as a fallen hero.

Sam adjusted his rearview while the sedan coughed out black exhaust, the engine rattling. A passing vehicle's headlights offered Sam his reflection. A bruised, bandaged face with a long cut over his left eye, held by twelve stitches. *Weaver gets killed, I get a nurse sewing me up.* Bannister had crashed that table leg through Weaver with enough force to imbed into the concrete wall. Took a crew of six workers three hours to unmount Weaver from the wall.

The gravel parking lot held various divots and puddles where the clay had sunken tire tracks deep beyond the surface. The meeting had been a quick set-up after Weaver's death. Agency group troopers were small on cooperation except that the top levels of the agency were upset. Now the agencies shared information Sam would have never discovered on his own. The Drug Enforcement Agency's information regarding the chemical known as Andro-Phosphate-Polimal that medical circles called A.P.P. The street names included Fireball, Pink Cadillac, Nuke, and Cherry Popper.

The D.E.A. provided small cases to Sam. A Delaware high school kid had used it to gain fifty pounds of muscle mass and garnered thirty-two Division I football scholarships for his play at defensive end, but died on the football field during homecoming of an A.P.P.-related seizure. Or the man who used A.P.P. as an alternative to cancer treatment, passing at least three doctor's exams saying he was cancer-free, then took a restaurant hostage with a semi-automatic. The scope had been limited until a local dealer synthesized the drug for mass production.

The D.E.A. had been working on the local A.P.P. operation case for two years. The agency claimed that an agent was lost during the undercover operation, but that they still had a contact on the inside. Sam was meeting with the contact after both the D.E.A. District Commander and the Drug Czar met with him about ending red tape. The brass wanted to put down whatever drug had helped make Chase Bannister into a madman. *A drug that makes a body builder slice his wrists and chew off his tongue in ritualistic suicide has every law enforcement agency nervous.* What happened with Darren Wright showed what a person on A.P.P. could do as well.

Darren Wright had been in surgery for sixteen hours. He woke up while his head was being stitched up by two nurses, the doctors declaring him brain dead after bone fragments from his cheek shot up into his skull. Wright decided to wake up in surgery, killing the two nurses and three security guards while wearing a hospital gown revealing his bare ass. *Man was a tank the same way Chase Bannister was.* They did their thing, raged on and destroyed anything in their path.

The back door of the sedan was opened, Peter Volov slid into the seat. Sam pulled the sedan away as the door slammed shut. His eyes forward on the road to keep anyone from assuming there was a passenger with him. Peter hid underneath the brim of the back windows. The low shadows gave him cover from passing cars in the next lane. Sam caught himself before he made a slight turn to talk, correcting his eyes so that they kept focused on the road.

"I hear you can help me," Sam said.

"Depends on what you do for me," Peter said. His accent sounded Russian, but light. *Americanized.*

Sam said, "The D.E.A. thinks so."

"Pigs and liars, I care nothing for them," Peter said. "They left me to die."

"How long you been in?"

"Sixteen months," Peter said. "I was recruited to help introduce an agent into the operation. Supposed to be a quick job and keep me from prison."

"What happened to the agent?"

Peter said, "They discovered him, put him in basement, high on that Pink Cadillac."

"And the D.E.A. left him there?"

"They did not believe me that he was there," Peter said. "The Serg's operation is hard to break into, so they said I could stay until I had proof of agent's whereabouts or I could walk."

"And why didn't you walk?"

"Where would I go?" Peter said. "I go anywhere, they find me. Only way out is to get agent from there. I saw the signal yesterday on the flowers by the road. Haven't seen that in seven months and thought I was left for dead."

"What do you have for me?"

Peter paused, then said, "Man named Turk keeps coming by, a new guy who sits around, drinks beer with The Serg. Old friends."

Sam smiled. "Turk Goyer. He's robbed a few in his time, half the jobs we suspect more than know. Keep listening to see if they are pulling a job soon." Sam made a turn off Division and headed onto Sharp. "What do you need from me?"

Peter slipped a folder to the front seat. "Make one of The Serg's men, Vitali, a paid informant."

"You want this leaked back to The Serg, help you go up the ranks."

"He controls the stash house, they will need someone to take his place after he is dismissed."

"How many guys is The Serg supplying with this A.P.P. shit?"

"Pink Cadillac?" Peter said. "Ten or fifteen. Serg uses them as enforcers for his operation or fighters down in the pits. They have a rage in them."

"Chase Bannister," Sam said. "Still looking for his pal, Darren Wright."

Peter laughed. "Stop looking. He was given to Brother Zachariah to stop violence."

"The Serg offers up his muscle boys as anyone else, huh?"

Peter shrugged. "Everyone to The Serg is a dog. But if you burn him, he will hunt you down, hold that grudge until he does. That is why I do not leave. Until he is in prison or dead, he would come find me."

"Okay, I will do the set-up on Vitali," Sam said. "If you need to get in contact with me, there is a business card on the seat next to you."

Peter showed the business card. "I will try to get Anthony out if possible."

"He's the only way you get a new identity for all of this, means you have to stay in until the job is done, sorry," Sam said.

Sam pulled the sedan over by an alley. Peter got out and disappeared into the shadows. Sam didn't attempt to watch him leave. He pulled the sedan away and merged into traffic. He eyed the folder in the front seat, ready to do his part. *If Peter's plan doesn't work, I'm going to be sitting here three months from now, nowhere on the case.*

10 The Blacklight club's life as a city hotspot ended after three months. A year had passed since its owner Sully Brooks was murdered in a senseless hit and run on the city streets, amid a drunk and his wife shooting up the club on Ash Wednesday. Brooks' body was left unclaimed at the city morgue, cut up by a university's medical students in the name of research. His establishment was a usual suspect of bullet fire, drug busts, and gang fights which created an atmosphere that the city's underworld thrived on. None of the locals stood in its lines anymore and waited to do anything to get inside. Even a former Academy Award winning actor directed his posse elsewhere in the city for their womanizing, drunken binges.

Dean Shockley had done bouncer work at the Blacklight for six months and figured the extra income helped keep his gym surviving when luxuries such as personal fitness soured with the bad economy. The moonlight money earned from the Blacklight grew less as a new club called Siam became the city's newest sensation. Siam had held off the vomit barn, boom-boom room mentality where the pours were long, the knives drawn quick. The Blacklight's alleyway increased commerce when the club started to fail; coke and meth deals went down outside as a constant.

Dean stood in the alley's shadows to beat off dealers and was heading back inside the club when Blye came to him. Blye had assumed operation responsibilities through attrition. He wore a Dallas Cowboys jersey which was tight at the seams because of his mass. Blye's left eye was permanently damaged from the drunk who busted up the club on Ash Wednesday. *Man came up with brass knuckles. Who still does that shit?* Blye turned his face so his right eye faced whoever he was talking to.

"Club's dead again," Blye said.

"It ain't like it used to be," Dean said.

Blye: "Gotta cut hours and you being the new guy, you get it first. Ain't fair but life ain't."

"I respect that," Dean said. "When you sending me home?"

"Right now."

Dean took Blye's out-stretched hand and shook it, smiling. They headed into the club, where bass pounded over an empty floor with club lights shining on no one. A few regulars attended The Blacklight over nostalgia. *How the owners haven't walked out on their lease and left the club shuttered by now is beyond me.* Dean eyed a former gangsta, Baron Gamble, sitting in a booth sulking over his drink without an entourage. Still mourning the loss of his friend, Junior. The gangster pulled his hat lower over his eyes with his hands resting in his lap.

Dean grabbed his windbreaker from underneath the bar counter and felt a woman's hands fold onto his arms. The touch was good enough that Dean smiled and watched his reflection in the bar's mirror. Diane Patterson was The Blacklight's remaining waitress from the good times. *Said she went with Sully Brooks back when he was alive, claimed he was taking her away from all of this.* Dean noted the wedding ring she wore that appeared to matter little to her. Diane went with a lot of guys including Dean. *She prefers men with big arms.* Diane's husband was off fighting alongside Uncle Sam over there while she gave a fist-bump to Tiger Woods on the home front.

"I'm off," Dean said. "You want to go with me?"

Diane shook her head, unhappy. "Can't, baby. Shift ends in five hours and I need the cash."

"Brenda doesn't pass her tips on to you, does she?"

"Blye said she didn't have to."

"That's bullshit."

The food industry's unwritten rule was that wait staff tipped back a bartender twenty percent from alcohol. *Brenda is above the law cause she is going with Blye.* She rubbed up against Dean once or twice to get her underage friends into the club. The enforcement by Spokane's finest died along with the crowds at The Blacklight. Diane kissed his right bicep, pulling away to pour him a shot of Dry Fly vodka. He downed it quick, letting the burn roll down his throat to settle his stomach. *You're still in off-season training right? Gonna beat Ulysses Turner no matter what, right?* He questioned that and wondered if he should quit. *Daddy can't take much more heartache from what I do to him.*

Daddy had neglected to return any of the five phone calls from Dean since the competition. *He needs time to himself to recover from what I've put him through. He wants a champion, not a runner-up.* Every call Dean made ended with him apologizing on his father's voicemail for what Dean had failed to do at the competition. *Because Daddy deserves to know he raised a winner.* Diane poured another Dry Fly shot that Dean contemplated drinking. *Alcohol isn't good for my training if I want to win this thing.* Dean winked at Diane, grabbing the shot to go down his hatch. Stew came from behind, and clutched Dean's wrist, preventing the drink from hitting his mouth.

"Hey," Stew said. "You're in training, remember?"

Dean's shrug drew a swift reaction from Stew, who frowned. The man's shaven head and large physique made him a natural specimen for body building. *I sit in my office sometimes and marvel at how massive he could get if he tried.* Stew's jaw clicked when he spoke, a remnant of the drunk with the brass knuckles. *How the hell did one guy do so much damage?* Stew appeared hesitant to approach patrons, worried they would offer a similar nasty surprise as the drunk. Stew yanked the shot of Dry Fly from Dean's hand and downed it, offering a shit-eating grin.

Stew: "You gotta stop trying to impress that asshole. Or get too down when you don't."

"Don't talk about him like that."

"My old man never hit me, but he was raised military," Stew said. "Gave me a dressing down each day that made me wish he would hit me. The shit you're going through, it ain't no different except that you don't see past his bullshit."

Dean stood straight and leaned in, eying his friend. It was the closest Stew had ever gotten to criticizing Daddy. *And I don't like it, not one bit.* Stew needed to realize how much Daddy meant to Dean. *How I need him to win this thing. I want to make him proud.* Stew moved back a step which caused Dean to relax but continue to stare. *No one should be able to criticize my father. Not even me.* At least Daddy didn't have to see it this time.

Two weeks prior to the competition, Daddy had been training Dean in the gym. There were exercises that Dean knew wouldn't work, but he wanted to show Daddy he could do them. *What did it hurt as long as my father was happy?* Daddy had been there with him, pointing out the flaws so he could correct them. *And Daddy finally cared about me.* Then Kyle stepped in and made

some remark. *Saying Daddy knew shit about weight-training.*
Got Daddy all heated and stormed out of the gym, Dean worried
he wouldn't see Daddy again. *Until I went to his house and
apologized to Daddy for what Kyle had said. Told him I would ban
Kyle from the gym if it ever happened again.*

"Turner's damn unbeatable," Dean said. "He crushed everyone
in that pose-down. Ripped it like a freak up there."

"Rivers End competition is three months out," Stew said. "Last
of the season, and you can do it if you train now."

"Thing's ain't equal," Dean said. "Turner let me in, says he's
using."

Stew's brow lifted. "Ain't pissed no positive. I was in his
grouping and would have seen something. Damn sure he ain't
found a way to beat it."

"Turner says he did, said it was called Fireball or some shit.
Told me he started using three back."

"You want to go down this road?" Stew said. "You piss a
positive, you lose everything."

Dean shrugged. "Haven't I already? All I got is a third place
trophy and a bunch of handshakes for being a good sport about
it. Turner's doing it, not getting caught. I want to see what's going
on."

"Are you serious about this?"

"If he's got an edge, I want it too. Aren't we already losing by not doing it?" Dean said. "All I'm saying is that third place is worse than pissing a positive."

Stew paused, thinking, then nodded. "Long as everyone goes all in. No one backs down when we take a needle, so if any of us piss positive, we all knew the risks."

"Let's talk to Blye and Kyle, see what they have to say."

Stew paused again, holding Dean's arm, staring at him as the big man probed his thoughts. "Are you sure about this?"

"Sure as anything."

Tony Hell tasted the darkness in the air with his lids closed. A fury charged through him as a flash lit up the night. A needle pierced his arm, slicing into his vein where it pushed a toxin that burned as he breathed through his nostrils. His heart pounded as thunder rode his arm to his shoulder. His breathing increased as pure energy bolted into his chest down his spine. His lids raised and the world came to him. *I am the destroyer of men.*

11

His room was crowded. Mikhail smirking in the corner shadows with eyes hid by dark amid the lone bulb that hung from a chain at the center of the room. Doctor Xhang stood at the door with a cigarette burning at the bend of his mouth, squinted eyes watering from the smoke. Fedor and Oleg stood guard gripping cattle prods. His room dank with water seeping from concrete slabs, bugs escaping out of cracks from nests. The music beat thumped bass from upstairs.

They keep you as a pet rat, Mikhail said.

"Shut up," Tony said in Russian.

They betrayed us, Mikhail said.

Tony moved his muscles to the bass rhythm and felt the rub of his chains that held him to the floor. Xhang spoke Chinese to Oleg and Fedor as they moved back. *Telling them not to be cowards, that two men can take one.* The fear was instinctive after the two

Russian goons had witnessed how capable Tony was in the ring. He cracked a smile and glared at Fedor, waiting to devour his eyes. Much time had passed since Tony and Mikhail had entered the ring. The past meant nothing but fragmented memories.

They held us down and put the fuel into us, Mikhail said. *Do you remember?*

"*Of course I remember*," Tony said, lying. His memory shallow, the last fight was recalled but little else prior.

You are a caged animal, Mikhail said.

"Someone had to keep us safe from the darkness," Tony said.

The two Russian men said nothing, nor Xhang. Mikhail was a critic who did not take the lashes or fights that Tony endured. *He is too weak to face them*. Tony wished Mikhail would be punished. *He is the one who betrayed The Serg. He is the reason we are down here as rats.*

"I am not a weak man," Tony said.

He spat at his brother, unimpeded by Fedor or Oleg. *They know better than to mess with siblings*. Mikhail sat on his stump and let the saliva hang off his brow. *Because he is weak and cannot fight for our survival as I do*. The thunder quaked in Tony's chest after churning through his torso, his legs and back. *I will destroy whatever The Serg brings me.*

You want their love when they want you to be destroyed, Mikhail said.

Tony ignored Mikhail and eyed a cracked mirror mounted on the concrete wall, brushing away the dirt. His reflection offered back a facial tattoo of a flaming skull. He lowered his head to rub his shaven scalp. His nude body did not offend him or the opposing fighters. He rubbed off the last beads of sweat and heart from his legs and torso while the club music's bass continued to beat. He laughed at Mikhail.

"You have none of these marks," Tony said. "No scars or ink to show you fight. You are nothing but a peasant's son."

Mikhail smiled. *Your delusion carries you far, dear brother.*

Tony beat his fists against his chest, glaring at Mikhail. "I fight with honor. You are a coward who refuses to fight with me despite sharing my bed and food."

Mikhail shrugged. *I survive regardless of my abilities.*

"Spoken as a coward would," Tony said.

Tony spied the reflection of his chest. The tattoo of the kremlin holding sixteen steeples laid ink across his skin. *Steeples representing time served in the room, each life sentences.* Mikhail bore no tattoos or markings. Tony turned his back sideways to see the reflection of several cats to illustrate the gang of thieves he belonged to. Words inked in Russian: *Prison is the Home of the*

Thief. He spat on Mikhail again.

"You betrayed us to The Serg and forced us into this room," Tony said.

Is that what you think? Mikhail said, laughing.

Tony eyed Fedor and Oleg. He gestured to Mikhail. "Put him out in my place. Let us see how long he stays alive."

The pair said nothing in response. *I have made similar offers only to see them exchange confused looks. They are idiots.* Tony grinned, falsely lunging at them. Both fell back off of their feet, stumbling toward the door. Xhang stood firm, calling them cowards. Oleg rose, aiming his cattle prod. The Russian glared at Tony, zapping him once in the torso for the prank. Tony shook from the electric shock but kept his eyes on Oleg while standing firm. Oleg pulled the cattle prod back, the smell of burnt flesh hung in the room. *I will kill him and devour his eyes.* Tony prepped to lunge at Oleg a second time when the room's metal door opened. The Serg entered, smiling.

"Come, Tony," The Serg said, in Russian. "It is time for you to destroy another man."

The glint of excitement filled Tony as he laughed, bouncing on his feet. His pupils dilated as the fuel smashed into his skull. Xhang yelled at Oleg and Fedor, saying in Chinese for them to remove Tony's bonds. The two men did with caution. He heard the clink of the bracelets breathe, the metal against his skin vanish. Tony moved his feet as blood circulation came back with numbness wearing off. Tony stopped moving and growled as a hound. The Serg stood in front of him and patted his cheek. The old Russian pulled out a small box from his coat pocket, opening the box to display a jellied human eyeball.

"A tribute before another victory," The Serg said.

You are no different than an animal, Mikhail said.

He ignored his brother's comment while snatching the eyeball and devouring it whole. His heart beat in fine rhythm as the pulsing eye fluid went through his veins. It transformed into liquid heat which rested in his stomach's pit and energized him. Tony closed his lids to fall into darkness as a man to be feared. Skin made of leather and the ability to murder five men at once. The room's occupants were moved into silence except for Mikhail whose breathing could be heard. *My brother finds ways to haunt me.*

He raised his lids as The Serg gestured for him to exit his room toward the pit. *Mikhail stays behind as a coward while I fight for both of us.* He passed the threshold of the metal door, eying the slot where Oleg would leave food and water. Tony rested himself against the door and stared through the opening whenever men came. *I listen to conversations to find my escape.* Mikhail refuses and waits to die. Tony gathered information or would have it translated from English to Georgian or Russian. *Always learning about this place where men come to challenge me.*

The pit was surrounded by benches filled with gamblers flashing paper bet slips, smoking cigars, holding plastic cups of booze. They displayed various currency of established and toppled governments while chanting for Tony's entrance into the sand pit. The humid pulse of people caused the temperature to rise by ten degrees. Mikhail sat with his back to the action to continue as a coward.

Tony returned his eyes to the crowd which held behind rotting wooden panels. Fat, pungent men glorified their lives through his success. The club basement was hot, thick and tense. Tony set eyes on four men standing to the side and caught their muscular frames. Their arms were folded across their chests, confident and impatient. *This is my challenge tonight.* Tony took a step toward the four men which sent the crowd moving a step back. The Serg snapped his fingers in front of Tony's face to gain his attention.

"They are audience," The Serg said.

His eyes went from the four muscular men to his challenger who stepped into the pit. A young man who Tony felt Mikhail could fight fair. *But I am not Mikhail.* Tony grinned as the challenger flexed small muscle tone to enliven gamblers. The crowd reacted poor to his cocky theatrics. The Serg gestured to the challenger, then to Tony. *I will harm his soul and destroy him.* Power coursed through Tony's system and slowed time. He noted beads of sweat hanging in the air as the young fighter shook his wet hair out. Tony's pupils dilated with excitement as he charged, leaping on the challenger's chest.

The crowd erupted with cheers as Tony tore his fingers deep into the challenger's flesh, latching in as the young man screamed. Tony delivered a series of blows to the man's face in quick succession causing him to wobble as he was released. Tony eyed him as he stumbled on his feet, unleashing a primal scream while beating his fists on his chest. His deafening cry silenced the crowd. *The Serg taught me to do that, to draw the gamblers in.*

The Serg requested Tony stretch-out fights in the pit regardless of his opponent. *Said the crowd wants to believe in you, but it hates clear winners.* He told Tony that the country roots against domination and enjoys underdogs who win despite the odds. The young challenger rose with a bloodied face, parts smashed in developing deep bruises. He spat out yellow shards of teeth mixed with blood and vomit. He offered a stare at Tony that made him excited to destroy the young man, but he resisted the urge. The challenger charged him, striking several times in the chest with his small fists. Tony fell into the pit, allowing the attack while the crowd burst into cheers.

The gamblers bet more on the underdog challenger who hit Tony with horrid soft shots that made the crowd cheer louder. The young man pounced onto Tony's chest while pounding away. Tony's eyes went from the challenger to the four muscular men standing in the crowd. He caught them appearing disgusted by his performance. *They think of me as a fool fighting this way*. He eyed the challenger while fending off two more soft blows by the young man who screamed that Tony was his bitch. *You think of me as a fool too*.

Tony fired his fist into the young man's throat which caused him to gasp for air. The challenger fell off of Tony while his eyes bulged. The crowd silenced by the attack in shock. Tony stumbled to his feet, emitting out a mix of blood and snot from his nostril. His tongue navigated his teeth to find none loose enough to yank out. The challenger coughed, choking as he rose up with eyes red. The young man offered a weak swing. The fuel's power allowed Tony to catch the challenger's fist mid-air and hold it. Tony snapped the challenger's arm down, breaking it over his knee. The young fighter squealed in pain.

Tony's eyes went to The Serg as the old Russian returned a nod of approval. Tony finished off the challenger, knocking him with a knee onto the ground, then pouncing on his chest. Tony's fingers gouged the young man's flesh. He smashed his head into the challenger's left shoulder, hearing the bone sever. The gamblers became a morgue of men who tore slips apart for betting against Tony Hell. The pieces of paper floated around Tony as he struck the challenger until the man's nose and mouth bled. Tony wanted to collect his tribute.

He brought the challenger's head up to him, staring into his eyes. They were beginning to yellow as death crept. Excitement coursed through Tony's veins as he licked his lips. Tony dove his fingers deep around the man's right eye socket. His fingers touched behind the eyeball, closing before he yanked away the delicious plunder. The young man screamed as the cord snapped. Tony consumed the eyeball, drinking its meaty cord. He ignored the collective groan from the gambling audience.

"He's a goddamn animal."

He searched the room for the source of the comment. The crowd beyond the pit tightened with fear at the expectation of what Tony might do. He examined the room and cut through the throng of spectators who knew better than to offer such a remark. His gaze fell upon the four muscular men who stood watching. Tony released the challenger who draped the ground in shock and shook. He vomited, dying. Tony focused on the four muscular men and hissed, unleashing a deafening scream.

The fuel raged in his stomach and overtook him with a primal intensity. *Devour their flesh while they scream. I am a powerful god who can destroy anyone.* Tony put out a step toward the four men. The crowd edged back. Tony smiled, taking another step while emitting a hound's growl as his eyes bore down on his targets. He flexed his arms ready to feed on their souls. He ignored the shouts from The Serg ordering him to stop. The Serg then yelled at Oleg and Fedor.

The two Russian goons closed in on Tony while screaming in broken English, wielding cattle prods. They had used these before to subdue him. Oleg's prod zapped a bolt less than a foot from Tony who turned and smiled a mouthful of blood at his adversary. Oleg backed away as Tony returned his focus on the four muscular men who stood silent and waited for him to approach. Another step closer meant Fedor came to Tony on the opposite side. Tony snatched Fedor's cattle prod away without looking and grabbed him into a headlock, squeezing off the man's air while staring at the four men. *Let them look at the domination I have waiting for them.* Fedor struggled to free himself without success.

He spat a gob of blood and eyeball fluid at their feet which caused the men to back toward the exit. Tony stepped forward while holding onto Fedor and drooling blood. Oleg screamed and charged Tony from behind, slamming the butt of the cattle prod into Tony's back. A surge of pain bit into Tony. He focused on Oleg, while holding onto Fedor, and missed Xhang as the doctor moved in with a syringe gun. Three shots from the blue vials were fired into Tony's neck. His body numbed, his grip limp, releasing Fedor.

He crashed in the pit as Oleg and Fedor zapped him with the cattle prods. Tony's lids closed into black as a quiet state cloaked his vision. He laid motionless on the ground, his ears picking up gamblers complaints and grumbles while milling about. The dense cigar smoke and sand did not hide the blood and vomit the challenger had left when they removed his body. His mind offered a faded image that he detested but it played regardless. *I am watching a woman blowing out candles on a cake, she is smiling at me.* The darkness returned, Tony confused by it. *I want to smash her face in.* Then, he decided that he didn't with an answer why.

Hands clutched his arms and legs without the ability to fend them off. He felt his body lifted from the sand pit and the air chill his chest. Tony's toes scraped the floor as he was dragged from the pit to his room. His mind displayed foreign images. *I am touching the woman's face as she cries, saying I love her.* Tony's mind attempted to answer his confusion but concluded minus results. He was dropped onto his stomach on the dank floor of his room where his lids remained closed. He heard Xhang talking Chinese, saying he would give Tony some fuel to revive. Another strange image played for him. *I am making love to a woman, gently*. Tony felt the sting of the syringe gun into his neck. The images of the woman watered away as the thunder rode down his body and Tony forgot them. He sulked in regret, wanting to know who the woman was that he loved. The metal door was slammed shut with the locking mechanisms bolted. Mikhail sat in his corner, breathing heavy.

She is no one, Mikhail said. *And if she was someone, she is no longer anyone who knows the beast you've become.*

Tony tried to scream at his brother for silence but could not move the muscles in his mouth. Drool and blood exited in a pool as he laid on the side of his face sucking in the floor's dank water. Mikhail is a coward who judges me but never fights for his survival. He leaves that to me, then mocks my efforts. A twinge in his fingers signaled rebirth. They curled, then his toes. The electrical charge from the cattle prods flushed from his system and was replaced by the fuel. A sound of thunder crashed through his veins as his senses enhanced.

They have made you into a junkie, Mikhail said.

The sound of random footsteps down the basement staircase

overtook the club's bass. The chatter came in lost voices speaking rapid English. Tony's lips moved as the taste of oil washed in his mouth from the floor. Water plopped down from the ceiling's pipes, pooling near his head. He kept his lids closed as he focused on hearing the shuffle of bodies in the next room as they exited up into the club. The weight of feet stomping down on decayed wooden steps was replaced by Oleg speaking to The Serg. *Said some people have asked for him, say a man named Turner told them about the fuel.*

Tony opened his lids and lifted himself off the ground. *That fuel is mine.* He struggled against the ache from the cattle prods and moved toward the metal door. He peered through the open slot, leaning against the door. His vision blurred, separated, then focused on the four muscular men. *The Serg will tell them that the fuel is not for sale. It is mine to be offered as a tribute.* They stood in the pit while Oleg spoke to The Serg in Russian.

"Turner sent them here?" The Serg said to Oleg.

Oleg saying to The Serg that Turner buys a forty milligram vial per day.

"He repays us with new customers," The Serg said, nodding.

They are taking your fuel from you, Mikhail said. *And telling others it is for sale.*

Tony hated Turner. The dark muscular god had entered the pit against Tony. *But only when they offer me the blue vials and I must fight without the fuel.* Turner beat him down in three fights. *He won my tribute by cheating me.* Tony glared at The Serg, hating him then. *He sells my fuel to whomever comes and asks for it. I need it in order to survive.* Tony spied the room, examining each of the four muscular men who stood waiting for The Serg's sale to continue.

Mikhail said, *soon they will ask to fight you in the ring, dear brother. What will you do when Xhang offers you blue vials instead of pink fuel?*

One of the four muscular men spoke to The Serg, saying that he wanted to know how much for what Turner was getting. The man had wavy hair, was shorter than the others. *Said his name was Dean, he thought I was an animal.* The Serg saying back, actually Tony is a bear.

Anger fueled him as the rage bore through his eyes. Tony licked his lips at the sight of Dean's pupils, wanting to choke them down, consume them whole. *I will feel their power when they settle in my stomach.* Tony eyed The Serg and questioned whether Dean would fight him fair. *Will they drug me to allow this fool to steal my tribute?* Tony grabbed the vent and twisted against it, unable to move it. He wanted to tear it off, toss it aside and crush Dean where he stood. Then destroy The Serg for his disloyalty.

Oleg handed The Serg a small crate of pink vials. *The Serg is giving away my fuel to these men who insult me.* Tony's anger built as Dean handed over currency in exchange. He shook at the door as if to tear it off with his teeth clenched, his mouth drooling foam that rolled onto his chin. Large saliva splats landed on the floor around his feet. Oleg moved to the door and pushed in the head of the cattle prod, zapping Tony until he released the door. The Russian goon laughed, begging Tony to come closer so he could do it again.

Mikhail said, *it is not the first time they betrayed us, dear brother. It is only the first time that you recognize that they have done so.*

Tony turned to Mikhail. "Shut up."

He collapsed onto his bed, contemplating revenge. *Everyone has betrayed me.* Tony eyed Mikhail who mocked in the corner shadows of the room while on his stump. *I will destroy you, my brother. You have not protected me anymore than The Serg has. For that, you will* pay. His mind went to the fuel and he was jealous of its distribution to anyone but him. *It is mine and I will do anything to protect it.*

12

"It's worse than I thought."

Rivers End GM Scott Tsosie eyed his hotel's largest luxury suite, a design he had personally overseen with some of the world's best architects and interior designers. Paintings valued at two million dollars were mounted on the walls. Tsosie had turned down the Philadelphia Museum of Art's request to loan the paintings for exhibition. The custom-made furniture in the suite cost four hundred thousand. The suite itself was saved for premiere Rivers End clients. It now resembled a disaster area.

The sofa cushions slashed were valued at twenty thousand dollars. The high-end plasmas had their screens kicked in. Water flowed on the expensive white carpet from a damaged private kitchen after its pipes were ripped out. Had guests on the floor below the suite not complained of dripping water from the ceiling, the damage might have gone unnoticed until check-out.

Scott's eyes fell to celebrity director Nicholas Van Meter who appeared unconcerned as he pouted on a destroyed couch with his hand resting on his jock. A shirtless mess, hair tangled, the man behind the cult film *Two Men, Two Guns* sighed at Scott's arrival. Van Meter sprawl across the torn couch with his eyes on a fractured plasma television. The visionary creative genius behind the summer blockbuster *Explosion City* glanced at Scott as if he were room service.

"Get out," Van Meter said.

He hurled his bottle of Jim Beam at Scott's head. Scott ducked into the hallway as he saw the bottle coming, closed his lids. The glass bottle shattered against the wall next to the door, spraying glass shards and booze. Scott opened his lids upon impact and turned to his head of security, Colonel George Civil-Fielder. The Brit stood prepared with his hand on his sidearm underneath his suit, offering Scott a questioning look as to how much force he should apply. Scott shook his head as Van Meter's manager Ryan Gonnath marched out of the elevator toward the suite. Gonnath's finger wagged at Scott as if he was at fault for the suite's destruction.

"Mister Tsosie, we had an arrangement," Gonnath said. "Disturbing Nick during his break is in violation of the contract we signed."

Scott gestured to the suite. "His break ends now. Ten minutes, he's out. Understood?"

"We have a deal," Gonnath said. "His image for casino advertising purposes for two full months of your luxury suite while he scouts locations for his next film. What part of this don't you understand?"

Scott grinned at Gonnath. *Brian Locklear made the deal with you, not me.* Scott enjoyed celebrities in his hotel but Van Meter's reputation as a carnal pillager had floated through the back channels of the hotel industry. Most inn keepers Scott had met refused to extend pleasantries to Van Meter. *Brian forced me to sign the contract after I told him what would happen here.* Scott had attempted to make Locklear happy. *Enough to keep him off my back after the meeting with Allen Nez and the Caha Tribe went sour.* Scott noticed the water on the carpet flowing from the suite into the hallway.

"This is unacceptable," Scott said, pointing to the water. "Ninety-eight percent capacity for our hotel and I might have to shut down the entire floor below you to play caretaker to some drunk fool."

"No, that is unacceptable," Van Meter said, his voice carrying from inside the room.

Scott heard another crunch as something was thrown against the wall. It was a plasma screen imbedded in the drywall with its cord plugged in, showing a news anchor's face, talking about the Middle East. Scott's eyes went to the Colonel who touched his sidearm again. Scott shook his head. *I don't want to kill anyone for this bullshit.*

Scott to Civil-Fielder: "Line everyone up in the suite, including Van Meter."

Civil-Fielder had lined the Van Meter entourage in the suite's living room in less than two minutes. Scott smiled as the group stood in water. He eyed twin eighteen-year-old girls emaciated to seventy pounds by coke and alcohol who rubbed at their noses while attempting to flirt with him. Scott guessed the balding guy with a rotund belly standing next to them was a drug dealer. He gestured to Civil-Fielder, receiving a nod. The man would be flagged by security, banned from the Rivers End for life, after he was tossed out of the hotel. Casino staff rushed into the suite, shutting off the water from the torn-out pipes. That coupled with an overflowing toilet jammed with three full rolls of tissue had caused the water that the entourage stood in. *I'm in control of the Rivers End, not Locklear or Van Meter.*

Nicholas Van Meter stood defiant, his arms draping the twins while offering Scott a cocky grin. *He's ready for a fight, thinking I can be pushed around.* The auteur director who had been an Academy Award for Best Screenplay nominee for penning the Viet Nam classic *Napalm Charlie* stuck out his tongue at Scott, then winked, grabbing his crotch while spitting at his feet. *He thinks he is above the law.* Scott turned to Gonnath who stood near, shaking his head at Van Meter. *Even he's sick of it.*

"He goes into a small suite while I get this mess repaired," Scott said. "His friends are not part of the contact so they are being escorted from the premises to go back to wherever the hell they came from."

"No," Van Meter said. "They stay put."

Van Meter moved to Scott and leaned in. He huffed out a dank odor of narcotics, booze. It offended Scott's nostrils. Van Meter grinned, putting his finger into Scott's abdomen. *He's touching my scar, same as the body builder from a few nights ago.* Scott grunted as Van Meter's finger pressed against him.

"You don't call the shots around here," Van Meter said. "I do."

A flashback of the old Rivers End operation cloaked Scott's thoughts. The image played in his head, him at the roulette wheel, greeting a few customers. Then he turned around, the white man leaning in with his knife, plunging it in deep. *I heard my heart beat in my ears and thought I was dying.* He remembered holding up his hand and seeing the blood. *Seeing everyone stare at me and Brian looking at me, scared to tell me what was happening.* The white man got away into the shadows. *No one knew why he stabbed me or if he was coming back.*

"You're just an asshole," Van Meter said, jamming his finger harder into Scott's wound. "I'm a celebrity. People care what happens to me."

"You're right." His heart beat in his ears, pounding. *Same as before when the other white man attacked me.* Scott examined

Van Meter as the director turned toward his entourage, mocking Scott and laughing. He could feel himself being scared with Nicholas' finger burrowing into his stomach, hurting him. *They think this is funny, that I am a joke.*

"Of course I'm right, Chief," Van Meter said.

Scott's eyes tightened in anger, when he heard *Chief.* He could feel the change come over him. Van Meter was having a show of it, enjoying the moment with his low-end buddies at Scott's expense. He listened to the man's laughter and hated him for it. Scott turned to Civil-Fielder, gesturing to Van Meter.

"Put him in the hall. Just him, and be gentle."

Civil-Fielder smiled, latching onto Van Meter's neck. The director was shocked by the assault and struggled but could not break free. The entourage stayed in place, frightened. Civil-Fielder pushed Van Meter into the hall. Scott heard a minor scuffle then nothing. Civil-Fielder returned to stand at Scott's side. Scott turned to Civil-Fielder, offering a grin.

"We can't hurt a celebrity because of the media exposure," Scott said. "But we can do whatever we want to these hangers-on."

"Orders, sir?" Civil-Fielder said.

"Each one gets their arm broke for this bullshit," Scott said. "Then get them off the premises."

"You can't do that," Gonnath said, protesting.

Scott smiled, cocky, nodding. "I believe... I just did."

He exited the suite as the rest of his security team came inside and descended upon the entourage. Screams and shouts came out of the suite into the hall. He heard bones *snap*, a woman howl in pain. Civil-Fielder follows orders. Scott walked down the hall, spotting Van Meter. The director sat in the hall, crouched while holding his head, pulling his hair, upset by the chorus of the venom his entourage was receiving. Scott got on his haunches in front of Van Meter, pointing.

"Still think I don't call the shots around here, white man," Scott said, he paused eying Van Meter. "Have you got nothing to say to the *Chief*?"

Van Meter offered Scott his eyes, filled with tears. Noise from the suite caused both Scott and Van Meter to focus on the suite. Out of the doorway crawled one of the twins. Bleeding from her skull, she cried with her left arm twisted, broken. She screamed while escaping, but was held at the ankle by one of Scott's security team. The girl dug her nails into the carpet but the security member yanked harder, breaking the nails off as she was dragged back into the suite, kicking, screaming. Van Meter sat frozen, unable to aid her. Scott slapped Van Meter's cheek, lightly, to gain the director's attention. Scott went eye-to-eye with him.

"I let one white man hurt me," Scott said. "And I told myself that

I would never let that happen again."

Scott rose, leaving Van Meter to sob with his head between his knees. The screams continued as the balding man was beaten. Scott entered the elevator and watched Van Meter. The man offered him a look of pity which was not returned. The elevator doors closed and Scott closed his lids. No one messes with this *Chief.* He closed his lids and sat in darkness, listening to the sounds of the music played as he descended the floors to the Rivers End.

Hours after the Van Meter incident, Scott's anger subsided into a new clarity. He received a copy of the contract with the director and respected its formation. The luxury suite would take three days to repair while Van Meter existed as a lone guest in one of the smaller suites, two floors down. While Scott expected to be told of a lawsuit stemming from the actions of his security team, an opposite revelation appeared. Van Meter's personal trainer had contacted Scott, thanking him for eliminating the entourage. The personal trainer had been on vacation after keeping the director from drugs and bad friends. *Said that Nicholas Van Meter would be better for what I had Civil-Fielder do to his crew of low-lifes.*

He was awake in his bed and stared at his reflection in the mirrored ceiling. Keisha Caron, Lance's wife, stirred with his arms around her. She had been a frequent visitor since Lance's visit to rehab. *He left us both for reasons I don't see. After Reggie Barber died, I needed help with the Rivers End, figured I could handle it and was knifed by that white man.* If Lance had been present, the man would have been caught. *I see that white man burying his blade in me and smiling.* Keisha had her own private reasons for infidelity that Scott never asked about.

Keisha snuggled him under satin sheets with her hand moving up from his thigh, to his groin, toward his abdomen. Her fingers touched his scar but did not rest, but he grunted as the piercing pain returned. Scott moved out of bed, letting the sheets slip from his naked body while heading to his bureau. *It hurts bad.* Scott opened the top drawer, removed a bottle of Maker's Mark and thumb-spun the cap off, taking a swig as the burn ran his throat. He closed his eyes, medicating the pain which stayed. Scott shook his head, grabbing a pinch of coke out of a small baggy. *I feel it no matter what the doctors say about it being in my head. It's there.* Scott devoured the cocaine pinch, his throat and belly numbed as the pain eased.

Keisha sat, staring at Scott, saying something about Lance he didn't catch.

"What about him?"

"You have that piano up here for him, don't you?"

Scott shrugged, saying what do you care?

Keisha stretched, yawning. "He stopped being there for me. We're just strangers who share something now."

"You knew who he was when you married him," Scott said. He downed another swig of Maker's Mark, to dull the pain.

"My father offered me money to break it off with him. I didn't realize until years later how honest my parents were with me," Keisha said. "He's worried about me having children with Lance."

"You could stay," Scott said. Keisha's silence offered his answer. "What? You don't love me?"

"He's my husband," she said.

"What does that mean anymore?" Scott said. "Do you love him?"

Keisha shrugged. "He never talks to me anymore."

"And you're just going to stay with him?"

Keisha: "Lance and I are married. That means forever in my book."

"What if he doesn't feel the same way?" he said.

"He doesn't get a choice in the matter," Keisha said. "And in a way, neither do I."

Scott watched Keisha, unsure what to say. He kept his mouth shut. His head charged with coke and booze. *I don't have an answer for you, Keisha. God help me, I wish I did.* Then the pain returned, causing him to grunt again. *She'll never let him go, no matter how much I try to love her.* He reached inside the drawer,

eating another pinch of cocaine to numb it. *I don't know whether*

it's the pain or the woman causing me to hurt this much.

Dean Shockley's heart thumped the second his truck parked in front of Daddy's house. *I have no idea how he will react to me showing up at his door.* Dean examined the perfect house, beset with an assortment of flowers that ran up a concrete step path to the porch. *You've never been invited here because you have shamed him.* Daddy's house sat in the summer's dwindling light and he attempted to remember his childhood home. His father never cared for the upkeep of an old house and sold out. *You cannot keep failing him. It's unacceptable.* Dean hung his head as he thought about his father.

Daddy never tolerated friends, disdainful of entertaining or the affinity for meeting people. *Daddy worries that they will ask him for things, loans in particular.* His father viewed begging for money as an ultimate weakness. *I swear I am not weak.* Dean held back tears that pooled over his pupils. *I have never asked him for anything in my life except to have him be a part of it.* If Dean asked for more, it would be the last time he would see his father. *Isn't that why you are here? To ask him what you should do about Fireball?* Dean was unsure he would want to hear Daddy's answer.

He gripped the steering wheel, the unknown outside his truck. *I want Daddy to see me up there, be proud. For once in his life,*

be proud of his son. Dean was unsure what Fireball did. Ulysses
Turner appeared to have excelled on the stuff. *Said he does his
forty milligrams and looks like that.* Dean shook his head, unsure
he wanted to confess to Daddy what he was prepared to do to
win. *If I do this, it would be for him.* Dean touched the vials given
by The Serg, his thumb rubbing the labels written in Russian.

All Dean wanted was to hear his father shout his praise at
the competition. Saying that's my boy from the crowd and clap,
cheer. Dean wondered if he owed it to himself to take Fireball. *If I
don't win, I hang it up but I gave everything I could to be a winner.*
Dean's eyes fell upon Daddy's house. *There's no going back. Third
place is a long distance between first place and Daddy's heart.*

He exited the truck, heading to the house which loomed over
him without lights burning inside. *This is a mistake, he's not
home.* Dean moved along the concrete step path. *If he's home, he
doesn't want to see the embarrassment you have become.* Dean
stepped up onto the porch. *I miss the house I grew up in, the one
off Ash.* He shook his head to erase the thought. *That's weakness
talking, I have to forget the past.* Dean found himself driving by
his childhood house, parking across the street with a bottle of
Muscle Milk. *Staring for hours at a place owned by people I don't
know.*

Dean tried to remember the happy times on that perfect lawn.

His mother's efforts at the flower garden, his father in the garage with his car hood open. *Before she got sick and Daddy couldn't handle the pain of seeing her that way anymore.* Dean would cry uncontrollably after staring at the house, shake it off and then cry some more. *I would never tell Daddy that. He never respects anyone who doesn't act like a man.*

Dean pushed the doorbell, listening to a chime cascade throughout the house's interior. *Daddy has his reasons for not inviting me here. He's not proud enough of me.* Dean stood there, waiting. *I've shamed him, never been good enough.* His eyes peered into a small window in the door, seeing a light turn on in the foyer. Footsteps came down the staircase. *I want him to invite me inside.* He saw Daddy's face appear in the door window, confused to see him. Dean hesitated as the door unlocked, opening.

Daddy stood majestic as he cracked the door enough to allow his face to show, blocking Dean from seeing the interior. *He's unsure why I've come.* Dean waited, seeing if Daddy would surprise him. *Maybe he will hug me, put me in those big arms, tell me that he is proud. Maybe he will do it just this once.* But Daddy didn't do that, he stood, waited for Dean to say his peace before shutting the door. *Because Daddy doesn't show weakness as I do.*

Daddy finally saying, what do you want?

"I'm starting up for the Rivers End," Dean said. "I want you to train me."

Daddy appeared surprised, saying he worked too hard for Dean to finish in third. It was embarrassing to him.

Dean saying he knew, but that won't happen again.

"I thought you knew better than to work that hard for third place," Daddy said.

"I'm winning this one," Dean said.

Daddy shook his head. "You can't beat Ulysses Turner. Why can't you see that? You didn't even beat Joe Maxon."

Dean begging please, I promise it won't happen again.

Daddy saying stop fooling yourself, wasting my time with third place finishes.

"I promise," Dean said.

Daddy leaned forward, pointing at Dean. "It's embarrassing to have a son who fails at everything. I can't keep this up, I'm not going through this again."

Dean watched his father pull his head out of the doorway, retiring back to sleep. Dean slid his right hand in the door, preventing it from closing. Dean leaned forward and eyed his father, intense. "I got an edge this time and I'm going to be better than Turner. You'll be proud of me, I swear."

"You don't have an edge," Daddy said. "Turner has an edge."

Dean said, "And I've got his edge too. He used it in the last competition, that's why he won. He had the edge all to himself, now we both have it, so I will out-work him in the gym to win."

Daddy stood there, examining his son for the truth. The door slacked, enough that Dean released his hand. *Even after everything I've put him through, he still cares about me after I've shamed him.* Daddy leaned forward, pointing at Dean.

"We'll start at seven if you want to beat him," Daddy said. "Bring this edge with you."

Dean nodded. "Thank you, sir. Thank you."

His father offered a faint grin. *He's unsure I can pull it off.* Daddy closed the front door. Dean smiled as he headed to his truck. *I won't embarrass him this time. Weakness doesn't sit well with Daddy. He's had to deal with a lot in his life, especially from me.* Dean left his father's house in his truck, knowing that he would not be a weak man. He had tried to follow his father's legacy with diminished results. Daddy had been a marine, so Dean had signed up only to wash out after a broken leg in boot camp. *That's not me anymore, I'm better than that.* Dean recalled fights his mother and father had over the shame that Dean had caused as a child. *Daddy is more sensitive than I give him credit for.*

When his mother's diagnosis of breast cancer arrived, it was Daddy who told her she would survive. He was so strong-minded she would beat it that he got discouraged when doctors kept informing him that she was terminal. That was why his father divorced her. *The heartache of suffering through the cancer was too much for Daddy to bear. He didn't want to continue hurting inside.* Weakness had a horrible effect on his father. *As my mother got worse, admitted into the hospital, Daddy visited less and less.*

An hour before her surgery, the divorce papers from Daddy arrived. *He wanted to move on and hurt too much to do it anymore.* Dean remembered his mother wheeling off into surgery for the final time, kissing her hand as she went away. She never signed the papers, but never made it out of the operating room alive. After her death, Daddy had Dean take care of her funeral arrangements to prove he was not weak. *I did everything he told me. I kept the funeral private, no newspaper notice, nothing to let the neighbors know that my parents had been divorcing. Because that was what a son does for a father. He makes his Daddy proud.*

It had been seven years of fighting to get back into Daddy's life. *I tried several times over the years, but always got a message machine when I called.* They were less than ten miles apart but Daddy never returned a call. Not for holidays or birthdays. *Daddy didn't want to remember that part of his life anymore because it hurt too much to think of my mother dying and a son he couldn't be proud of.*

Their relationship changed when Dean took up body building, performing at competitions and improving his finishes. Dean finished fifth at The Rivers End Competition three years back and Daddy picked up the phone, congratulations. *Saw it in the newspaper and wanted to know if I was interested in getting better.* Daddy showed up to congratulate Dean during the trophy ceremony. *Shaking my hand, something he didn't do when I graduated from high school.* He shook off those memories. *I can't blame him for not being at my graduation.* His schedule at the aluminum plant was hectic. *Things are different this time.*

Dean drove back to the gym smiling, knowing Daddy would be there at seven in the morning, ready to go. Night was creeping in as he pulled into the alleyway. He noted the gym lights shining out the store front. He left the truck, taking the vials and entered the gym to see Kyle, Blye and Stew waiting for him in their workout gear. They were sitting around the benches, talking stupid shit. *Saying how a flight meant a grouping of more than two, so if a guy says a flight of wine and means measurement, he's wrong.*

They all eyed him with intense focus, curious on his decision. After leaving Exit One, Dean told them he had to think about whether he wanted to do Fireball. They respected that, saying if not, they would flush it down the john and laugh about the whole thing later. *Saying they would remember that maniac fighter down in the basement.* The three men appeared ready to accept a negative decision from Dean and move on. *I have to do this now, I can't disappoint Daddy again.* Dean tossed the vials to Stew, who caught them.

"Let's do this shit," Dean said.

The three men erupted in cheers. Each had assignments formed in symmetry. Dean locked the front door. Blye dropped the store front blinds. Stew prepared the vials, handing them to Kyle who readied the syringes. Each man peeled off their clothes, nude with preening muscles pumped as they stood in line to Kyle, who aimed for the fat of their buttocks. Stew received the first dose of forty milligrams, then Blye. Both headed away without dressing, grabbing the weights for their lifts. Kyle eyed Dean.

"Do me after I do you," Kyle said.

Dean saying sure as Kyle shot him up with the dose.

Disappointment cloaked as his head lowered to his torso when the needle bit through his skin. Nothing was going to happen. Blye and Stew did repetitions with dumbbells in common form. *The juice has no effect on us.* Dean dropped his lids as he stood. *What the hell have I done?* Then, energy passed through his system. He squinted as thunder rode up his spine, into his head. *I see lightning against black.*

Dean felt gooseflesh on his skin, opening his eyes. Kyle said something but Dean didn't catch it. He handed Dean a syringe full of juice, bent over and received a shot. Dean caught his reflection in one of the wall mirrors. His eyes singed red with burning madness. *But it feels so good.* Kyle stood next to him, catching the thunder as it quaked through his body. They went to join Stew and Blye, grabbing weights.

The world slowed as beads of perspiration floated through the sky around him, hanging in suspension as time inched forward while the four naked men pumped iron in front of the mirror that extended the wall. Dean felt lightning ride up his arms, legs as his heart quaked. *I'm winning this thing for you, Daddy. No matter what it costs, I'm doing it. So you can be proud of me.* Dean grabbed a barbell ticket with weights on both end. The other three laughed with him in a fluid madness. *The power is coursing through all of us. Nothing is impossible now.*

The group pumped, releasing in lock-step motion with a rhythm of nude rage flowing through them. Sweat dripped off mountains of mass and pooled around their feet. The Fireball sensation crystallized in workout form. Dean felt his mind free, charged by the idea of burning off repetitions because he could. His muscles scream but instead of stopping, he grinned. His senses removed as humanity voided a presence in his body. Each man served as an assembly line of form, precision. They emitted out involuntary screams unconscious they were doing so.

The limitless charges drove them to do another repetition, then another while staring mindless into their mirror reflections. The gym temperature rose from body heat and fogged the mirror. The workout never stopped, none of the men desiring a break. That was what Fireball did for each of them. The drive to burn off more fuel became them. The Fireball quaked inside them, alive and raging through the night.

"How serious is this?"

Lance Caron sat across Richard Yazzie's desk in the Rivers End's Tribal Gaming Agency. The man who told his friends to call him "Yaz" said it was important to meet with Lance. The old native with a long, white mane hanging on his shoulders adjusted his glasses sizing Lance up. *He's pissed I'm asking questions*. T.G.A. didn't like inquiries, especially from inside the organization.

"Phil Quentin can no longer stay at his current position," Yazzie said.

Yazzie had suggested Quentin was sleeping with the assistant director of food and beverage, Holly Murphy. *If it's true, Phil should know better*. Yazzie wanted Quentin demoted from director of hospitality to avoid a sexual harassment suit. *It's funny how Holly doesn't get punished for her involvement*. Yazzie grinned at Lance.

The Yamenhi elder was acting suspicious. *He wants to hoodwink a guy like me in order to stay ahead in the game*. Lance avoided conversations with Yazzie, unwilling to comfort the native's racist views on whites. *It doesn't stop the Yamenhi from taking their money*. Yazzie had kept to himself in the last few months, attempting to broker a deal with the Caha to keep the tribe out of the casino business. *He should be focusing on the survival of the Rivers End, rather than who Phil Quentin decides to sleep with.*

"Title thirty-one means something, Lance," Yazzie said.

He's trying too hard to convince me. Employee fraternization would not bring a Title 31 investigation. *I've never seen one in the years at the Rivers End.* But T.G.A. wielded that sword whenever the agency saw fit. *Yazzie uses it when he needs to shut people up.* No one wanted to risk an I.R.S. investigation and possible casino shutdown. *Phil is a pawn for whatever Yazzie's true reasonings are.*

"Yaz, I thought you liked Phil," Lance said.

Yazzie shrugged. "I like the rules better."

He's hiding something. "This doesn't have to do with Phil's report, does it?"

Yazzie's demeanor changed. "T.G.A. is reviewing that report to highlight some of the disputes he decided were facts."

Bingo. Yazzie appeared agitated about the report that Phil Quentin had presented to Lance last week. Quentin had discovered several Rivers End fund accounts were diverting gaming revenues that showed the different divisions as being unprofitable in the last few months. This despite the Rivers End generating millions per day. Lance had forwarded it onto Yazzie three days ago in order to have T.G.A. perform an investigation.

And now Quentin is the bad guy. Someone that Yazzie is trying to discredit. Lance didn't buy any of it from Yazzie.

Yazzie pointed at Lance: "Phil Quentin goes to slots, end of story."

"Why isn't Brian or Scott here to help decide this?"

"They are being kept out of it," Yazzie said. "It's none of their concern."

"You might want to talk to them about that."

Yazzie grinned. "Scott listens to me. I've almost got an agreement with the Caha tribe that will keep them out of the casino business. I helped you out with your drinking problem, didn't go to Brian or Scott. Just said 'get help, see you in a month and a half.' Don't question my methods as a way of repaying me."

Lance held up his hands. He knew how Brian Locklear would have handled Lance's alcoholism. *Would have fired me for it, I owe Yazzie for not telling anyone.* "I know what you did for me. I appreciate it."

Yazzie: "T.G.A. enforces security here. We see everything. Secrets can be found out. Especially ones from the past on tapes that you thought might be erased. Don't have me search archives to find some of the things you did back when you weren't on the wagon."

Lance nodded. *I have no idea what I did back before I stopped drinking.* "You know how Scott feels about not being included."

Yazzie shrugged. "The Italian tried to involve himself in security matters too. That's why he's collecting social security."

Gispie Carlino had been known as the Italian by the Rivers End staff. He was a businessman from New York who had crafted the Rivers End casino loan with Las Vegas. Carlino ran casino operations as the Rivers End general manager for ten years until he was ousted and replaced when T.G.A. Security had noticed high class call girls entering the casino, heading up to Carlino's apartment. Unaccounted for expense reports in the millions also earned Carlino his walking papers. Since then, Scott Tsosie had served as general manager. *It's a fight I won't win with Yazzie. If he looks deep enough, I'm sure he will find something to get rid of me.* Yazzie smiled, letting Lance think over his options.

"What do I do about Holly Murphy?" Lance said. "She can't move up the ladder while everyone she sleeps with falls down it."

Yazzie paused, thinking, then nodded in agreement. "Transfer her to TGA. She gets a cubicle and a hint that she needs to find other employment."

Lance felt lucky to exit Yazzie's office with a job. *The old native knows how to turn the screws on someone, doesn't he?* Lance passed by the T.G.A. reception desk, grabbing a mint from a little woven basket on the head receptionist's desk. Miss Lacey smiled at Lance. *She treats us as her extended family, since she has none of her own.* Miss Lacey had served as head of reception since the Rivers End's opening. Next to her was her assistant, Samantha Greene. The pair were known as "the girls."

The adage went that others disliking someone may mean nothing, but if Miss Lacey did not care for them, it meant they were an asshole. One of T.G.A.'s accountants, Wilson Bright, had treated Miss Lacey bad. She complained to Richard Yazzie and Bright was terminated. Samantha Greene was thirty years younger than Miss Lacey but a similar demeanor. *She's a muffin-top with a car that looks like a green booger.* Both "girls" giggled, laughing regardless of the mundane tasks they were assigned.

"When does the spa reopen?" Miss Lacey said.

"Soon, I hope," Lance said.

The Rivers End spa had been shut down yesterday after the county health board's investigation proved water used for soaking feet was not tossed by the staff. Lance terminated the three Korean workers who ran the spa after customers reported a tuberculosis outbreak after their pampering sessions. He was scheduled to meet with the county health board in a week for recertification. Lance shook his head at Miss Lacey.

"I have no idea why the staff wasn't dumping the water," he said.

Miss Lacey made a face. "Gross."

"The county has photos of what the guests with TB look like," Lance said. "Not pretty."

He left T.G.A.'s offices, heading down to the casino floor as the afternoon sun shined through the glass entrance onto the guests playing slots, craps or pai gow poker. Lance offered a handshake to a former Division-I quarterback who was playing in a Texas Hold'em game right before the turn revealed he had three deuces. Lance saying he always knew he was good luck, then moved on right before the next hand was dealt as two men decided to go all-in.

Lance moved to the slots, finding his path blocked by Sizzle who stood up from one of the machines. Lance tried not to grimace. Jon "Sizzle" Stempton drank diet soda out of a straw while playing a five-dollar progressive. Sizzle had been a top draw in the local Mixed Martial Arts community for three years. Then, a positive H.I.V. test took the fighter down last year and lost his state certification. Sizzle offered Lance a hand to shake, but Lance waved instead.

"I want you to put me up on one of your cards," Sizzle said. "Lot better than that body building shit you got in a few months. That shit died in the seventies when Arnold retired; you got it up on the marquee like it's new, or making a comeback."

Lance's eyes went to Sizzle's arms, seeing bruises running up each limb, looking back. *He still refuses medication.* "Entertainment is Scott Tsosie's decision."

Sizzle shook his head. Lance noted the fighter's sunken cheeks. "He doesn't take my calls anymore."

"You know we loved having your fights out here," Lance said. "But the state has to clear it."

"State won't let me until I do more blood tests."

Lance shrugged. "Rules are rules."

"This is tribal land, shit doesn't need state to certify me to fight. I looked it up," Sizzle said. He looked around, then leaned in toward Lance, lowering his voice. "If it's that virus bullshit, you can relax. I don't have it. Professor down in Berkeley says it's a myth, misdiagnosed. And I ain't got no signs of being ill."

Guess he has to believe in something to keep himself going. Lance threw up his hands. "Casino policy says we follow state and county health certifications."

Sizzle shook his head, defeated. "Disappointing, that's all. I could have done some great stuff with you guys."

"I know," Lance said, nodding.

Lance's eyes drifted from Sizzle over to a row of slot machines. Three junkies sat around another one who held all of the money. They were watching him play. This doesn't look good. Lance had seen this scam before. Lance smiled at Sizzle, saying he had to do something. Sizzle saying understandable, but hey, think about it. *Sizzle found an opponent he can't beat.* Lance radioed for casino security to take care of the junkies before their scam started.

The junkie playing the slots cashed out his five cent money ticket, then inserted it back into the slot's print dispenser. All four junkies sat at slots around the original slot machine, leaving it open. Sure enough, less than a minute lapsed before a guest sat down at the vacated machine to be the mark. The guest slipped in a twenty. Lance watched as casino security approached, surrounding the junkies and escorting them off the premises.

He had witnessed the slot scam before. The mark would play, then cash out any winnings, taking the five cent money ticket rather than the actual money ticket which took a few seconds to print. The junkies would steal the new money ticket for a profit. Guest services handled the mark, explained the scam that had been prevented, then offered him a free hotel stay as well as two free dinners at the Rivers End buffet for his trouble. He wondered why TGA's surveillance wasn't monitoring that situation instead of employee fraternization.

Lance headed over to the off-track betting area. Plasmas showed horses racing across simulcasts while old men on fixed incomes offered up three-dollar-trifectas while arguing about the seventeen percent take with the cashiers. Lance decided long ago the off-track betting center was home of the degenerate gambler; a coot with shocks of white hair comb-over smoking cheap cigarettes burning long on the ash between two twisted, wrinkled fingers while thumbing between a racing form and a five-dollar guide trying to determine running times of Aqueduct and Tampa Bay. Some gamblers stayed after the America track posts ended for the day at five Pacific, laying down cheap bets on Australian tracks which offered little information on each of the ponies running.

The off-track betting lounge's employees had filed reports about possible union moles working undercover. It was not the first time that unions had attempted to infiltrate the Rivers End. T.G.A. frowned about unionization, terminating employees attempting to breach its unwritten policy. Some employees were denounced by their co-workers as a way to ensure movement up the company's ranks. *There is more than one way to become a Holly Murphy at the Rivers End.*

The eclectic tastes of styles, servers and guests made the off-track betting lounge unique to the rest of the casino. The bartender, Fly, was a bisexual with a goatee and ponytail who prided himself on deflowering married men, calling guests "baby" when taking their order. That included some of the eighty-year-old burn-outs who had retired from the local gravel factory, or the car dealers who occupied the hotel every Tuesday to buy at the regional auction. Fly was tending bar with only two customers, Coach Haskins and Judge Herbert Roth.

Lance eased himself to the side of the bar, watching Coach continue to act surly as hell while sucking down bottle Heinekens to celebrate his German ancestry. Roth sat next to Coach, nursing three-dollar Godfathers with a cherry on top of a berg of ice, poured stronger by Fly who offered a wink while he did it. Both men were edging the octogenarian mark. Coach was a retired tenth grade math teacher who had guided the West Valley girl's team to fourteen state tournaments, winning seven titles before hanging it up so his son could take the reigns over the team. Judge Roth sat on the U.S. District Court bench for over thirty years as a stalwart of the community, rumored to retire at the end of the next summer to finally spend his time fishing off Badger Lake as he had promised his wife for the last ten years.

"I get this kid in my court, up on three counts," Roth said. "People keep calling him 'Tick' in my court room. Even the prosecutor does this. Saying 'Tick did this,' or 'Tick did that.' I tell the stenographer, 'honey, call this kid by his name cause I don't want him off on some shady appeal.' And she looks at me and says, 'I don't know what his name is.' Neither did the prosecutor.

Assholes at the Feds arrested him and just got 'Tick' out of him, no record or nothing."

"He has to have a name," Coach said. "Every asshole has a name."

"Yeah, they found it, his name was Pat," Roth said, sharing a laugh. "Your tax dollars at work."

"What did they pick him up for?"

"Kid washed five dollar Lincolns, made them into hundred dollar Franklins," Roth said. "Dirty notes passed counterfeit pens. He got caught on a routine traffic stop with a bunch in his pockets, tried to pay off a cop arresting him."

"You sent him up, right?"

Roth shook his head. "Didn't get a chance after some prosecutor came in, made the kid an informant against the guys making the bills. Guy walks with a spotless record."

"Well, at least you know his name," Coach said, shaking his head. "That's the system we live in, right? All this paperwork, rules, and no damn common sense."

"Every place is screwed up, even Canada," Roth said. "Brought me back three cases of wine crossing the border, cost me six-and-a-quarter in duty, gave the customs lady a ten dollar bill to cover. She had to fill out fifteen pages of paperwork for it. Lady gave me her cell, said if I was crossing again to give her a call, she would take a vacation day to keep from being there next time."

Coach sucked down the rest of his Heineken. He tapped two fingers on the bar. Fly exchanged the empty green bottle for a fresh one without comment. "System ain't changed for the standards people got now. Saw two fat, ugly people biker-tongue kiss outside the clubhouse bathroom on the eighth hole out of Loon Point last week. Almost turned in my membership, cause no field marshal would have put up with that in the past and would have kicked them off the course, nothing flat. Not now, cause anything goes."

The two old men nodded at their revelations. Roth gestured with his glass at a working girl who entered the lounge. "Speaking of which." Both old men had their eyes following the working girl as she drifted through the betting area, up toward the lounge. The woman wore cheap jewelry, shiny toe rings between flip flops, doing her job for a meal while trying to forget the roughness of her occupation. She cut between them at the bar counter, ordering a Bloody Mary from Fly while trying to gauge interest from the two men at the prospect of her services.

Fly did up the Bloody Mary. Some of the mix shot up from the glass into his nostrils. He screamed, heading off to the bathroom crying. Lance moved behind the bar to cover and started mixing the Bloody Mary. He wondered if it was a good idea, given his history. *I can handle it.* The working girl dropped a dirty, wrinkled five dollar Lincoln on the counter, exiting without her drink. Lance smelled the vodka on his hands, and wanted to lick it off. He washed his hands in the sink. Roth and Coach eyed the working girl as she left.

"Glad I never had kids," Coach said. "My son was an adult the second he was born."

"My Abby, she's special," Roth said. He offered up a creased photo from his wallet, showing Lance and Coach. It showed Roth and his daughter smiling. Roth saying she graduated from the police academy a week ago, got assigned the downtown city beat with the department. Coach saying good, nothing ever happens in the downtown district, she will be safe. Roth nodding, saying that was why he called up her captain, asked as a favor for her to be placed there. Roth sipped at his Godfather, complaining that it was watered down. Coach laughed at him.

"Stop being a pussy," Coach said. "I spent seventeen months in-county during that green jungle expedition they refuse to call a war. Drank nothing but room-temperature-beer. Whatever you got ain't worth bitching about."

Roth shrugged, mentioned he had to go over to the cashier, put down a bet on a horse running Emerald Downs in the seventh, before the race closed. Coach saying how the horses were weaker nowadays, all of the bets are bullshit, cause the ponies don't run like they used to.

Roth laughed at Coach. "Abby used to say when she was a kid, 'Daddy, when someone says something you don't agree with, ask to see their data.' So, asshole, where's your data?"

Coach offered up his middle finger. The old man gunned down his beer before tabbing out the second Fly returned from the bathroom, prepping for entry into the poker tournament. Fly's nose and eyes bore red from the mix sauce. He apologized to Lance for the exit, receiving a laugh, saying no worries. Fly looked around, confused why the working girl had not stayed for her drink. Lance excused himself, heading to the second floor of the hotel. TGA surveillance was hooked into his office. The area was primed to monitor guests, card tables, and ensure the House was not being cheated.

Lance sat at his desk and eyed the monitor until the cameras found the working girl. She was in the hotel lobby bar, but exiting. He questioned calling security to have her removed, only to see the working girl exit the hotel for the parking lot. *The economy must be bad when she leaves without work.* Lance sat there, watching the monitor as people went through the hotel lobby. He was about to turn it off when he noticed his wife Keisha entering. He smiled at the thoughtful surprise. *Maybe she wants to fix whatever has been going on between us.*

Keisha went to the elevators, waiting. *I've been coming home late, not paying attention to her.* Lance found her asleep, smelling wine on her breath, not wanting to get into a fight by waking her up. *I see post-it notes from her in the morning because she's left for the law firm.* He fought the urge to sit up at night, drinking by himself. *That's no longer what I do. But sometimes it's harder to resist than it should be.*

Keisha entered the elevator. *I haven't been fair to her, shutting her out of what I'm going through.* Then, Lance watched as Keisha inserted a key into the elevator control panel and hit the button for the top floor. *How did she get a key to Scott's floor?* Lance watched his wife on surveillance; she stood there, patient and waiting. *This must be some mistake. She can't be doing this.* Keisha exited the elevators as soon as the lift stopped, the doors opening.

The door to Tsosie's suite opened as Keisha moved through the hall. Scott Tsosie walked out, naked with his hair hanging around his shoulders and back. The two embraced, kissing. They turned quick, heading inside, shutting the door behind them. Lance collapsed in his chair, sulking. *What the hell have you done, Scott?* Lance shook his head, holding his face, wanting to cry.

15

The four men became a machine of muscle. The first injection of Fireball overtook the builders, fusing them into giants. The standard fourteen week steroid cycle was useless to Dean Shockley. Fireball showed results in three days of training, flushing their system quick to renew calls for a fresh delivery for the chemical The Serg's men called Pink Cadillac. Steroid vials of Brown Sugar or D-Bol had the power to stop a charging bull, but they were minor compared to one hit of Fireball.

It's a wide turn right when everyone else is going left. The pink stuff worked magic in a week as the forty milligram dose no longer sufficed. The thunder subsided quick with a mass growth that was noticeable. The hunger for another dose came as the last hit wore off. The need crawled in Dean's belly. He noted how each builder talked of upping their dose beyond forty. *If Ulysses Turner only does forty, think of how big I can be by doing eighty.*

Kyle was designated in charge of the builders' communion. Each builder assembled by Kyle to reveal their buttocks for an electrical charge pushing everything into focus. Kyle's injections for each builder jumped from eighty to three hundred milligrams per dose daily. The doses in four weeks had stretched out to five thousand milligrams. But it was never enough. Each builder lifted, rode that lightning through the day. The focus brought a state of awareness where Dean heard static sounds and Kyle complained of catching conversations without a source.

They became a gang of muscle where Fireball separated them from everything else. Dean's life fell into deep focus as the color of the world brightened while receiving his morning dose. Sleep meant dreams of contentment. Each shot begat requests for another. *All I want is to rep more weight, get bigger, and get another dose in my system.* His mind stopped processing the world passing his store front window. *Everything is warp speed; it's all fine, taken care of.*

Three hour training sessions meant a thousand reps from six hundred pounds of weight. The crash after was slight then lingered. All of the builders complained about hitting the wall. Kyle upped the dose to six thousand milligrams after the fifth week which allowed the strangeness of Pink Cadillac to take hold. Dean caught an odd buzzing sound in his ears when he woke each morning, or footsteps running away. He dismissed it and continued to train, seeing growth in each muscle.

The builders would gather in the shower at the end of the day and brace the wall, letting water caress their skin. Dean's eyes would catch his hands, mistake them as foreign. His fingernails split as the width of his digits increased. Everything grew. His gums showed more as his teeth separated into larger gaps.

Dean questioned raising concerns to the other builders until he received another dose of Pink Cadillac. Then those concerns *washed* away from him.

I can handle whatever is happening to me. He repeated that mantra lying in bed as he waited for sleep to take him. The weeks of intense training made it harder to shut his lids, turn his mind off. *I can rip a man apart.* He questioned the brutal thoughts that were as foreign as moments of reflection where he would catch himself weeping. Then he would hear his mother calling him in the next room, realizing she was dead. Sleep meant dreams of lifting a thousand pounds with one hand.

A drawback to dosing Fireball was that it made Blye a chatterbox. *He's a child eating a sugar diet.* The randomness of his conversations caused the builders to avoid being spotted by him. Kyle found himself choking with a four-hundred-pound barbell across his throat while Blye gave a half-cocked opinion on world politics. Kyle threw a two-hundred pound dumbbell at Blye's head in retaliation. Blye caught it midair with one hand, smiling.

Dean embraced the drug's ability to supply euphoria. Daddy stopped being a concern after dosing Pink Cadillac. *My father's help is irrelevant.* Dean performed his father's exercise schedule despite it ineffectiveness while the other builders snickered.

My father doesn't know what he is doing. Once the Pink Cadillac settled in, Dean freed himself of worrying about the other builders. Nights would have him stir awake, imagining Daddy was sitting at the edge of his bed. He would return to sleep and register his father's appearance as a dream the next morning.

Between training times became obtuse. Gym memberships dropped to nothing and expenses rose. The builders rationalized the losses after the city shut down the street in front of his gym for repairs. Stew saying the city is blowing up streets better than Al-Qaeda. Dean agreeing, saying the city is better at it too. They laughed until Stew yanked his front tooth out, handing it to Dean, showing him that another tooth was edging out the bloody gum ready to come in.

"It's making us bigger, better," Stew said. Two weeks later, the builder's tooth sat perfect in his gum as if nothing had happened.

The Exit One visits increased for resupply. The builders were entertained by the underground fighting while Oleg got a crate of Pink Cadillac. The doses were cheap enough that they purchased higher amounts each time. A second mortgage went into the gym. Blye and Kyle sold their motorcycles. Stew skimmed from the cash register at the Blacklight. All went toward Pink Cadillac. Venturing to Exit One drew them closer to the fighting which entranced Dean toward watching two fighters attack each other in a pit surrounded by a hundred gamblers offering screams, taunts. Tony Hell's moves captured Dean's attention as the maniac won. He took his tribune of the opponent's eyes and then was forced back into his cell with the zap of Oleg's cattle prod.

Dean approached Oleg one night. "Let me fight."

Oleg curled his brow, unsure if it was a joke. "Why would you want this?"

"Look around," Dean said. "No one wants to leave after Tony does his thing. Give me a shot."

The Serg moved behind Oleg, staring at Dean. The old Russian mobster smiled, nodding.

"We will bring man out for you to fight," he said.

Dean's first challenger was a man out of the crowd. The idiot charged him and was beaten to a pulp. The match's quick end kept gamblers from reacting. The only person who caught the battle's entirety stood behind the metal door, his arms hanging out of the slot while peering through the darkness. *He wants to destroy me.* The crowd soaked Dean in applause. He eyed The Serg who sat beyond the pit, lighting his rolled cigarette while nodding at the victory. Tony Hell screamed from his cell which quieted the crowd, each watching the metal door. *The animal hates competition for affection.*

A freeing rush overtook Dean each time he did one-hundred-seventy-five reps with two dumbbells in two hour sessions. The first few weeks meant managing one or two sessions per day. At the end of the sixth week he was doing three hundred reps with two dumbbells per hour. The training allowed him a sense of contentment; none of the financial worries of the gym fazed him. Daddy stood behind him sometimes, offering negative statements. Dean woke in the night to see his father standing in the far corner shadows of his bedroom, saying horrible things. But as the training continued, Daddy's comments were lost.

All I want to do is rep, burn a few more after that, smile and think about getting another dose. Dean kept going to Exit One, fighting opponents in the pit. He overpowered each with a pounding forearm or a swift kick. He turned into an attraction for The Serg who brought him into one of the VIP rooms, letting twin plastics fondle his muscles, kiss his chest while the old Russian congratulated him by offering tribute crates of Pink Cadillac. The Serg saying Dean had the instinct of a great warrior.

"Whatever it is, you have it that makes the crowd love you," he said. "The one downstairs does not."

"But he loves you," Dean said.

"He betrayed me, that is why he stays down there," The Serg said. "You are a champion."

Dean enjoyed the electricity in the middle of the pit, raising his arms in victory while receiving adulation. *I am a god.* Kyle attended fights but kept clear of the crowd. Conversations with Kyle depended on the day; some days he spoke as an uneducated teenager or mentioned doing his timesheet for the airport parking lot. *When I mention this to him later, Kyle doesn't remember the conversations.* Stew started conquering women as part of his training. One woman coughed and received a white dragon for her troubles. Flesh unavailable prior to Pink Cadillac came easy after but the builders held little interest as training wore on.

Their mass had been questionable before using Fireball. *My build had been better than average but never great.* Ulysses Turner had great mass. Dean's physique altered when Pink Cadillac ripped through his system. His good weight rose ten pounds each week. His joints never dried, injuries were evaded as lifts became easier. Dean twisted his ankle lifting after ten weeks of training. The soreness vacated ten minutes later as the ankle healed. *I can do all of Daddy's counter-productive exercises and not worry.* Pink Cadillac would protect him from harm.

Daddy insisted on ineffective training methods that Fireball made work for Dean's body. He moved through the program, did his reps and ignored Daddy's advice. The old man's reflection sat in the wall mirror as Daddy stood by, sulking as his commands were left unheeded. *My father is a coward who cannot do this himself.* Dean's view of his father became negative now. *He puts me down because he despises the competition.* Dean noted his father's displeasure with his son's behavior but the old man said nothing. The mass came, definition followed, and Daddy wanted to be a part of Dean's success.

Ulysses Turner began to train at Shockley's gym as the training headed into the home stretch. The other builders welcomed Ulysses; he received his forty milligram dose from Kyle each morning while everyone shot up with eight thousand milligrams. Every builder called Turner "a pussy" for not increasing his dose, but he got a pass because he arrived each week with more crates of Pink Cadillac provided by The Serg as gifts to his "muscle boys."

The first time Daddy entered the gym after Turner started training, he approached Dean about providing an introduction to the championship builder. Dean obliged, regretting it as Daddy fawned over Turner, who said nothing. After that training session, Turner, Stew and Dean went out to a local dive for a dollar-fifty-two pint draft. Turner eyed Dean.

"You got issues with that man," Turner said.

Stew butted in. "You saying he's alone?"

Turner shook his head. "My old man never gave a shit, dime or phone call. He dies a couple years back, my aunt sends me a clip of his obituary from the paper. Lists all these things about him, interests I didn't share. I came to the conclusion that he wasn't part of me at all."

Stew laughed, shaking his head. "My dad was an ass that I got away from as soon as possible. Never beat me but came from a military background. Liked to stand me and my sister in the living room, give us a dressing down until we broke. My sis hated him. He dropped dead from a bad ticker, she cremated him, lined his ashes in her kitty's litter box. Fed little Bugsy enough chocolate he used up all our dad's remains in one night."

Daddy's visits at the gym shortened. Dean noted Daddy's habit of ten minutes of training, then drifting to watch Turner lift. Daddy would smile, talk to Turner about how difficult a child Dean was. How he was never a "gamer" like Turner. Dean shut out Daddy's voice when he would tell Turner that Daddy should train him for a while. *Saying I can't focus like Turner can.*

Strange nights began following training. *I dream of being a child, picked up, held by my father.* These foreign ideas evaporated as Dean woke, returning when he shut his lids. He found himself waking with tears, unable to remember what he had dreamt. Except the sensation of wet that covered his skin. He would fixate on the dreamscape during his morning shower, then it would erase when that dose of Fireball hit his system.

Dean had sixty-seven pounds of good, solid mass in eleven weeks of training. Daddy patted his shoulders, telling him he was a good boy. Then Dean would grimace as he watched Daddy drift over to Ulysses Turner to spot his lifts. He brushed off the hurt, standing in front of the mirror, eying his posed reflection, newfound accomplishments. Lifts at six hundred pounds per rep were easy. *My previous high was two-fifty. The Fireball is working.* His strength overpowered concerns about Daddy spending time helping Turner. *You have to pretend he doesn't exist. That he's a stranger to you.*

Fatigue hit after training sessions causing him to collapse into bed with dreams of lying in red wet that haunted him. *I am standing over someone but can't see anything else.* Each morning shower, followed by a dose of Fireball, erased his troubles. He ignored the extra hair clogging the shower drain, the new clumps of follicles growing on his shoulders, chest. Dean noted how Kyle shaved three times daily to keep up. Kyle complaining about cutting himself while using a disposable razor, marveling how the skin healed itself with a thin layer in less than a minute.

The Fireball enhanced Dean's mind enough that he forgot Daddy's role in training. His father spent time with Turner, and Dean had trouble remembering his name some days. Nightmares haunted Dean's sleep as the image of being covered in red, wet blood while holding something in his hands became more defined. *I smile and believe I'm an animal.* Dean woke up crying several times as he rose from his bed, waiting for a Fireball dose. The other builders kept dreams or thoughts to themselves. Kyle never commented on the enlarged bone above his brow. Stew's jaw stopped clicking when he spoke and his chin cleft deepened.

The builders took shit from no one at the Blacklight. Dean moved toward customer fights to finish them, excited. Anger pumped hard through his system. *And I like it.* The builders hung around the Blacklight after their shifts ended to eye opportunities to hurt someone. People got tossed for giving a look. Stew provided confirmation to the others by giving a yank of his thumb. The customer was thrown out on his ass, then got pummeled by three builders in the alleyway.

If Stew didn't care for the looks of an asshole, or wanted his girl, the man got tossed. The builder broke the man's right eye orbit because he thought the guy talked back. *Beat that guy in the alley, screaming for the guy to stop talking shit even though Kyle and I saw he was passed out.* Stew remained over the guy, grabbing his collar, screaming at the unconscious man to shut up. *I would have stopped him for punching the guy if I cared.* Inside of them, something had awoken.

Kyle served as Fireball delivery boy. Dean gave the lease to his gym after The Serg's fighting tributes were not enough for the ten thousand milligram daily doses they each received. Turner stayed at his forty milligrams per day while the other builders craved, needed more. When the Fireball had flushed out quick or Kyle was late with resupplies, Dean thought of slicing his throat in the gym shower. When the Fireball was not riding high in his system, Dean noted Daddy did not sit in his corner anymore. But after the dose came, Daddy would return, watching his boy from the shadows, proud.

He began to welcome his dream of standing covered in red, wet blood. The further he rode the dreamscape, the more he saw of standing over Daddy's body. *I'm holding my father's heart in my hand, devouring it like an animal. And I like it.* Dean woke from his dreams no longer in tears, seeing Daddy in the corner shadows. He nodded to his father in cold fashion and saw the man stay at his side during his training. *He sits there with only time for me while a stranger helps Turner, saying that he trains me too.* Daddy came to all of the Exit One fights, cheering on his son. *He loves me.*

The stranger at the gym came over sometimes, saying do you want help, son?

Dean asking what good would it do me?

The stranger frowned, but Dean shrugged it off, doing his reps while ignoring the man who was nothing. *I don't need anyone else. My father loves me now.* Daddy stood off in the corner shadows, applauding his son's training. The stranger stayed by Dean instead of heading back to Turner.

The builders existed as gods of Exit One's fighting pit. Kyle, Turner, Stew took turns beating back opponents who found themselves over-matched by the fusion of mass and force. Dean attacked three men at one time. Each victory meant finding The Serg who would pat Dean's cheeks as a proud father. *He loves me.* His eyes drifted after each fight to Tony Hell's metal door, seeing the fighter's tattooed arms hanging out of the slot. *He's waiting his turn.* Oleg would zap Tony back into his cage with the cattle prod, enjoying it.

The completion of the fourteenth week showed the builders as men chiseled from rock. The massive growth expended beyond expectations. Kyle and Blye each held their own with twenty-five inch arms, and improved their mass to two hundred-ten. Stew's arms measured at twenty-eight and three-quarters, waist at twenty-nine and a half. His chest was fifty-six inches wide carrying about two-hundred-fifty-four in weight for his six-seven height. Dean made the most improvement, his arms going thirty-three and one half, waist at thirty-one even with a chest that expanded sixty-one inches across his two hundred-seventy-two weight while growing to six-two.

The Rivers End competition approached with each builder mentally ready. None worried about a positive test. Daddy sat in the corner shadows waiting to shake Dean's hand, saying how proud he was of his son. *How much he loves me and always has been proud of me.* The stranger tried to pat Dean on the shoulders, but Dean had none of it. All five builders posed in the mirror, marveling at their reflections. *Fireball was the best decision I've ever made.*

16 Lance Caron had known for years that his wife's social dinners gave her something he could not. *She can be herself with them. Sometimes I'm too white for her.* He tried to ignore that feeling but could not after each Sunday dinner session with local community members, artists or culture eclectics came to his home. He spent the last few months wondering when he should mention her trysts with Scott Tsosie, but said nothing. *It's my fault that they came together. Had I been more open, Keisha would have never slept with Scott.* Lance kept quiet, lying with his back turned to her in bed while she sat up with the light on, organizing newspaper clippings of area socialites she wished to invite three Sundays in advance.

Keisha kept the parties small, to three or four couples. It accommodated conversations while segmenting the topics to something she felt comfortable hearing about. He would eye that glass of red in her hand and want it. She would have him smell the cork every time she opened a new bottle. *She thinks this is a phase I'm going through, that I will be drinking again.* Her world was smaller than his. The conversations surrounded books or films, community events, disdainful of the Rivers End. *Yet all of these places fill out non-profit grants to get money from the Yamenhi tribe.*

"Gambling is a burden on society," Keisha told him once.

"These non-profits enjoy taking money made from it."

Keisha: "Because they can do something good with it."

Lance found himself nodding slow and thinking about when to mention her affair. *Do you really want to lose her?* He thought about the Fells Point Hotel in Baltimore where they married. *She did it despite her parents refusing to attend because I wasn't black enough for them.* Lance wondered if Keisha had drifted from him. The party conversations surrounded common things he had not experienced. But he still tried to be a part of it. Often a guest would gesture toward the grand piano that Lance had had shipped from New York to Spokane that sat in the den. Lance would smile, replying that he no longer played. *Keisha said I needed to stop living in the past and quit music like she had.*

His wife's guest lists were offered the few minorities who resided in the city. *She feels she has color when she's with them.* Lance welcomed the opportunity to meet others with an ethnic background. His father was a black man from New York, his mother was white from Kansas. It left him devoid of conversations surrounding skin color, racism. Lance cringed whenever the subjects came up. He remembered when Reverend Archibald from the Lower Mission Union had come to Keisha's social dinner one Sunday. *He spoke to us about the advancement of African-Americans in the executive level of local businesses.*

"It will get easier for us," Lance said.

The Reverend eyed Lance, then smiled: "Us?"

Keisha laughed because she knew I wasn't black enough for the Reverend or her. I didn't count. He had experienced the cliquish nature of minorities before, trying to best each other in blackness. *I'm a true minority; neither blacks nor whites claim me.* Conversations about race between Lance and a social guest caused Keisha to show signs of discomfort. *She believes I have no right to speak on the matter.*

He dated Keisha for two years before she said that her parents would not meet him. *They refused to believe it wasn't a phase Keisha was going through, unwilling to accept a grandchild who might be lily white.* During their marriage they had spoken about having children. *Thought we were actually trying to, until I found birth control pills in the bathroom.* It was before he went away to deal with his drinking problem. *I've never talked to her about it, same as with her affair with Scott Tsosie.*

Lance resigned himself to sitting alone during Keisha's dinner parties after he returned from his rehabilitation. Meals served at their large dinner table were tolerable but he felt ignored. *They chatter about things but no one engages me one-on-one.* He had spoken up once or twice only to see Keisha cringe with embarrassment at his inclusion about a topic. One guest asked him to play the piano in the den, so he obliged. Halfway through his first stanza, Keisha came and asked him to stop playing.

"It's hard for us to hear each other," she said.

He nodded, regretting that he stopped. Two days after that social dinner with the piano, Keisha had it moved from the den and to the back of the house. *None of them respect the piano because it sounds too white to them.* Lance would sit in the garage by himself during her parties; his fingers gliding over the keys. *Gave me a chance to hide and miss the entire night.* He heard muffled conversations, laughter and enjoyment which he could not share.

Keisha spoke ignorance with guests at her social dinners. Her upper class education devolved into a lower class vernacular to fit their expectations. Lance was mistaken for an affluent background because he played the piano and spoke accordingly, a result of his father and mother having him read the dictionary aloud at dinner in their middle income home. *It's Keisha who hides where she came from to blend in with her guests.* She spoke ghetto slang around minority guests using "ax" instead of "ask" and suggest that everyone "keep it real." Her guests nodded as if Keisha had received her bona fides.

She doesn't tell them she was an only child from two physicians or that her first car was a BMW. Keisha refrained from reminiscing about meeting Lance at Julliard while she studied violin alongside his piano. *When I proposed, she said we would have to give up our childish dreams of music to go into practical careers.* Colombia offered Lance an MBA while Keisha studied at its law school. *She hides our degrees in the bedroom away from guests who might believe we sold out by receiving an advanced education.*

The social party that Keisha held tonight had been long, dragging on because the interstate was closed. Another mega-load truck haul shut down the city as the cargo crossed through to Idaho. Lance listened to Keisha's way of speaking, bothered by the Reverend Archibald's hand sliding down her back, and the fact that the night went longer than it should have. He was tired, letting his guard down. Sometimes I say what's on my mind when I'm not careful. When they prepared for bed, Lance looked at his wife as they rolled back the comforter.

"Why do you speak that way in front of our guests?" he said.

Keisha eyed him while removing her brass earrings, confused. "What?"

"When you are around those people, you speak uneducated. Why?"

"Those people, huh?" Keisha said. "Sounds as if you don't

believe you are one of them."

"Depends on who is in the room."

Keisha shook her head, heading into the bathroom. "I don't get you, sometimes."

"Maybe I'm not black enough for you."

Keisha turned on the basin water, washing off her makeup, then shrugged. "Why are you starting a fight?"

Lance imitated his wife's shrug. "Maybe we need one."

"What's going on?" Keisha looked into the mirror at Lance, nervous. *She wonders what I know.* He watched her dry her face with a towel, then return to the bedroom. His eyes followed her, unwilling to concede so quick.

"Am I not black enough for you?"

"What kind of question is that?"

Lance: "A legitimate one."

Keisha paused, then said: "You could sound less white."

"You believe I sound white?" Lance said. "What does white sound like?"

Keisha's eyes focused on Lance, examining him. She appeared too confident, then looked away from him. "My parents said you were raised too white for them."

"My circumstances were worse than yours," Lance said. "How does speaking well make me white?"

"Your name is white for god sake," Keisha said. "What does it matter anyway? I married you, didn't I? Despite what my parents said."

He offered her a slow nod in response. "I guess I needed to know how you felt."

Keisha pointed to the bed. "I would suggest we kiss and make up, but by now, I should expect that not to happen."

"And why do you think that is?"

"How should I know?" Keisha said. "For the past few months, you haven't touched me. Ever since you came back from wherever it was that you went."

"I quit drinking," Lance said. "I called you every day and I did it for us."

"So you say," she said. "But you didn't go to some rehab clinic. You went away to some cabin somewhere, without me."

"It was the best I could do."

Keisha shook her head. "Well, sometimes that isn't good enough, Lance." She added emphasis when she said his name. *As if she's ashamed to say it.*

Lance dressed and left her in the bedroom. He grabbed his keys, driving his Lexus back to the Rivers End. *Do some work at the office, get this anger out of me.* Lance wanted to throw the affair in her face. *Make her hurt bad for what she did to me.* But the more he thought about it, the more he justified what she had done. *I left her behind to help myself but that's no excuse.* He felt guilty that he picked up and left one day, tired of drinking his life away. *And look at everything its cost me.*

He sat in his office less than an hour later, thinking in the dark. *I love her so much.* He didn't want to talk to her about the affair. *Maybe she can end it, we can go back to loving each other.* Lance didn't know if that was possible. *All we seem to do now is fight.* Lance eyed the open desk drawer, the divorce papers sat there with a few print-outs of Scott Tsosie and Keisha together. *I don't know if I want to keep living this lie anymore.* On his desk was an open Coors Light bottle. *Waiting for me to get back to who I was before I decided to get sober and ruin my life.* Lance's eyes drifted from the bottle to his office door.

"Not good for your eyes, man," Scott Tsosie stood in the threshold, flipped on the light which caused Lance to squint. "What are you doing here on your day off?"

"Thinking," he said. *I should knock out your teeth, cheater.* Lance shut the desk drawer, hiding the divorce papers and photos from Tsosie.

"Is Reggie still on your mind?"

No, but you and Keisha are. "I don't want to talk about it."

"I miss him too," Tsosie said. "But he's gone."

Reggie Barber's influence at the Rivers End had kept the casino intact after Gispie Carlino's ouster. He fought the Caha tribe's influence at brokering a deal. *Said we could go to the Feds, convince them not to give the Caha's a chance to build.* Then that morning came when the news came out. Barber found dead at his farm house. *None of us knew Reggie as much as we thought we did.* The Rivers End changed after that moment. *Richard Yazzie came to me only a few days later, offered me the chance to get rehab and keep my job if I left right away.* Lance eyed Tsosie, wondering if he had made the right decision.

Tsosie pointed to the Coors on Lance's desk. "You ending this sobriety bullshit?"

"Not yet," Lance said, grabbing the bottle by the neck, dropping it in the waste basket next to his desk. The foam bubbled out the bottle, soaking the plastic bag. The scent of beer hit his nose and he wanted to drink it.

"Reggie did it to himself with that crowd he was running with. Didn't know anything about it myself, always thought the guy was credible," Tsosie said. "Life is shitty and things happen no matter which way you think they should go."

Lance: "You sound fatalistic."

"People shit on everyone else. Can't prove it otherwise," Tsosie said. "I passed Len Bias in the dorms back when I was at

Maryland in the mid-80's. Had a coke party after he was drafted, came out feet first, down six feet below ground before he played a minute in the NBA. That's when I knew life was shit. No matter what, it happens to everyone. Get used to it."

"Never heard of him," Lance said.

"He's as much of a household name as this asshole here," Tsosie said, producing a letter from his coat, handing it to Lance.

The letter was addressed to a Stewart Reading and informed him of banishment from the Rivers End casino premises for the next thirty days. Lance shrugged, returning the letter to Tsosie. "We ban cheats from this place all of the time."

Tsosie smiled, shaking his head. "He hasn't been around in months, but life is going to shit on him hard. I had to pay a private eye two grand to hunt him down so he could get this letter."

"Why ban someone who hasn't been coming to the casino?" Lance said.

Tsosie winked. "He comes back next week, part of the body building competition. Already called the event director, made sure he isn't welcome here."

"It sounds like you."

"Are you saying I like to piss people off?"

"Scott, for all of the time I've known you, I'd swear you revel in it."

Tsosie paused, thinking. He said, "The Cahas and this goon gotta learn not to make it tribal. This man rolled up while I was watching the Celtics, got in my grill, poking me in my chest. Said we should have fought harder. Now, he gets to learn how hard my team fights."

"Your team needs to calm down, Scott," he said. "We have ten complaints from the suite incident, including a lawyer threatening to sue us."

"I can have the Colonel chat with him. Toss him off the Falls if needed, make it look like an accident."

Lance eyed Tsosie, unsure about his friend. "You serious right now?"

Tsosie shook his head, grinning. Lance felt relieved. "People just gotta stop messing with me. They do it and they get what's coming to them."

"We're running low, man. We gotta do something."

17

Stew had tried this approach several times with the other builders. *Trying to build that urgency and get them in the mood for pulling a job.* None of them bit. He was standing in front of Ulysses Turner after working out in Shockley's gym. The ebony nightmare was someone that Stew didn't care for much. *I think less of him after knowing that his mass is drug-made.* If it ever came to blows, Stew knew he could take Turner. The massive black stallion eyed Stew for a few seconds, running his eyes over him. *He's sizing me up, trying to see if I'm serious.* Stew had seen guys like Turner do that with him before. *Everyone thinking I'm kidding when I eye a place, say it can be taken down.* Only Kyle was smart enough to value his skills.

Turner gauged Stew as being serious, frowning, shaking his head. "No, that ain't me, man. Maybe you, but not me."

"What do you mean it ain't you?"

What's Turner mean by that? Man was creepy. *He gives me a weird vibe, like guys I met back at The Sides.* Cons who acted like friends and narc'd-out the group for good time when the heat came down. Guys like that got in good with the group, then stabbed them. Turner had been lifting with the other builders the last few weeks. *But I've always been suspicious of his intentions.*

Especially after the way he's acting now.

"I do my forty," Turner said. "That's enough."

Stew saying, you serious right now? Turner nodding, yes he was. Stew disbelieving.

Turner doesn't have the need for Pink Cadillac like the rest of us. Man is content with his forty milligrams. Stew watched Turner receive his shot each morning from *Kyle. Watching him get in line, taking it like everyone else, but reminding Kyle to only give him forty milligrams.* A demand that caught Kyle off-guard, but he complied with. *Man wanted forty, nothing you could do about it. It meant more to go around for the rest of us.* But Stew thought it was strange. *Turner thinks he's better than us.*

Can't remember the last time I only did forty. Hell, Kyle popped a dose of two hundred milligrams an hour once. *Felt like I was weak, dying. I made him juice it up to two thousand a day.* That was the type of juice Stew was used to. *My body flushes forty in ten minutes, guaranteed.* But here was Turner, sticking to his system and not begging for more. *Everyone thinks it's strange.* Stew would watch Turner get his forty from Kyle, who reacted by giving Stew a look. *Saying, he's kidding, right?*

But the supply is getting low. After a day of pounding the iron, the rest of the builders would need two hundred milligrams to get through the night. Turner never worried about cash. *He's different than us.* Stew wondered if he should have approached the black champion at all. *Man seems not to be getting with the program. We need more shit.* Stew ended up saying he could get more Pink Cadillac for the group, help their mass grow, but cash was needed fast.

Turner shook his head, saying he was fine with forty, the rest of them should be too.

Stew leaned in to Turner. Tried stuff he learned back at *The Sides. Get up in a guy's grill, talk low tones, give them that serious look meaning business to get a point across, catch his eyes looking in yours, see who blinks first.* "Rest of us aren't like you. And what we got don't cut it anymore."

Turner saying too damn bad, ready to take Stew down. Stew thought of slamming his forearm into the man's throat. *See how fast he moves without wind.* Turner shrugged, saying nothing but giving that stare to Stew, ready to throw down if real trouble comes. *Man is all about himself. He ain't one of us.*

Stew backed off, not wanting to press Turner. *Left him at the mirror, letting him pose his mass while doing only forty.* Stew shook his head. *Winning takes more than doing forty.* His eyes searched the gym for Dean Shockley, seeing him cooling down with his old man by his side, at the end of the gym. Dean was slated for another battle underneath Exit One tonight. The Serg's tributes of Pink Cadillac are getting smaller. *He wants us all to be his pets, work in the pits like that maniac he's got behind the metal door.*

Blye and Kyle had left the gym. Blye off to do bouncer work at The Blacklight which needed little muscle now that the crowds had thinned to nothing. Kyle back at the pad he shared with Stew. *He's waiting to see if I can get the green light from Dean or Turner on the Rivers End job.* Stew wanted to take down that casino, hard. *Get that native asshole back for the shit he pulled on me.* Since the incident, Stew had not been back. *Let them forget my face, my reasons why. So I can pull up and steal his shit proper.*

Shockley was posing with his father standing behind him. Old man was being silent and knowing his place around his son. *Dean acts different around his dad now. Like the old guy is some hanger-on and not his son's idol anymore.* When Stew first met Shockley, all the man talked about was the greatness of his old man. *Dean's father gives two shits less about his kid, treats him like dirt.* Now the tables were turned where the old man had to beg to be part of Shockley's life.

Stew eyed the old man. *See he's passive, can't figure out how Dean got him needy.* Stew grinned. *That's how you get someone on your side. Indifference, mess with their head.* The old man said goodbye to Shockley who grunted. Stew watched Shockley's father head for the exit, hurt and perplexed. *He never expected to fight for Dean's affection. Good for you, bro. Good for you.* Stew leaned in to Dean, giving him a hard look that Turner blew off.

"We gotta get more stuff," Stew said. "Got a plan for us to get the cash."

Dean stopped posing, paying full attention. "What you got in mind?"

Stew grinned wider, knowing he had Shockley in his pocket. Saying I got some ideas, seeing Shockley grin back, nodding, ready.

That was what made Shockley enjoyable since they trained with Pink Cadillac. *Man gets interested real quick. Not the pussy he used to be.* Shockley used to be afraid. He wouldn't smack up some asshole giving trouble unless ordered to. *Now, Dean does what he wants. Goes up, hits guys with his fists if it suits him.* Old Shockley used to hear a guy out, kept his opinions to himself. *Not no more, he's one of us.* He wanted to go all-in regardless who was dealing. *Get the same vibe from Dean that I get from Kyle. They want to follow my lead.*

Shockley was smarter than Kyle. *If he can run a gym, he can handle a gun.* Kyle was different. *Man wants to do but never trusts himself.* Stew thought about the airport parking lot job in Boise. *Would have done that cop, never stepped foot in The Sides, had*

Kyle not insisted we not load the guns. Stew lost three years, got a record, cause Kyle was being Kyle. *Water under the bridge, Kyle served time too.* But the issue still resided between the two. *I've never said nothing even when Kyle tries to talk up the subject of our arrest.*

"Kyle and I scoped out a casino," Stew said. He laid out Kyle's name, so it sounded bigger than him casing the joint by himself.

Shockley saying casinos don't sound like a good choice to rob. *He sounds interested in pulling a job.*

Stew shrugged. "Two days from now, we pose there, Rivers End. Got a man I want to burn with this one."

Shockley raised his eyebrow, saying oh really?

That was when Turner stepped in, right between Shockley and Stew. *Giving us no space to talk, no privacy, man not offering me a look of respect.* With a move that got a beat-down at *The Sides* if a con was stupid to pull it. Turner glaring at Shockley, saying he's got to trust what Turner says. "You don't need this, man. This ain't you."

Shockley surprised, a pussy around Turner. *Hearing big brother telling you what's what.* Asking Turner, you ain't in?

Turner shaking no while Stew eyed the back of the black man's neck, thinking of grabbing it, seeing whether he can be taken. "You got the edge now. Don't lose it for this asshole." Turner using his thumb, referring to Stew as if he was some cardboard cut-out. *Saying this asshole gets you sent up for ten, maybe twenty years if you kill someone.*

Stew watched Shockley nod his head, knowing he lost him. Hearing Shockley say, what about getting more stuff?

Turner laying down the heavy, what Stew felt was coming. Hearing the man say to Shockley, how you think your old man's gonna feel about you being a con?

He sold Dean on that one. Shockley's eyes watered. He shook his head, worried and a pussy. Stew watched Shockley turn, eyeing a shadowy corner of the gym. Nothing was there, but Dean stared at it for a moment. He nodded, as if agreeing with some ball of dust lying in the corner that he was talking to. Shockley faced Turner again, sniffling. "He wouldn't want me to do that."

Turner glared at Stew. *Saying that he can take me if he needs to, we can meet outside in five.* "Do stupid shit without us. No one here needs to be in lock-up with you."

Stew backed off. Turner and Shockley chatted, mumbled about him. *Stuff I'm not supposed to hear.* Stew had known guys like Turner before. *Type thinking they're better than you cause they got that piece of paper from a school that costs more in a year than you make in a lifetime.* Stew had handled those cocky assholes before. *Bust a lead pipe across his face, man learns he don't know shit.* Stew shook his head at the prospect of getting Shockley into the mix. *Long as Turner is around, Dean ain't interested in doing the casino job.*

Turner was a tight-ass. *Man up in my face, talking like I ain't nothing in the scheme of things.* Stew remembered how Turner acted when they first met. *Man was almost cool, till he found out Kyle and I did time.* Turner first thought it meant serving in the military, then learned it meant at *The Sides. We did our time, not like we were going to do him with a shiv right there.* But Turner acted strange after he learned about *The Sides. He's distant when Kyle or I speak up about anything.* Stew saw Turner giving Shockley the what-for talk about the casino plans. *Saying I'm trouble, trying to boot me from the gym for good.*

Stew grabbed his bag, exited the gym, heading down the street. Took him ten minutes to get to the pad he shared with Kyle. Door left unlocked, open. *Who's going to mess with a guy my size?* Stew entered the living room. Place consisted of two old, stained mattresses from a second-hand store. Bunch of food boxes, beer cans left from before they started training; it was a mess but who cared? Stew grabbed a dirty glass out of the kitchen sink, filled it with iron-white water, drank it down, pissed. *Turner has Dean wrapped around his little finger, don't he?*

Kyle entered the kitchen, fresh from a shower, wearing nothing but a towel around his junk, half his ass. He eyed Stew, leaning up against the stove, thinking. "What about Turner?"

Stew shook his head, saying man was an asshole.

Kyle shrugged. "Dean?"

Stew saying it was a work in progress, don't worry, shit will get worked out.

Kyle saying we could do it together, two of us, old times.

That's what I'm worried about. Stew saying we can get everyone in, go big or go home.

Kyle pointed to the mattress in the living room. "You got a letter."

"Who sends letters anymore?"

Kyle saying, whoever knows you sends letters. "Mailman made me sign for it; must be important."

Stew eyed Kyle, unsure. "You think it's parole?"

Kyle gestured to the mattress where Stew saw the registered letter sitting. Kyle saying parole was done two and half months ago, that cops don't ask you polite to come back. Stew laughed, saying yeah, that would be kinda funny to have prison time be voluntary, but what con would go? Kyle saying sugar dealers, mostly, getting a nod of agreement from Stew.

Stew grabbed the letter off the mattress, tore it open. Read it for ten seconds, seeing it was payback from that native asshole.

Man at the Rivers End got him good. *Found me first, got me banned, knowing the competition was coming up.* Stew hid his anger from Kyle. Seeing his friend standing there holding his towel, dripping wet, waiting to see what was in the letter.

Stew shrugged. "Survey, wants to know what I like on my pizza." Kyle laughed, exiting to the bedroom to dress. Stew hid the letter in his gym bag, headed to the door, telling Kyle not to wait up, he was going to see Shockley fight at Exit One. Kyle yelling for Stew to tell Shockley that he said good luck.

The Exit One parking lot was filling up with customers when Stew rolled up in a car he lifted from The Blacklight parking lot. Threw his fist through the window, felt his hand bust with the glass, hotwired the ride as Ben Salters had taught him back at *The Sides.* Engine purred while Stew had flexed his hand, feeling the bones heal in seconds. Hand good as new. *Damn, this Pink Cadillac shit works wonders.* He chuckled at the sight of the Exit One crowd. *All going in to see an underground fight that ain't supposed to be happening.*

The Serg had developed a good following. Men wanting to see someone get their ass beat. Women left at home while their asshole ex stands in the crowd, thinking he's better than the guys in the pit. *Asshole ex finding he's wrong, too late when he's signed up to face Dean or that maniac locked in the cell who eats fighters' eyes after he beats them to death.* Stew eyed cops off-duty, knowing they were there as customers, not undercover. *Even the blue knows better than to mess with The Serg's operation.*

The plastic thing at the door removed the oily velvet rope so Stew could cross. Oleg approached, smiling with his hand on Stew's massive shoulder. Russian goon leaned in, talking in Stew's ear to get heard over the loud dance music. Saying Serg wanted to see Stew in private, chat in the back. Stew worried, but refused to show it. *Am I getting my throat sliced tonight?* Stew wondering if Shockley wanted him done for the casino job approach.

Oleg led Stew to the back room. Seeing the Russian goon's nickel-plated .45 holstered at his side. Stew wondered if Oleg shot people he knew. *The man does what he's told, no questions asked.* Stew was escorted into the back, sat down with a plastic thing who curled up to him. The Serg entered, sitting across, holding a bottle of cheap vodka that he strangled by the neck, winking at Stew. *This is where it gets done. I get a .45 in my face for approaching Dean.*

"My pet wishes to fight your friend," The Serg said. "I am granting request."

Stew saying, what do you want from me?

The Serg saying, depends on whether your friend can win,

without interference.

"You got something in mind, to help my friend?"

The Serg grinned, eyes up to Oleg, speaking fast Russian. Oleg left on the orders, returning with vials of blue liquid and a syringe gun. The Serg saying if Stew laid down bets for the old Russian on the underdog Shockley to win, Tony got iced with the blue stuff, fights bad tonight.

Stew nodding, liking those odds, hoping this would work.

The agreement made The Serg thirty thousand in wadded cash by the end of the fight. Dean pounded Tony with a fury. The man's eyes got groggy, he fell into the pit within five minutes. Dean stopped before killing him. Let the maniac be carried away by Oleg and another henchman named Peter. Stew handed the winnings to The Serg. Old Russian thanked him for his help, gave him a crate of Pink Cadillac and two grand in cash for his efforts.

Stew smiled, enjoying the business venture. Wanting to do more, but afraid to ask and ruin the possibilities. Stew moved to Tony's cell. Oleg was zapping the unconscious maniac in his back with a cattle prod, laughing. Stew asking why you hate him so much? Oleg calling Tony a betrayer, a man who is not what he seems. *Says Tony talks to ghosts now, drives Oleg nuts to listen to, chatting with a brother that ain't there. Says that's what he got for crossing The Serg.*

Stew nodded, trying to understand. He produced the two grand in cash, showing it to Oleg. "You got more of that blue shit?"

Oleg saying yeah, got a supply that Dr. Xhang made up when Tony takes a dive.

"How much more?"

Oleg stopped, stroking his chin. Xhang dilutes them, stretches out their strength, counteracts effects of Pink Cadillac. *Saying one fighter took a whole pure vial, had seizure in the pit, dead.*

Stew offered the cash to Oleg for a pure vial. *Just one is all I need.*

Oleg grinned. "Stuff is dangerous."

Stew grinned back, nodding, grabbing the pure blue vial. *Ulysses Turner ain't gonna know what hit him.* "I like the sound of that."

18

The morning communion went fast the day of the competition. All of the builders lined up in front of Kyle who gave the shots. Dean Shockley went first, feeling the charge run through his body. Stew shook his head, saying he wasn't ready for the competition. Dean shook his head. *He still wants to take that casino down, willing to hurt himself by not letting them get a look at his face on stage.* Dean smiled at Ulysses Turner, thankful. *The man was thinking about my best interests, kept me from going down that dark path.*

Turner was next with the shot as Kyle prepped his syringe. Dean noted the blue vial that Kyle drew from, Turner not paying any attention. *Is this some new stuff that they got from The Serg?* Dean wanted to know why he didn't get any of it during his shot, jealous. Dean moved to say something, then saw Blye rush past, whipping off his towel, showing his ass to Kyle. *Chatterbox was in a hurry, jumped in front of Turner for the shot.* Dean caught the look at the Kyle offered Stew, who shrugged back. *What's going on, huh?*

Blye took his shot, but Kyle kept some of the blue stuff in the syringe stem. Moved in, poked Turner's buttocks with the shot, draining the bluish dose into the body building champion. *Saying that the shot looked like forty milligrams.* Turner wasn't paying attention to Kyle from what Dean noticed. *Turner's eying Stew, ready to fight if needed to keep the man from approaching me again about doing criminal shit.* Turner had talked to Dean, tonight after the Rivers End competition, Stew was going to be out of the gym for good. The ban could include Kyle too, if he didn't want to follow the rules. *Ulysses is looking out for me, making sure I don't embarrass Daddy.*

None of the builders talked on the way to the competition. They each got there in separate ways. Kyle in a brown car with Blye. Turner and Dean rode together. *Ulysses saying that this is for the best, kicking Stew out, making him see that criminal shit isn't what this sport is about.* Dean nodded, agreeing. He enjoyed fighting under the Exit One club, but it never felt illegal. The bruises and cuts on his hands healed overnight. Good as new. *Taking down a casino with guns and shit, that isn't me, it's a whole different ballgame.*

They waited in a traffic jam while a large mega-load caravan rode by. State patrols flashing police lights as the flight of vehicles moved across I-90 in the Saturday morning heat. Temperature was expected to hit ninety-five or higher. Little wind to speak of. Dean turned to Turner who was gripping the wheel, saying thank you for all of this, no matter how it turns out. Turner nodding, saying no need, it all works out in the end.

They arrived at the Rivers End, parking in the back. Dean and Turner walked inside. Daddy sat in the corner shadows near Dean's bench. *He made it.* Dean was thrilled, leaving Turner to the gray-haired stranger who came into the gym each day. Dean heard the stranger say something, but ignored it. He set down his gym bag, watching his father rise from the corner shadow. Daddy putting his hand on Dean's shoulder, then pulled him forward for a hug. Dean shut his lids. *Don't let this moment end.*

I'm so proud of you, Daddy said.

Dean opened his lids, seeing the stranger had joined them. He wanted to be left with his father. *But Daddy would think I was rude.* So the stranger stayed. The back room was starting to fill up with builders getting ready. Dean stripped to his trunks, preening as a God. The doses of Pink Cadillac pushed out enough glycogen to cut the muscles. *The first time I've never needed to pig out on donuts the night before a competition.* Daddy and the stranger each grabbed one of his arms, oiling him, massaging the muscles while he let his lids down, meditating.

My father is proud of me, he actually said that. Dean had waited so long to hear that from Daddy. For the first time, he wants to be with me, no one else, not even Ulysses Turner. Dean smiled with his lids shut, ready to win. He imagined his body chiseled from rock. *I want to say something back to Daddy, tell him how much*

I love him. Dean kept silent. *Daddy wouldn't like that. He would walk out on me for being weak.*

I'm going to win this thing, for Daddy and me. Nothing stopped him, not even the random piss test that came from the competition officials less than two hours prior to the event. *Didn't even flinch when they asked me to drop my trunks, piss right in front of them.* Dean did it like a man, test came clean, no issues. *Turner was right about Fireball.* He felt confident, firm. *Daddy being proud of me has been worth it. I can't thank Turner enough for helping me. He's a true friend.*

"You ready, son?"

Dean opened his lids, looking at Daddy. *He called me "son."* Dean couldn't remember the last time that Daddy had called him that. Even the stranger noticed how Dean reacted. He fought back tears, knowing Daddy wouldn't accept that. Dean's eyes went from Daddy to beyond the stranger who helped massage him, focusing on Turner. The massive champion appeared no longer the giant. Turner had his head lowered, standing on the base of the stage steps, deep in thought. Dean pulled away from Daddy and the stranger, leaving their hands vacant and headed to Turner.

The man was concentrating, getting into his vibe. *He wants to be alone. I shouldn't bother him after all he's done for me.* Dean approached quiet and stood behind his friend. Turner lifted his head, smiling at him. The two grabbed each other's forearm, locking. *I'm part of the club now. I'm no longer some third place finisher.*

"Thank you for this," Dean said.

Turner smiled. "What are you thanking me for?"

"Everything," Dean said, gesturing over to Daddy and the gray-haired stranger. Both waved back, smiling. "Thank you for that, especially."

"What you did was on your own," Turner said. "I pointed you in the right direction."

"Have it your way," Dean said, then shrugged. "Never felt better than I do now. Everything's coming together."

Turner nodded. "Addictive, ain't it?"

"Sometimes I don't realize how many reps I've done. Just keep blasting away until I pass out."

Turner was about to say something, then blinked. Dean caught it. Turner held his head, squinting. Turner swayed as if he was going to fall. Dean caught him. Turner shook it off, looking at Dean with his eyes red. "Thanks, I don't know what happened."

"You should sit down, rest a minute," Dean said.

Turner's name came over the loud speakers. Both builders eyed each other. Once a competitor's name was called, they had twenty-five seconds to go on stage. Otherwise they were disqualified. *No time for rest, at least not yet.* Turner went up the stage steps. Dean watched him, wishing him well. *Man did a lot for me. But this is my time to win, not Ulysses Turner's.* Blye's name was called over the loud speakers. The builder rushed past, Dean, smiling. It was Blye's display of teeth that made Dean uneasy. *That guy has the devil's smile.*

Blye did not respond, looking toward the stage and ran up it, eager. Two competitors followed Blye as their name was called for the front double bicep category. *This is my time, my moment.* Dean eyed Turner's arms spread out in straight form. *I can beat that.* The crowd ogled Turner's physical form, erupting in cheers as the champion posed. *No more third place finishes. Tonight, it's all or nothing.*

The lights shined down hot on the stage competitors, sparking a sheen of strength, captivating the audience with an allure of impossible power. Dean eyed Turner's motion as the champion's pose enamored the judges while he finished his set. After him was Blye who stepped forward. *Go get him, man, show Ulysses Turner how hard we worked this time around.* Blye moved in front of Turner while displaying that wicked grin locking his teeth together. *He ain't grabbing the audience smiling like that.* Blye posed into the front double biceps. Dean's eyes drifted to the crowd, faces that offered uncertainty toward Blye.

A collective gasp from the crowd caused Dean to look back at Blye. The man shook as he stood on stage, while keeping his pose. Blye's muscles stretched in a flex, skin expanding until it burst apart in small pockets. Blye continued his pose. Blood dripped from his muscle tears. Blye unleashed a scream, something that all the builders had done in the gym since they had started using Fireball. A woman screamed from the crowd, fainting. The audience watched as more skin tore on Blye's chests, his legs ripping open.

The gasps grew louder as camera flashes ignited. It covered Blye in blinding, white bursts. Dean froze, resisting the urge to leap on stage and help his friend. Blye shook, gritting his teeth until porcelain chunks dropped from his mouth. His eyes fluttered, rolled into his head's far reaches. A muscle god chatterbox was reduced to an invalid with a seizure. Blye collapsed, hitting the stage with a thud. His body unleashed tremors as casino emergency crews raced out of the audience to aid him. The house speaker attempted to calm the crowd. The casino EMTs surrounded Blye, stabilizing while prying his mouth open. Blye had bitten off a small piece of his tongue.

Dean stood there, doing nothing to aid his friend. Watching it happen in front of me, it's too unreal. Casino E.M.T.s administered restraints on Blye, then placed him on a wooden slab. His body was awash in blood from multiple wounds. The casino E.M.T.s carted him off stage, through a crowd which parted to give them access, gawking as the fallen hero passed by. The house announcer's voice carried over the loud speakers, informing the public to depart the Palladium Auditorium due to the event's suspension. *No, this isn't happening.*

Dean closed his lids, the world became black. He stood patient, listening to his heart thump. The rustle of people moving out of the auditorium carried to his ears. *My dream is over. All of that work was for nothing.* He thought of the pain in the gym, wondering how Daddy felt about the situation. *I had Daddy's love for a moment, just one. I thought I could hold onto it forever.* What was Dean to his father if never a champion? *Another shameful coward Daddy would ignore.*

He wanted to leap on stage, yell at the judges, scream at the crowd. *Tell them that we have to continue. Whatever happened to Blye, it has nothing to do with us.* Dean shook his head with his lids shut tight, knowing that his display would not happen. *I never got to show off my new mass or got a chance to win this thing once and for all.* Dean wondered why Blye's exit suspended the competition. *He wasn't going to win it anyway, you could see it in his face. The man was weak.*

"No. We keep going."

Turner's scream punctured through Dean's ears, causing his lids to open. Ulysses Turner stood in his place on stage, lights shining off his mass. He pointed at the judges in the crowd. *Man's face is covered in white, hot anger. Pupils dilated, ready to burst.* Turner gnashed teeth, flexing muscles with veins popping off his neck, arms while screaming at the judges. Each of the five judges squirmed, backing from the stage in fear. The house announcer's voice carried over the loud speakers again, repeating that the event was being suspended.

"You can't take this from me," Turner said, screaming. "I won't let you."

Turner moved quick, leaping from the stage into the crowd. The audience members panicked, screaming as they scrambled from him. Turner reached, grabbing hold of one judge by the throat, drawing the balding man toward him. The crowd edged into a large circle, leaving Turner and the judge in the center. Dean stood frozen as he had with Blye's convulsions.

Dean wasn't sympathetic to the judge as he was to Blye. *Kill him, Turner.* Dean curled his lips into a bloodlust smile. *Do it for all of us.* The rage burned deep inside Dean's belly. It charged up his chest, pounding anger in his head. Dean clutched his fists, excited. *Do it for all of the hours we put in. Every one of us who has to go home empty handed because this asshole took it away from us. Make him pay for what he's done to us.*

Turner pulled the judge forward, into a head-lock. He tossed the balding man's back up, then brought him down with a sharp *snap* as his vertebrae broke. The judge's body limped, dead as Turner released him into a heap. *Man got what he deserved.* Turner eyed the crowd members who stared at the massive murder. No barrier stood between them and a molten beast of muscle. *Do it, Ulysses. Make them all pay for what they've done.* Turner stepped forward, the crowd edged back in response. Another step by Turner caused a panic to spread through the auditorium, the audience rushing toward the doors for escape.

The stampede caused its own victims. Old crowd members fell onto the ground, trampled by younger as people escaped through the exits. Turner latched onto the nape of a young woman's neck. He pulled the screaming young woman in the sundress toward him, lifted her above his head. Turner roared, tossing her toward the auditorium entrance, the young woman's arms and legs kicked air as she landed fifteen feet away, colliding with a man rushing for the exit. Both were brought to the ground. The woman's right leg shattered, twisted, broken. The man was unconscious beneath her.

"We need to leave."

Dean felt a hand on his shoulder. He looked, seeing the gray-haired stranger touching him. Dean wanted to rip that hand off and kill the man. He glared at the stranger, who jerked his hand away, repulsed by Dean's smile. *Yes, that's right, I'm enjoying this. Turner needs to make them all pay for what they've done.* The stranger looked from Dean to Turner, seeing that both had transformed into monsters. *You don't know what lies inside us.*

The stranger backed away from Dean, afraid. *That's right, escape with the rest of the chattel while you still have a chance.* The stranger pivoted, running out the back door of the auditorium. Dean expected no different from the gray-haired stranger. *That's what hangers-on do, ride you until they can't get any more out of you.* Dean's eyes went to Daddy who sat in the corner shadows. His father smiled at him, nodding at the violence.

I'm so proud of you, son, Daddy said.

"Thank you," Dean said.

Dean's focus left Daddy to eye the auditorium. Most of the crowd had scattered from the building, into the casino. Bodies were spread on the ground, some trampled unconscious, limbs broken which rendered them unable to move. Turner stepped toward a man lying on his back, a bloody wound on his skull. Turner slammed fists into the man's chest, receiving a meager defense. The man's broken right arm hung dead while he protected himself with his left. It was no use. Turner beat on the man with a fury, screaming in rage. The auditorium doors opened, drawing the attention of Turner and Dean, as four armed men in expensive suits entered.

The security force wore black berets, appearing primed for war with faces chiseled in hate, brandishing M4 carbine rifles strapped at their shoulders. Dean eyed Turner, who stopped beating on the unconscious man and stood, ready to face the security force. The security team drew out in a line twenty feet from Turner, including an older man with a white mustache and cold eyes, who led the group. *They mean business.* Turner braced, flexing his muscles while his hands formed claws. The security staff did not rush to aid fallen audience members. Each focused on Turner. The older man gestured at some of the wounded lying in the auditorium.

"Now, what's all this then?" The older man spoke with an English accent.

Turner pointed at the older man, screaming. "This is mine. We keep going. I'm winning this thing."

The older man saying the show was over. Turner saying gibberish, his speech slurred. The Fireball is wearing off inside him. The massive muscle man was tiring, arms slumped, dropped down hanging slabs of meat at his torso. Turner's chin touched his chest, the man ready to pass out. *I've been there before with a Fireball burn. Once it runs thin, I become weak as a child.* Dean eyed the security team which stood prepared to attack, wild animals waiting for orders to stop him.

The older man saying Turner needed to surrender. More gibberish came from Turner in a weak voiced reply. Anger quaked inside Dean. *Go stand with your friend, fight them off together.* Dean wanted to beat the shit out of the security guards. A fusion of rage poured out through his veins. Dean resisted the rage. His eyes went to Turner who began to scream, returning to juggernaut form. Turner's voice echoed the auditorium, clanking off the marble columns. Turner stepped toward the security men, laughing.

The security force appeared resolved, pointing their M4 carbine barrels at Turner's chest. Saliva foamed from the champion's mouth. The older man smiled, ordering his men to prepare to fire. Turner pounded his fists against his chest, ready to charge. The security force emptied rounds into his chest less than five yards from them. Turner's body danced from the bullets until the carbines were spent. He fell back into a pool of blood, light vanishing from his eyes.

Kill them all for your fallen friend. Dean pushed back the rage until the quake simmered. The security force holstered their M4 carbines. Casino E.M.T.s rushed inside the auditorium, aiding wounded attendees. The older man led the security force out of the exit. Dean stood there in the shadows behind the stage. The great Ulysses Turner expended a final breath, his soul escaping. Dean eyed the corner shadows, seeing Daddy was there, smiling.

I'm proud of you, son, Daddy said.

"I would do anything for you, Daddy. Anything."

19 Peter Volov put the distance of time between his meetings with F.B.I. Agent Sam Brown. He remembered what Anthony Batellini had taught him. *Go in easy, don't give people a chance to see a pattern, and hope that you come out alive.* Peter wondered if Anthony would ever come out of the detail alive. *He sits there in madness, drooling to himself in that cell, waiting to fight another person to devour their eyes.* Peter didn't know if finding The Serg's stash house would make a difference. *Even if I get more of the blue vials, how will I know if it has any effect? Anthony's mind may have cracked.*

The meeting was called ten days prior. Peter grabbed a burner cell phone he purchased in cash out of a convenience store around Five Mile while running some illegal guns for The Serg up to gang-banging La939 boys. He sent a text with a GPS location for the meet to Sam Brown, then stomped the phone, trashing it to cover his tracks. *How Anthony Batellini instructed me to do. Said to stay around, act as if you got nothing else but the undercover job going for you.* Peter was bemused by that thought. *My only way out of this is to get Anthony Batellini out, free. If The Serg finds out I betrayed him, he will have Oleg deal with me.*

I'm doomed. Peter had been inside so long, back when Uri was running operations for The Serg. Uri was a big ox of a man, a goon cruel and cunning. Uri was killed over a year ago by a man named Frank who came down into the pits underneath Exit One, stabbed him with a switchblade, breaking it off. Peter had not witnessed Uri's murder. He had been on a delivery errand, came back to help Oleg heft Uri's body from the pits. *Dug his grave in a field, Oleg covered him in lye. In The Serg's operation, the only way to be promoted is by the death of the person ahead of you.*

The GPS coordinates were for an abandoned warehouse on route eleven which used to house a beer distributor. Place was empty, desolate with nothing but trees, overgrown golden fields, and two rusted buildings of sheet metal and iron standing around cracked asphalt with faded white parking lines. Peter had eyed this place twice before in the last two months. *Perfect if I had to meet Sam Brown again. Anthony Batellini told me not to trust too many Feds. Said they will burn you in order to make a higher pay grade.*

The Serg led a rough operation at Exit One compared to the Russians in Oregon that Peter had worked for. Meth labs had rat-looking cookers, slimy from breathing in those fumes. Exit One boasted a clientele of men getting ripped off by the dancers ready to slice someone without reason. Peter checked the rearview of the stolen sedan he drove, uneasy about being followed. He went down wrong roads, did double-backs to lose people. The abandoned lot was about thirty minutes out from Exit One, but Peter took three and a half hours, making sure he would not be followed.

After Vitali, you have reason to be worried. Peter had given the information for Sam Brown to burn Vitali. He didn't know how quick The Serg would discover Vitali's inclusion on the FBI payroll. It was a matter of weeks. Vitali was invited out by Fedor and Oleg, while the Russian goons hung around the Exit One parking lot. Oleg had come up to Peter, saying to come along. Peter had nodded, getting in the back of the cream colored van, sitting on the back benches across from Vitali. *Man acted as if he were part of the crew, nothing wrong.*

Vitali talking up a storm to Peter, offering swigs from his vodka bottle. *Man joking about how hard those muscle boys worked for pink shit.* Damned if Dean wasn't making Tony Hell jealous in his cage. Vitali taking verbal jabs at Oleg, saying he's gonna have to treat Dean like shit too. *Said otherwise, Tony will feel it's personal between the two.* Peter recalled eying the front seats. No reaction from Oleg as if Vitali weren't talking at all. Eyeing a shovel and bucket of lye strapped underneath Vitali's feet, wondering if he was being burned by the FBI. Peter catching something was happening, watching Vitali smoke his fine cigar stub. *Talking about some plastic number back at Exit One that he bent over in the parking lot one night, back when she asked for a ride home and Vitali gave her a different type.*

Oleg stopped the cream colored van at a stoplight in the middle of an empty intersection. He foot braked quick, which pushed everyone forward. Vitali cursed Oleg, calling him an idiot. Vitali puffed his cigar stub, laughing while eying Peter, calling Oleg a horse's ass. In the corner of his eye, Peter caught Oleg moving around.

Vitali laughing, holding his bottle, puffing white smoke while Oleg aimed his nickel-plated .45, squeezing off a round that slapped the right side of Vitali's head. A ringing sound sat in Peter's ears for thirty minutes after. He coughed, choked on gun powder while the rancid odor burned his eyes. Oleg refused to roll down the windows. Vitali lay dead, eyes open, face relaxed as the van sped off to a field, to be covered in lye and erased away.

I want no part of that end, that's why I'm cautious. Peter switched two more routes on his way to the meeting. Peter drove inside the abandoned structure in the parking lot, hiding his car in the shadows. Sam Brown flashed his headlights, sitting at the end in a beat-up sedan, idling. Evening was beginning to hit. Peter rolled up alongside him, holding an 8-cell Maglite for little protection. *If I have to, I can get a good whack in if the guy is here to burn me.* He rolled the car window down slow, easing himself low behind the wheel to ensure no random person would catch him speaking to Brown. They sat in the darkness in their rides.

"You called this," Brown said. "What's going down?"

"Movement, close to finding stash house."

Brown paused, then said, "You know what happened at the casino?"

"Ulysses was ours, but was never junkie," Peter said.

"So far, I'm rolling up with the casino operation," Brown said. "See what happens when I shake the tree."

Peter grabbed a USB drive, handed it to Brown. "This may help you."

Brown looked at the drive. "Oh?"

"Native man, indios, he deals with Oleg a lot," Peter said. "Had us do a fire five months ago. I knew nothing about the people inside until too late."

Brown smiled. "Not every native operates out of a casino."

Peter shrugged. "Worth a shot."

Brown: "What else you got? Vitali getting burned helped, right?"

Peter nodded. "Got me closer, doing more."

Brown got interested, scratching his chin, saying oh really?

Peter handed him a file of reports. "Serg has us tail clients, do up reports. Did it on the muscle boys, got their gym, details on them. Some is in Russian. I made you copy."

Brown appeared impressed, raising an eyebrow. "And the stash house? That and Anthony Batellini get you out of this thing."

"Working on it," Peter said. "Will be in touch."

Peter put the sedan in drive, leaving without letting Brown reply. *Man gets the location when I know it.* Peter headed back to Exit One, doing a switch of routes to make sure no one could tail him. *Following what Anthony Batellini taught me.* Peter's cell chimed a text from Oleg: *Meet in parking lot, one hour.* Peter sent back: *k.*

Peter cut his travel time from three hours to one, getting into the lot to see Oleg standing there by the cream colored van, waiting for him. *Man appeared as if he had something to discuss.* It made Peter nervous. *Maybe he knows.* Oleg was smoking those stupid, hand-rolled nails that The Serg gave him. *The ones I hate smelling, keeps in your clothes for days.* He eyed Oleg as he parked the sedan. *Man has his .45 holstered, hanging from its side, ready to use on me if I run.* Peter fought back the thought of running. *Where are you going to go, anyway?*

"Got job for us to do," Oleg said.

Peter said fine, but I need to take a piss. He debated running. Figured Oleg was onto him, the way he looked through him. *Somebody followed me, saw me heading out and tailed me. Caught me with Brown and now I'm gonna wind up in a field, covered in lye next to whatever remains of Vitali.*

Oleg shook his head. "No time, hold water until we get where we're going."

Oh, shit. "Where are we going?"

Oleg winked, saying you'll see. *Oh, shit, what I am going to do?* Peter's heart sank.

When Anthony Batellini had trained him to work undercover, the instructions were brief. *Act cool, do the job, come out of it fine. Said most agents have their cover blown when they start acting uncool, trying to talk themselves out a situation without cause.* Peter had done the job so long he didn't believe he could blow his cover. *I've done a lot of stuff for The Serg, proved my worth by taking a clean Browning Semi to the Garland District, squeezing off two into Freeway Phil's chest after he tried to swindle The Serg on some diamonds.* Peter calmed his nerves and waited for Oleg's instructions. *He don't know shit, unless you tell him.*

Peter eyed Oleg's .45 hanging off his holster, dangling ready to fire when needed. *Same when he did Vitali in the back of the van.* Peter waited for Oleg to yank out his gun, end him for not following orders. *Keep your cool, he knows nothing. You're a trusted man in this organization.* He had felt that The Serg's trust could become indifference within minutes. Vitali was trusted too.

It didn't stop The Serg from having him eliminated. Peter felt sick, knowing that he had earned trust through his actions.

The native man with white hair was Peter's test of loyalty. Oleg and the native man talked without Peter in the Exit One parking lot. Then Oleg drove Peter in the van out to a farmland home beyond Nine Mile Falls. They put two pounds of heroin in the trunk of the owner's car, an illegal gun to keep suspicion from the native man. *We unloaded plywood, gas cans, making quiet while we walked around the house at three in the morning.* Oleg and Peter sealed windows, doors with plywood sheets and nail guns. *Then Oleg cracked the flare, tossed it on the grass, place went up in seconds.* The screams from inside the house haunted Peter long after the fire was set. They burned alive, pounding on the plywood, trying to escape. The smell lingered in his mind long after leaving his nose. *I earned The Serg's trust that day but he never stopped asking for me to prove my worth again and again.*

When the native man with white hair came a second time, Oleg brought Peter to meet him. *Said call me "Yaz." Gave me a tribal knife, told me to stick another native running the casino, scare him but don't kill him.* Peter had walked into the Rivers End, clutching the knife's handle as he eyed the casino's man. *Grabbed his shoulder, spun him around, his smile dropped, the fear in his eyes, burying the knife deep.* Peter had seen that look before with

Anthony when they first shot him up with Pink Cadillac. *It's the loss of innocence.*

Peter eyed Oleg in the parking lot. *Just go with him, be ready to leap from the van if he drives somewhere strange.* Peter went to ride shotgun. Oleg waved him off, pointed for Peter to go behind the wheel, saying no, you drive. That stopped Peter. Oleg never let anyone drive him around. *Rule the Russian goon had, you either like it, say nothing, or you don't come along.* Now things were different. *Change is not good in our line of work.* Peter eyed the .45 again, waiting to have it pointed at him during a stoplight. *Am I driving to my own grave somewhere east of Idaho?*

Peter saying, what's going on here?

Oleg volatile, yelling at him in Russian fast, Peter only catching the words "shut up and drive."

Oleg had acted that way before when Anthony Batellini had been discovered as a D.E.A. agent. An operational contact named Turk had come to Exit One to see The Serg on business and fingered Anthony as the guy who took down five crooks in Tacoma trying to sell him five thousand Oxy pills. Oleg was pissed after trusting Anthony, whose undercover name was "Mikhail." Peter was brought into the basement. *Saw Anthony held by Fedor and Oleg in the pit, waiting for me.* The Serg handed Peter a Glock to prove himself. Anthony was defiant, willing to take a bullet by not outing Peter.

That's why I have to get him out. He kept quiet for me, I owe him my life. Peter had aimed the Glock at Anthony's head, ready to squeeze the trigger. Then Doctor Xhang spoke to The Serg in a hybrid of fast Russian-Chinese, saying to let Anthony fight to the death in the pit. The Serg needed a show after the cock-fighting ended. His delivery boy Dmitri had built the pit, laid the sand, drew the gamblers. A rooster leapt backward, stabbing its metal talon in his left leg artery. Dmitri bled out in the pit, creating an opening. Fighting in the basement made more than the naked girls dancing upstairs.

They stripped Anthony of his clothes, drugged him. Fedor took out his tattoo kit, decorating Anthony's face with tattoos of a Russian criminal. *Saying if he wishes to be a Butyrka Prison criminal, then he should act like one.* Xhang loaded ten vials of Pink Cadillac and shot Anthony up with the junk. Peter heard the screams echo downstairs in the supply closet where he was held. Oleg welded on a large metal door to keep him caged. Peter remembered Anthony's eyes when he woke. The insanity had milked over his pupils, madness running free. During the fights, The Serg listed Anthony's name for the gamblers. He could not spell Batellini and thought he wrote "Bell". The gamblers read Anthony's fighting name as "Tony Hell."

Oleg got in the passenger's seat, eying Peter behind the wheel. Both sat for a moment in silence, while Oleg checked his cell phone, reading something, laughing. *What the hell could he laughing at?* Peter was too scared to ask. *Things would be different if The Serg trusted me to carry a piece.* The Serg handed out guns only in times of trouble. Oleg was different because he had earned The Serg's trust by taking down Anthony Batellini even though Anthony was his friend. *That's why he gets to carry the nickel-plated .45, so he can blast anyone who gives The Serg trouble.*

Oleg fixated on his cell phone, checking it for information. *Have they found me out through Anthony?* Oleg sat in deep thought while scrunching his brow, trying to read off the reflective smart phone screen as dusk settled in. *Oh, shit.* Oleg never acted this way, soaking information, putting the news together. *He knows something.* Peter thought back, wondering if he had been spotted meeting with Brown. Oleg coughed, breaking silence but when Peter attempted to use the IPod for tunes, he saw it was gone.

Peter was instructed down the Interstate going east, twenty exits into the top half of the state, running toward Bonners Ferry. Oleg pointed him off a quiet exit phalanxed by trees. If they got a flat tire out there, it would take forever to walk back to civilization. Peter eyed the area, seeing a dirt road cut through the edge of twin hills. He looked off the right side of the windshield, seeing the small community of Rathdrum in the valley below. *The Sides'* footprint was visible. All of the boys removed from the yard, place resembling a bunch of warehouses with a lot of electric, barbed-wired fencing around it. Some of the Russian goons had been to the place once or twice, laughing about doing American time where the brutality was shorter than it was in the motherland.

The country road the van went along edged over the other side of the hill, twisting enough that the right front tire was a third off the hill's cliff, sending dirt tumbling down the side. Peter maneuvered the van, slamming his foot on the gas until they went over the other side toward an opposite valley. The road transformed into two dirt strips for tires, with a green grass berm that kissed the undercarriage as they rode through a mass of evergreens which held by the dwindling sky. Headlights on, Peter eyed the thicket of woods on each side, finding no option of escape.

The road stopped at a large tree laid across the path. Peter applied brakes, killing the engine, then eyed Oleg, ready to have the .45 pointed back at him, to get the thing over with. Oleg sat cursing in Russian, checking his cell phone, smacking it with the butt of his hand to make the cell service improve. *You are in the middle of nothing. He finds you, no escape.* Peter chose to sit, waiting it out, seeing if he was wrong. Oleg turned, stared at him with cold blue eyes.

"We get out here."

Peter asked where are we going? Oleg cursed Russian at his cell phone, ignored Peter as they exited the van. Oleg's cell chimed, he spoke fast Russian to the person at the other end, then the service dropped. Oleg screamed in the mouthpiece a few times, then tucked it back in his pocket. He shrugged at Peter, who didn't know what to think. *Man thinks his cell works anywhere, don't he?*

Oleg gestured to a small single trail with Peter in the lead. Peter eyed the trees, wondering if he would be blasted from behind by the .45, contemplating begging for his life. He felt sweat on his neck, chest, his heart ready to jump out. Peter's feet crunched hard grass. *Should I run?* Oleg stomped the grass behind him keeping pace. *He knows something, been onto me.* Peter saw the sky turn a pinkish hue and wondering if it was over.

"This is place," Oleg said.

Peter stopped, seeing nothing until his eyes adjusted to the creeping darkness. He made out a small cabin lying cold in the darkness. Oleg moved past him, cursing Russian gibberish that glanced off Peter's ears about the cell phone service. Oleg turned, gesturing with his arms for Peter to follow, saying they didn't have all night for this shit. Peter nodded, moving forward, unsure what to make of the cabin.

"You got directions correct?" Oleg said. "Paid attention, no telling you again, no?"

Peter saying yea, piece of cake once you drive it.

Oleg nodded, saying that's why I came with you. No map needed.

Peter saying cool, keeping to himself that he almost blew his cover by freaking out over directions.

Oleg kicked open the cabin's front door. The rotting wood splintered swinging open, offering a dank mold odor. A raccoon screamed, scooting from across the floor as Oleg turned on the lights. He drew out his .45, following the raccoon with the barrel, squeezing off two shots into a rotten couch. Tuffs of diseased fabric floated out of the furniture's wounds. Peter was unsure Oleg had hit the raccoon. *He could shoot anything out here, no one would hear it.* Oleg winked at Peter.

"Vitali never cleaned," Oleg said.

Oleg led Peter to the back of the cabin, stepping into a small bedroom devoid of furniture. The room held large caches of three-foot green and white crates on the floor, along with a large blue tarp covering other gear. Oleg knocked his foot against a white crate.

"Andrei needs more for fighters and Mikhail." Oleg spat on the ground as he said Anthony's undercover name.

Peter lifted the white crate's lid. Vials of pink, blue and purple fluid chilled in an insulated crate. He asked Oleg why only take one, why not take them all. Oleg shaking him off, saying no, the fighters would steal it, they are junkies. Oleg pointed to the purple vials, saying they were dangerous, make men into animals or worse. Peter didn't ask what worse was, guessing what happened at the Rivers End probably played a part in it.

Peter pointed to the green crates, watching Oleg grin. He removed the blue tarp, revealing Kevlar vests, sleeves, leggings and other military gear. Peter lifted the green crate's lid, seeing grenades, carbine rifles and about ten thousand rounds inside. Another green crate held mortar shells, another held a large round gun called a Vulcan. Oleg laughed, shaking his head at Peter's discovery.

"Vitali and Fedor, they steal cigarette truck, kill driver," Oleg said. "Back of truck has no cigarettes, has this headed to military base in Nevada."

Peter saying, what is the plan, a war?

Oleg smiled. "You never know what Andrei has planned."

Oh, shit. Yamenhi Tribal Leader Brian Locklear sensed trouble the second Rivers End GM Scott Tsosie entered the Coho Room for their scheduled meeting with the F.B.I. *He's all gung-ho, ready to go. Tsosie reminded Brian of a lot of young natives who were mad at the world for crimes committed in generations past.* Next to Brian was assistant GM Lance Caron. *I may have to suspend Scott if he cannot act right. I don't know if Lance is ready to take over the reigns of the Rivers End.*

20

Brian eyed Richard Yazzie across the table from him. *He brings out the worst in Tsosie, makes him see demons that aren't there, especially white ones.* Tsosie moved into the room with his body guard Col. Civil-Fielder, moving as a bully with a large stick, waiting to use it if anyone crossed his path. *And he did, which is how we got into this mess.*

The F.B.I. had brought in a field agent to discuss the matter. Sam Brown, a young man who sat at the far end of the table, away from Yazzie, Tsosie and Brian. He did not rise to extend his hand for Tsosie when the general manager entered the room. He sat, stared, examining a dossier in front of him. Brown wore a cheap suit, hair cropped close, and eyed the Rivers End executives until everyone except for Civil-Fielder sat down. The bodyguard stood next to the door. Brian eyed the sidearm which bulged from the holster of the Colonel's suit coat, then looked at Brown, seeing a scar which ran over his right eye that still appeared fresh.

Brian noted the look of smug arrogance across Tsosie's face. *Brown and Scott are going to be adversaries from the start, using the Rivers End as their pissing ground.* Yazzie appeared unconcerned. Brian felt worried, eying his young general manager in the expensive suit. Brian wished Reggie Barber were still alive. *I would have made him general manager, groomed Scott for a while until he was ready.* Whatever happened out at Reggie Barber's farm house, it appeared there was a side to the man that Brian didn't know. *Cops think Reggie and his family were murdered in a drug deal dispute by a local gang, burned them alive while they slept in their house.*

"Two hundred, sixty-nine," Brown said, without looking up from his dossier.

Everyone in the room eyed Brown at the end of the table. The summer sun caught the back of his shoulders from the windows. Brown leaned in. "Two hundred, sixty-nine. Now that's impressive."

"Excuse me?" Brian said, curious what the number represented.

Brown: "That's how many rounds were used to suppress a half-naked body builder."

"It was necessary," Tsosie said, uninterested. "Guy went nuts."

"His body was almost torn in half by the time it got down to the city morgue."

Brian looked at the other Rivers End executives, shocked. "Did you each know about this?"

Tsosie, Yazzie and Civil-Fielder appeared unconcerned, indifferent. Lance Caron appeared as surprised as Brian felt. *Yazzie's having a bad effect on Scott. Making him cold, calculated.* Brown waited, then smiled, shaking his head. *Now he's going to use Scott's reaction against us.*

"He had it coming," Tsosie said to Brown. "I have a right to protect my guests."

"Don't you think it's a tad over-kill?" Brown said.

"One woman is paralyzed, a man is dead, others injured," Tsosie said. When he stood, pointing at Brown, Tsosie reminded Brian of Tsosie's father, Russell. *That fiery asshole who took on anyone if you gave him a chance, saying stand for what you believe in, be damned the consequences.* "I don't know why the F.B.I. feels they should criticize us for protecting the public from a maniac."

Brown smirked at Tsosie. "This is not tribal sovereign ground. It's United States soil."

"A few of your Supreme Court rulings disagree with you," Yazzie said. "We have the right to operate here, manage this facility as we see fit."

Brian glared at Yazzie. *What is he doing? He knows what this could cost the Rivers End and the Yamenhi tribe if the F.B.I. gets upset at us.* Yazzie did not make eye contact with Brian. *Too busy fighting some type of tribal issue with the F.B.I.* Brian didn't want to go back to having nothing if the F.B.I. attempted to shut down the Rivers End. *Where the only F.B.I. man you see is a Flat Broke Indian.*

"You do have the right to operate," Brown said, conceding. "But killing people means a formal inquiry."

Yazzie: "Our tribal council performs criminal inquiries, not the F.B.I."

"Do they also monitor alcohol consumption?" Brown said.

Tsosie, Yazzie, Caron and Brian exchanged confused glances. Brian to Tsosie: "What the hell is he talking about?"

"Local police say you've had three guests arrested for D.U.I. suspicion on Bayliss Road, not two miles from here," Brown said. "That's just in the last two weeks."

Tsosie shrugged. "We've got five thousand people through here each day, you bring up three. That's not even a percentage."

"That's the beauty of the law. Nuance," Brown said. "If I want to blow it out of proportion, I can. Takes five minutes to recommend a full review of the casino's serving license by the state liquor board."

Enough is enough. Tsosie can be frustrating, but Brown is trying to gut the casino with a bureaucratic knife. Brian shook his head. "You can't pull our liquor license."

"Full review doesn't mean pulling it," Brown said. "But that suspends all facility alcohol sales while it sits in turnaround for thirty to ninety days."

Tsosie: "Thirty to ninety days?"

The revelation shocked all of the Rivers End executives. A liquor license suspension would kill the casino operation. *Hell, our study of not selling alcohol between the hours of two and six in the morning showed we lost ten million annually because sober people do not gamble as much as those drunk.* Losing the ability to sell alcohol for thirty days would cost the Rivers End a fortune. *But I know the United States bureaucratic nightmare would be sixty-five days or more.* The Rivers End would be a ghost town, eliminated by virtue of revenue never coming back. *The negative publicity would kill us afterward, even if we started serving alcohol during that time.*

"Your liquor license is issued by the state," Brown said. "If the F.B.I. asks the liquor board to issue a full review, it will happen."

Yazzie: "We are standing on tribal land up to five feet beyond the casino's parking lot. That's all tribal, only after that is the United States. Where we stand here, it's our laws, our rules."

"The land was parceled by agreement with the United States and the State of Washington," Brown said. "All individuals with United States citizenship are subject to U.S. laws. I can haul any of them into Federal Court, put them in front of Judge Roth, to get to what happened to Ulysses Turner."

Yazzie said, "Our security staff who confronted Turner are not United States citizens."

Brown shrugged. "They have visas to enter this country. Therefore, I can bring them up on charges if I need to."

Tsosie was about to say something when Yazzie put his hand up, silencing the general manager. *I wish I knew why he had so much control over Scott.* Yazzie pointed at Brown. "I think this discussion is over." Tsosie, Yazzie and Civil-Fielder exited the Coho Room. Lance Caron and Brian stayed behind with Brown. *Yazzie seems hell-bent on destroying the Rivers End to make a point with the F.B.I.*

"Who was that older man?"

Brian eyed Brown, curious. *Are you going to persecute him for talking back to you?* "He runs the tribal gaming agency."

Brown paused, appearing to think. He said, "I've seen him somewhere before. But I can't tell you where at the moment."

Brian: "Lucky us."

"I need your group here to understand something," Brown said.

"The Rivers End is fifty miles beyond your tribal borders, thanks to the state and federal government. I want you to understand that, because if you don't, I'll have your gaming licenses transferred back to Yamenhi tribal grounds. This place will be an empty shell in two months with a mountain of debt."

Brian had dealt with people like Sam Brown. *A tribal chief is nothing more than the complaint department of his people. Hear them out, let their anger simmer, relax them, then calmly speak a solution.* Brian cared little for threats. Usually from the I.R.S. about Title 31 violations. *We don't want this F.B.I. agent going away deciding to do us harm.* Brian knew he would have to agree to something in this meeting in order to keep the Rivers End from being targeted.

"How do I comply with the F.B.I. enough to keep the Rivers End going?" Brian said. "No liquor board inquiries, no gaming licenses transferred."

"The F.B.I. would be happier if there weren't a paramilitary force acting as bodyguards for the general manager," Brown said.

Brian nodded. "It happened after he was attacked. Now he thinks he needs round-the-clock protection." *All of that blood coming out of Scott. I thought he was going to die in my arms.*

"What is this?" Brown said. "Some new age murkiness where you own up to something only to silence questions while doing whatever you damn well please no matter who you end up hurting?"

"I was telling you why he feels he needs the bodyguards."

"Regardless of the reasoning, I would like to know how he pays for it," Brown said. "He makes an annual salary in the low one hundreds and I don't see a discretionary fund set-up for their payroll."

"How would you suggest I go about doing this?" Brian said. "He's the GM, I can't pull casino staff together without having questions asked out in the open."

Brown shrugged. "Hire a private auditor, off the books, who is doing it at the request of the F.B.I. to ensure all employee overtime is being paid. We've got a hellish lawsuit we are investigating the Bureau of Indian Affairs on, so it has credibility."

Brian: "And that's it? You won't try to suspend licenses or anything that hurts the Rivers End?"

Brown shook his head. "If the Rivers End becomes more cooperative in the death of Mister Ulysses Turner, then I don't have a problem with the operation. That being said, find a way to tone down the bodyguards. None of them should carry high-caliber weapons on your premises."

Stew arrived at Exit One because The Serg had called a meeting and was unsure he should be there without back-up. Oleg had contacted him on a cell, he didn't know that the Russian goon had his number. *Said Andrei wanted to talk after I told him he backs us with guns and juice, we go in heavy at the Rivers End casino.* Stew failed to mention his intent on shooting the native asshole Scott Tsosie in the face. Not for what the guy had his security team do to Ulysses Turner. *No, this shit is personal.* Stew was still pissed about being banned from the Rivers End competition. *That asshole took away everything I worked so hard for.* The Serg wouldn't understand, thinking it was a petty vendetta rather than a skilled robbery.

The builder entered the strip club, seeing it turned down in the morning hour. Door was open, summer light spilled in behind him, extending his shadow deep. Stew eyed it, seeing no one waiting to brawl him, though he half expected it. Stew wondered if Oleg had burned him after selling him some purple vials. *That shit worked wonders, took Ulysses Turner out quick, same with Blye.* Stew wanted to feel bad about Blye. *Guy wouldn't shut up, had to be first for his shot. Some guys are lucky, Blye wasn't one of them.*

Eying the place, Stew noted The Serg with his back to the door,

21

sitting in one of the stained lounge chairs near the main stage, sipping on tea or some shit out of a small cup. *It's weird seeing this dive without people in it.* No dancers parading plastic work of a downtown surgery while prepping a five-dollar-dive across the couch. Oleg and Peter came out from the basement, greeting Stew with a nod but not doing anything to stop him from entering.

Stew eyed both with suspicion as Oleg approached, leaving Peter by the basement door. Stew lifted his huge arms, letting Oleg feel his mass for weapons. The Russian goon grinned when Stew came up clean, winking at him, gesturing for Stew to see The Serg by the stage. Stew leaned forward, giving Oleg a look. *If you want to go, we can go.* Not being too serious, but standing his ground to keep the Russian from taking him light. Oleg stood firm but respected Stew's posture saying nothing. Stew glanced at Peter, but that goon said nothing either.

Stew went to The Serg, catching a mixture of thirty different cheap perfumes in his nostrils. Spent liquor, body fluids and stale cigarette smoke in the furniture. The Serg was not alone, sitting with a balding guy with a ponytail. Trying to catch the 1980s and his youth as best as he could. Stew sat across from the two men, offering his mitt to the ponytail dude. Stew gave The Serg a false smile, saying this man the reason you called me here?

The Serg nodded. Saying yes, name was Turk, old friend. Stew sized Turk up, seeing the man giving him back a cheap, big box store grin from a cashier lady right before they check your receipt to see if you stole anything on the way out. Turk was five-ten, lean, riding the age of forty-five north to fifty with a weathered face.

Stew shared eyes with Turk, getting that chance to find out who people are before they open their mouth. *Wondering if you are getting fed the truth or a line of shit.* Stew could tell the guy had done time. *Not serious enough to branch out over county stays, maybe a state vacation of less than two.* Stew figured asking a guy if they did time gave the answer quick. *It's bullshit if they want to talk about it. Guys who say nothing they were the ones who did serious stretches. That stiffness in the brain, remembering all of those mindless hours in turn-your-life-around sessions with ten other cons, some dink shrink thinking he's saving the world wearing a sweatervest.* Turk acted prepped to be attacked by watching the place at all points as any con in *The Sides* would.

"Andrei says you got ideas," Turk said.

The way Turk called The Serg by his first name, he was trusted. No one used The Serg's first name without permission or being part of his inner circle. *Seen guys try to pull it, knocked out with Oleg's .45 imprinted against their skull.* The Serg never gave the order to attack. Guys did it as a matter of principle for disrespecting the old Russian. *Anyone who knows The Serg enough to call him by his first name has the old man's backing.*

Stew started by telling Turk that his idea depended on Pink Cadillac before and after the job was done. The Serg nodded. *Saying yeah, he's willing to provide on that end of the deal.* Stew grinned.

"Rivers End Casino," Stew said. "Scoped it out, looks good if we hit it hard and figure it can be taken down. Security is a mess; both teams answer to the same guy."

Turk laughed, masking it as a huff, eyeing The Serg, sharing a silent moment. *Maybe I made a mistake with this man, thinking I could count on him.* Stew glared at Turk. *Don't do that, thinking I can't have a plan, don't know how to bust something down when I want to.* He watched the cheap crook across from him shake his head and wanted to yank on the man's ponytail, hard.

"Place took down one of your boys," Turk said. "They got you on camera, in mind, they know who you are."

"We hit them hard, they don't know shit," Stew said. "I ain't avenging anyone. Turner was an asshole. Blye was just a dumbshit."

Turk: "But they put them down, right? Security there has enough hardware to do it without prep and answering to the same guy."

"What are you getting at?"

This asshole ain't taking me serious. He thinks I'm some dumb con out on vacation. That I can't pull off a job. That I want to go back to The Sides. Stew wanted to rip the man from his seat, strangle him. *But you gotta show respect, he's with The Serg. All of the builders needed more Pink Cadillac. What we have ain't cutting it anymore. We keep getting weaker.* Stew didn't know what would happen if The Serg cut all of the builders off.

"I got a better plan," Turk said. "More pay, but I need muscle, which is why Andrei said you would be the one I talked to."

"I want the Rivers End," Stew said. *I get the feeling I'm dealing with another Ulysses Turner in this Turk asshole.* He figured taking Dean and Kyle, they could rage the cashier cage, be out with two hundred grand while putting a few holes in the ceiling. *That's my plan, even if Turk doesn't jive with it, thinks I need him and shit.* The Rivers End meant something to Stew and Kyle. Dean was coming around a little ever since Turner got shot up. *Paying back that native asshole Tsosie is too important. Taking his shit from him is way too sweet to pass up too.*

The Serg noticed Stew's reaction, even if the old Russian said nothing about it. *Asked me to hear Turk out, he knows what he's doing.* Stew sat, wondering if The Serg didn't take Stew serious either.

"Pitchfork Alley is the downtown district's version of a gold mine going along Riverside, yet no one hits it," Turk said.

Stew: "No one hits it because its three blocks from the police department. More blue action than a thief can handle."

Turk nodded, agreeing with Stew. *Then why are we discussing it? Case closed. There's too much blue coming down your throat to comprehend a plan actually working.*

"Four banks, two diamond stores, about five hundred feet of gold connected by alleyway system," Turk said. "Got two guys working as armored truck carriers for four months, waiting for this score to come together, cause it's easy if we do it right."

Stew asking where the muscle fits in, or do we?

"Muscle's gotta handle the heat and there will be some," Turk said. "We come down the other alley, make sure that any blue arrives gets it hard while my boys steal the loot. Andrei says you don't have an issue giving some blue a few toe tags."

Stew shook his head. "I came to talk about doing the Rivers End."

The Serg placed his hand on Stew's massive arm, calming him and giving him a serious look. Stew eying The Serg's calloused, cigarette-stained hand on his arm. *Wanting to rip it off, kill the old man but knowing you can't because he has the Pink Cadillac. You do it, you get drained to nothing.* The Serg's glare dropped Stew's anger, letting the temperature simmer. *I know who gives the orders.* Stew glanced beyond The Serg to Oleg, seeing the man draw out his .45 from its holster. *In case he needs to put me down with seven shots to the chest.*

"There a problem?" Turk said.

Stew shook his head, saying no problem.

"I back Pitchfork plan," The Serg said. "If it goes well, we do casino after."

Stew nodded, liking the idea. "What do you need from us?"

"Two, maybe three muscle boys," Turk said. "Andrei says one of the guys you have fights well, got some raw talent."

Stew sat wondering if Dean would do the job. *If Dean's not in, I'm guessing Turk and The Serg won't be willing to go ahead either. We need this to get more Pink Cadillac.* Stew saw how low the funds were getting. *Kyle and I are losing our pad, Dean's gym is going under in two months. How long before we got nothing left, no Pink Cadillac to keep us going?* Stew figured Dean would have listened more if they would have hit the Rivers End. *Man is still mourning the loss of that asshole Turner.* Now that Ulysses Turner was out of the picture, it might be easier to get Dean into the fold. *Get him holding a piece, knowing it's for his own survival.*

Stew noted that both The Serg and Turk were eying him, trying to figure out if there was an issue.

Stew to The Serg: "Give me some Pink Cadillac, enough for me and Kyle for a week. Cut Dean off so he drops that moral code. Then we'll be ready to go."

The Serg nodded, grinning at the idea. The Serg had Oleg offer up a white crate of Pink Cadillac. The Serg told Stew he would have Oleg deliver hardware for the Pitchfork job.

"I want to be going a week from tomorrow," Turk said. "Hit guys on a Friday, with blue having their pants down ready for the weekend fishing plans, no one expects it. My boys will be moving their armored truck in for a deposit, on schedule, not even raising a red flag before we hit them."

Stew smiled, liking what he was hearing. Things were going down good. He had prepped on taking something down. If it meant doing the Pitchfork before screwing over that native asshole at The Rivers End, so be it. *But I'm going to get Scott Tsosie. Whether it be next week or three months from now, that asshole's place is going down.* Stew could already see the shocked look on that native man's face as he envisioned putting a gun up against the man's head, pulling the trigger. *Now I get to show you how hard I fight.*

"Have you guys had success in quitting?"

It had been two weeks since Turner's death.

22

Dean Shockley had tried quitting the Pink Cadillac about ten times since then. *Each time, I find myself going back to get another dose.* The three builders sat in Dean's office. Kyle and Stew offered blank looks to each other, then offered a shroud of worry to Dean. *They don't have it as bad as I do.* He felt like crying. Daddy was no longer in the corner shadows waiting for him. *Everyone but Stew and Kyle has left me.*

Kyle raised his hand. "I tried to, but it ain't worth it."

Stew nodded. "Got the shakes, couldn't feel my right arm for a couple hours, got through about half a day before I found myself needing it. Couldn't get out of my own chair I was so weak."

"Yeah," Kyle said. "Couldn't eat, sleep. I'd lie there on my mattress for hours, couldn't even think. It was scary, man."

Dean: "And now The Serg don't want to supply us, does he?"

"He got us good," Kyle said. "I ain't ending my days like Blye."

The rest of the builders nodded at that sentiment. No one wanted to lie for years in a hospital bed, brain dead with a feeding tube shoved down their throat. *All because momma's got religion, can't pull the plug cause her little boy won't get to heaven if he don't go naturally.* The living death that Blye was enduring scared Dean. *There has to be way to get more stuff.*

"We could do a job for him," Stew said. "Man backs people who earn."

"How many more fights can I do like this?" Dean lifted his arm, which took effort. "He's thinned us out to the point where we have next to nothing."

Stew shook his head. "Not a fight. We pull a job."

Kyle nodded. "Pay for enough shit we don't have to worry about The Serg for a while."

Dean felt uneasy about the two builders. Turner was right, they were two cold-blooded killers hiding as my friends. Dean eyed the corner shadows, not seeing Daddy there to tell him what to do. *Where are you, Daddy? I need you to tell me what to do. His father had been gone since the Rivers End competition.* Sometimes Dean would stir awake at night and expect Daddy to be sitting at the foot of his bed. *He's abandoned me, as he did before.*

"I can't be a part of it," Dean said.

Stew leaned in. "You serious right now?"

Dean didn't want to offer an answer. *There's that feeling of no return from this, because I'm sitting with two felons.* Dean wished Daddy were there to make them go away. *If Turner was here, I wouldn't have to be alone in this. He would step in, tell them to leave and that would be that.* Dean didn't want to be alone anymore. *Everyone else has left me except for Kyle and Stew.*

Dean shook his head. "There has to be another way. Something to tide us over until The Serg starts giving us more."

"What do you possibly have that he wants other than us pulling a job?" Stew said. "Look around you. The gym's going under in a month, you got nothing, Dean. Not even your old man wants to talk to you."

The debt of the gym was weighing on Dean's mind. *I kept thinking that the winnings from the Rivers End competition would cover anything we did. It would be the price of admission to take home first place.* The gym memberships were morbid. *We kept kicking people out, giving them refunds, so we could work out in private. The bank keeps calling on the two mortgages, gonna close me down in a week.*

He had tapered off of the Pink Cadillac, watching Stew and Kyle not need it to keep going. *I tried doing forty milligrams same as what Turner did.* But it never worked. *I felt zapped by the thought of working out.* Something inside him desired Fireball. *Get that plug of the needle into my ass, do reps all day until I go to bed at night. What do you have to lose now if you pull a job? Not the gym, not Daddy.* Dean found himself nodding. Stew and Kyle smiled at him.

"Okay," Dean said. "Let's go see The Serg."

23 Tony Hell opened his lids. Air breathed onto his pupils as he saw foreign images in his head. *A woman hugging me, saying she loved me. And I love her.* Tony winced, wanting to hurt the woman. Then, he decided he did not. He looked to the corner shadows, expecting to see Mikhail, who was gone. Tony moved off his mattress in the dark, feeling his muscles sing to him. *I need the fuel to survive.* A piercing sound made him squint. *Another image of this woman I love. I slip a ring on her finger and look into her eyes.* Tony wanted to devour those beautiful blue orbs she carried, then decided he did not.

"I am D.E.A.," Tony said.

He did not know what that meant. The words recessed in his mind, causing him to speak. *What is D.E.A.?* Another image played for him. *I am receiving my credentials from a man in a suit. Saying congratulations on making the team, his name is Weaver.* Tony slapped his head, screaming. *What are these thoughts that have been injected into my head?* Tony eyed the corner shadows, seeing a faint version of a stranger sitting there. There were seconds in which the stranger's presence would flicker, then vanish before reappearing.

"Peter?" Tony said. "Are you, Peter?"

No, I am Mikhail, the stranger said. *I am you.*

Mikhail's voice dipped, drowning as he spoke. Tony sat up, his head groggy, tired. "Who are you?"

Tony ached for the fire that ran through his veins. *I need the fuel to survive.* It had flushed from his system. He imagined a gigantic drain, the energy drowning away, sucking him dry. Tony let out an exhaustive huff, seeing Mikhail vanish from the corner shadows. *Who is this ghost who haunts me?* Tony heard shuffling from the metal door. He looked through the slot, seeing a face staring back at him in the dark. *Who is this with such beautiful eyes?* Tony edged forward.

"Anthony, are you in there?"

The person moved back as Tony approached. *Afraid of what I will do to him if I grab hold.* He stopped, noting how the person looked. Nervous, apprehensive about whatever he was doing. *Are you another ghost, same as my brother Mikhail?* Tony wiped his own face, feeling the sweat come down on him. Another image stalked his mind. *I am telling a man that I am Anthony Batellini, D.E.A. What is D.E.A.?* Tony shook it off, blinking at the person beyond the metal door.

"Who are you?" Tony said to the corner shadow where a stranger appeared again. "Who are you, really?"

The person beyond the door spoke, gaining Tony's attention. "I am Peter Volov, don't you remember?"

Tony: "I am D.E.A."

"You are Anthony Batellini, D.E.A., that's right," Peter said. "That means the drug is working. I've come down here before, tried to get you to talk before."

"Anthony Batellini," Tony said, repeating what the person had said.

Peter nodded, excited. "Yes, you are Anthony. That means the blue vials are working. They get you clean."

He is lying, Mikhail said in the corner shadows. *He is trying to trick you.*

Tony eyed his brother whose image flickered in the corner. Mikhail appeared translucent but content in the shadows. "Who is Mikhail?"

Peter slammed against the metal door, gaining Tony's attention. "It is the drugs they have given you. Mikhail was your undercover name here. There is no Mikhail."

Tony peered through the metal door. "What do you want?"

"To get you free of here," Peter said. "But we don't have time, soon though. Give me your arm."

Don't do it, brother, Mikhail said. *He will betray you.*

Tony spat in Mikhail's direction, watching his image flicker. Another image attacked his mind. *I have a wife named Andrea. She loves me very much.* Tony wanted to see this Andrea. *She is so beautiful that I cried when she said yes to me*. Tony's eyes fell upon the metal door. "Where is Andrea? What have you done with her?"

"Nothing," Peter said. "Give me your arm and I will help you."

Tony stuck his arm through the metal door slot. He felt a bee sting slice into him. He pulled back his arm, feeling the fuel pound through his veins. *I want it, but I don't*. The image of Andrea watered, leaving him. Tony felt his eyes milk with hatred, seeing Mikhail return fully-formed. *He betrayed me*. Tony gnarled his teeth as he moved forward, sticking his arms through the slot in the metal door to grab Peter. The man backed up, escaping Tony's grasp.

"I will come back for you soon," Peter said, leaving.

You have been made into an addict, dear brother, Mikhail said, laughing at Tony.

"I am a God," Tony said, kicking at Mikhail to no affect.

Do you know your real name? Mikhail said.

Tony heard water droplets crashing into floor puddles along with the beat of the club above his head. His nostrils picked up the enhanced scents of blood, pus and decay fermenting in his room. The fuel was alive in his system. Tony wiped the caked dirt from his skin. The Serg loves me, enjoys my brutality, it is my gift back to him.

You are his dog, Mikhail said. *An animal put to sleep after it can no longer fight.*

"I am still a warrior," Tony said. "It is you who are not the favorite here."

I am you, Mikhail said.

"Stop saying that," Tony said, screaming.

I taunt you because I can, dear brother, Mikhail said.

Tony pulled back his right fist, swinging it to pummel Mikhail. The attack missed, Tony's hand swinging free through the air. Mikhail laughed, begging to be punished. Tony readied to attack again when he heard footsteps coming down the staircase toward his room. Tony eyed the metal door, seeing the light illuminate over the fighting pit. *Do I have another challenger?* Tony's mouth foamed saliva, waiting for more fuel to charge through his system. Mikhail laughed in the corner shadows, drawing Tony's attention.

Your master is here to sell you out and give away more of your precious fuel to those undeserving, Mikhail said.

"You lie."

Look for yourself and see the betrayal firsthand, Mikhail said, gesturing toward the metal door's slot.

"His business does not concern me," Tony said, waving his brother off. He spat on Mikhail's face. His brother grinned as the slime ran down his cheeks, indifferent.

Tonight it does, Mikhail said.

"Welcome back, my friends."

Tony heard The Serg's voice speaking in slow Russian outside his door. He heard the shuffling of footsteps. Tony peered through the metal slot. The Serg stood with Fedor, who acted as translator. The Serg said to Fedor, "Stew wants us to keep his friend weak. Tell them that I will only supply them if they do the job."

Fedor spoke in English to the visitors who Tony could not see. The words were spoken fast enough that Tony could not understand what was being said back and forth. Fedor focused on The Serg and said, "Dean says we tricked them into being junkies. They will die without fuel."

They are your replacements, Mikhail said.

"No," Tony said, screaming. His fingers clutched the door's slot, yanking to rip it free. Oleg headed over to the door, zapping Tony with a cattle prod. Tony released the slot, falling back. He watched Oleg grin, zapping the door a couple more times, eager to hurt Tony again. *I will kill you, Oleg, and devour your eyes*. Oleg moved away from the slot. Tony crept closer, watching as Dean stood near The Serg and Fedor in the pit.

"Tell them no trick, they have what they have," The Serg said.

"They help me, I give them more."

Fedor relayed the information to the builders. Dean reacted with anger while the other two appeared content. *They want to do what The Serg asks. It is Dean who is keeping them from it.* The Serg leaned in as Fedor spoke English, waving him off to halt his conversation with the builders. The Serg gestured at Dean. "I have associate who needs your services. I will offer you much more Fireball in exchange."

Tony watched Dean, seeing the man stand, thinking. The two other builders moved behind him, speaking English. *Convincing him that he has no choice; the job must be done to obtain more.* Dean gestured to The Serg. "What are we going to do?"

The Serg's eyes ignited at the builders' interest. "Rob downtown district tomorrow. Turk calls it 'Pitchfork Alley.' Needs muscle for job. For this, I give you as much Fireball as you want."

Of the three men, Dean was the only one recoiling at the suggestion of a robbery. The two other builders leaned in, interested, smiling. The two builders closed in on Dean, convincing him. *The Serg will get what he wants from these men.* Tony shook his head, angry.

He has given away your fuel, brother, Mikhail said. *This man treats you as if you are nothing.*

A froth boiled from Tony's mouth. It foamed huge goblets that fell from his lips, descending onto the ground in large splats. *I swear vengeance against you, Serg, who have stolen my fuel, and given it to my enemies.* Tony's eyes went to Dean, who stood with a grin on his face, with the two other men. *You will feast on my supply for only a short time. But once I break free of this prison, I will devour your eyes.*

24

"I love her, that's all you gotta know."

Lance Caron sat his desk, amazed. Reverend Archibald sat in Lance's office, confessing his love for Lance's wife, Keisha. *I should reach across and beat him to death.* Archibald had arrived unannounced, speaking to guest services to navigate back to Lance. *I expected him to approach me on having the Rivers End casino provide a grant for his mission, but not this.* Lance had suppressed the feelings about Scott Tsosie's involvement with Keisha. *There are things I cannot do anything about, but this is a different matter.*

The Reverend had offered up dates when Keisha had met him at the Lower Union Mission. Where they had first kissed, contemplating that they would be together. All of those little things that Lance had ignored appeared obvious now. When she would work late at the office or never come home at all. *I felt guilty that I had pushed her away because I left to gain sobriety.* But this had a far sinister feel to it. *She's with him because he's darker than I am.*

"I don't expect you to understand," Archibald said.

"What's that supposed to mean?" Lance said. "What about this can't I fully comprehend?"

"Well…" Archibald said, stammering. "I'm a better fit for her."

Lance: "What she tells you, and what she is, are two different things."

Lance grinned with a slow nod of his head. *He thinks I'm too white for her. He doesn't realize that her parents would kill her if she got a divorce.* If there was one thing he had learned about Keisha's family, after she was married, the family begrudgingly accepted Lance. To a point, because neither of her parents believe divorce is an option. Keisha's cousin divorced her husband who was beating on her and her children. Keisha's parents refused to attend gatherings if the cousin was there.

"Have you told Keisha you were coming to see me?"

"I didn't want to interfere in your marriage."

Lance stunned, laughed. "Didn't want to interfere?"

Archibald grew angry, pointing at Lance. "Now, just hold up a damn minute."

"Wait," Lance said, holding up his hands. "I'll discuss it with Keisha tonight. If she wants a divorce, we will get one. Are you satisfied?"

Archibald appeared confused. "Why are you giving up so easy on her?"

Lance drew divorce papers out of his desk. He handed them to Archibald, who looked them over, curious. "I have been considering this for a while. But I've tried to get her to sign them, it hasn't worked."

"What does that mean?"

"I tried two years ago," Lance said. "She tried to slit her wrists in the bathroom. Spent sixteen hours in the emergency room regretting having the papers."

"That isn't the Keisha I know," Archibald said. *He's in denial because he only sees what Keisha wants him to see. Not the cold woman, frail and willing to harm herself to keep me from leaving.*

"I guess we'll find out, won't we?"

Archibald handed the papers back to Lance. "I'm glad that you understand my position in this."

"Oh, I do, Reverend," Lance said. "I do."

Lance called Keisha as soon as Archibald left his office. Arranged for them to meet at Wen's Diner on Elm, the first place they ate when they had come into the city. The food was never good, the waitresses crass, but they held anniversary meals there as a way of remembering the past. Lance sat in his booth waiting for Keisha as the clock hit a little after five with the sun still up and summer holding on as best as it could to light. He remembered how she had been hired with the U.S. Attorney General's office, was relocated to Spokane, and how even when he was unemployed, she saw something in him that kept them together.

I know her father offered her money to prevent her from marrying me. Lance decided he needed to see what Keisha wanted to do. *Let her know that I love her. That it's okay to be wrong.* He remembered the move to the city being one of silence. Her family wasn't speaking to her, hoping she would come back from a summer fling with me and tell them that we had broken up. Lance and Keisha had thought of eloping in Aspen or heading off to Europe.

But in the end, we attempted to make right by planning to come back to Baltimore, to marry in front of our parents in order to give them an olive branch. Keisha's parents attempted to be civil to Lance, but nothing more. *I was too white for them, not good enough for their daughter. If they could only see their little girl now.*

When they had arrived in the city, Lance had been unemployed after leaving a junior executive position with a tire manufacturer in New York. *Spent months applying for the wrong jobs.* A classmate from Columbia told him about the Rivers End Casino. *Said he knew a man named Reggie Barber from high school, talked to him about me, wanted to meet me about a position they had open in the hospitality division.* The meeting went well between Reggie Barber and Lance. Scott Tsosie joined them at some point, each drinking, enjoying each other's company. *That's when I knew*

I was finally a part of something big. Finally one of the group.

Keisha arrived at the diner, looking around then found Lance in the booth tucked in the back. Better to give us privacy to talk. She walked over, took off her coat and sat across from him. She smiled, pointing to the menu. "I'm having fish and chips."

Lance grinned. *She always orders that when we come here.* "Sounds fair."

Keisha gestured to the menu. "You know I hate red meat, but I'm sure you'll have the burger and fries anyway."

Lance shrugged. "Old habits, huh?"

They laughed. Lance eyed the manila folder next to him, wondering if he should offer it to her. His eyes went to Keisha's left wrist, seeing scars below the palm running down into her sleeve. *She wouldn't let me go then, even when I told her I knew about the other men.* He looked at those eyes of Keisha's. *What's she going to do when I tell her it's over?* The two of them alone in the back of the diner, aside from a waitress pouring black coffee for a man at the counter, hovering around the fifty-cent cup while keeping his eye on the tube anytime CNN had a new update on the Middle East. *Archibald came to me without discussing it with her, so she might not want to leave me.*

Lance smiled. "How is everything at work?"

"Fine," she said. "Judge Roth needs to retire."

"He comes into the casino a lot."

Keisha: "His wife died a few years ago, I think it took a lot out of him."

"Cancer?"

Keisha shook her head. "Elective surgery, getting her stomach stapled. You never know what might happen when you go into the hospital."

Lance nodded. He remembered his mother passing. She had gone into the doctor for a routine check-up and that's when they found the tumor. "He never talks about it?"

"I wouldn't expect him to," Keisha said. "He spends his time on the bench issuing tangents about lack of law enforcement. He sees criminals everywhere."

"He's been talking about his daughter on the police force, how proud he is of her."

Keisha: "She's an idiot who got pushed through the academy because of him. I had to work for what I had, fight that good ole black tax."

Lance ignored what Keisha said. He smiled wider, staring into her eyes. Keisha focused back on him, blushing. Lance looked down at the manila folder, moving it back into his bag. *If Archibald wants to push it, he can. But I'm not going to lose her unless I have to.*

"What?"

"I enjoy being with you." Lance reached across the table, putting his hand on Keisha's. She did not move away from him. *There's still something here between us. No matter what Archibald or anyone else wants to think, she loves me.* "And I want to apologize."

Keisha's eyes welled with tears. "You need to involve me, Lance. Whatever you're going through, that needs to be it."

"I have thought about it a lot," Lance said. "I should have asked you to come with me."

"The truth is, I don't even know where you went," Keisha said. "Or with whom."

The way she spoke stopped him. *Does she really think I would betray her trust?* The comment burned him, especially after the meeting with Archibald. *How many more men has she been with?* Lance didn't want the answer. "I went to dry out and did it the best way I could."

"I don't know if that's good enough."

They ate their meal in silence. Lance's eyes drifted away from Keisha, over to the guy at the counter who had left without giving a tip. *She acts as if she is a saint.* His cell phone chimed a text. It was from Locklear: *Emergency meeting in twenty minutes, Coho Room.*

"I have to go back to work," Lance said.

He pushed his burger away, slid out of the booth, heading toward the door. *Keisha doesn't want to forgive me.* Halfway down the diner floor, he heard Keisha say something back to him. *She will stay to punish me and keep sleeping with Archibald as if nothing is wrong.* He turned to see her moving out of the booth, grabbing something off the floor. The manila folder must have fallen out of his bag.

"You dropped something," Keisha said.

Lance watched her reach for the manila folder, opening it, reading the contents of the divorce papers, seeing the printed-out photos from the security camera shots of Keisha and Scott Tsosie kissing in the suite hallway. Keisha looked up at him, surprised.

Lance shook his head. "We can't keep doing this, Keisha. I don't care what you try to do to yourself, I can't live this way anymore."

25 Dean Shockley sat on his father's porch holding his face in his hands. Tears soaked through the cracks of his fingers. *I have shamed my father to this point of my life. I've never been good enough for what Daddy deserves.* Dean fought temptation to confess what had happened at the Exit One to his father. *Daddy won't understand, he'll think I'm weak, that I want to be a criminal.* Dean moved his arms and strained against the weakness. *I'm nothing but a slave to my habit.*

He looked at his trembling hands as the last vestiges of Fireball flushed from his system. *I need it so bad. I don't want to be weak anymore.* Kyle and Stew were prepping for tomorrow back at the gym. *I've been made a thief by Fireball.* The Serg had made it clear they would be cut off from the drug. Kyle and Stew had left him alone, letting him decide whether he was in or not. *I need the juice in order to exist.*

Dean's eyes went to his red beat-up Ford truck parked across the street from his father's house. *I could sell it, maybe get some other builder to go in, by some shit off The Serg.* His mind went to his gym. *Maybe sell the equipment before the repo men collect next week.* None of that sounded appealing. *I can maybe buy enough to last me two or three days. Then I'm back to this.* Dean saw no other choice but to go ahead with the Pitchfork plan.

He felt the urge to leave as the sun was dropping from the sky, a light pink hue turning black into the night. Dean checked his cell, seeing that it was after eight. *If we take down the Pitchfork, I'll get what I need. Get back to making Daddy proud of me again.* Dean shook his head, wishing that his father would talk to him. *I wish I hadn't listened to Ulysses Turner back at the first competition. Things would be so much easier now.* He dismissed those thoughts, knowing his father was never going to be happy with his son. *Not after what I have become.*

If I help take down the Pitchfork, maybe we'll get away with it. So Daddy won't have to see his embarrassment of a son on the eleven o'clock news. He sat there on his father's porch waiting for his strength to come back to him. *I took a complimentary dose in the Exit One parking lot after meeting The Serg. But the burn hasn't come like it used to.* His body remained sick, misshapen as the drug remained dormant in his system. *I remember how good that first dose was, best I ever had, way back when we juiced up and rode out the night lifting during a hardcore burn. Where's that feeling now?* Every dose he took after that first one felt as if he were trying to climb back to the original feeling.

Dean lifted himself off his father's porch. *Leave Daddy alone now.* He eyed his truck, ready to head back to the gym. *Begin my life as a criminal to support my habit.* Stew and Kyle were unloading the body armor and weapons that The Serg had supplied them with. *He's been prepping for this for a long time.* The porch light flickered on behind Dean as he headed away from Daddy's house.

"What are you doing here?"

Dean turned, hearing Daddy's voice. The light burned, causing him to shield his eyes with his hands. He saw a shadowy figure standing at the front door, watching him. Dean wanted to run to his father, hold him, cry on his chest, be told that everything would be okay. *Please, Daddy, tell me what to do, help me, I don't want to be a crook stealing for my fix. Help me, Daddy, help me.*

"I need you," Dean said, voice croaking, weak.

He stumbled on the path, moving forward to the porch. *The Fireball isn't working.* His legs were exhausted, tired from the lack of fuel riding through his system. *I'm a child again, weak, useless to my father.* Dean's stomach groaned as he collapsed onto the porch. He rubbed his hand through his hair, finding clumps coming out. *What's happening to me?* Dean eyed the front door, seeing that his father was not there. The gray-haired stranger stood in his father's doorway, watching him.

"I don't want your problems here," the stranger said.

"Who are you?" Dean said, reaching out for help.

"Did you hear me?" the stranger said. "You need to leave. Don't ever come back."

Drool came from Dean's mouth as he laid his head on the porch, weak, exhausted. His lids dropped, his muscles lax as he felt his heart beat calm. *I need Daddy to help me. Where is my Daddy?* He dreamt of his father coming over to him, picking him up in those great big arms, carrying him into the house past the gray-haired stranger. *He used to hold me when I was a child, in those arms that could lift anything.* Dean smiled, delirious at the false dream.

"Whatever you're on," the stranger said. "I can't help you."

Dean cried soft tears that welled in his eyes, tumbling off his cheeks. "Where's my Daddy?"

The stranger laughed at him. "I knew it would come to this, at some point, I just knew it. Your *Daddy* doesn't want you anymore."

The front door slammed shut, the wind causing Dean's hair to sway as the porch light extinguished. The stranger had convinced Daddy not to speak to Dean. *He has taken my father away from me, kept him hidden from helping.* Dean's sobs tapered off, then ceased. *The stranger has kidnapped my father.* A change churned inside his brain. The feeling of an intensity that started to rage, slow at first, then quicker, forming in his mind. The burn ran the edges of his arms, bowels, legs. *No one hurts my Daddy.*

Dean's teeth clench as he stood. *I'm not an embarrassment.*
The Fireball shot fueled his rise to his feet as he flexed his back,
moving his arms. Dean eyed his muscles as they grew. The charge
pounded through his veins, pulsing. Dean eyed the front door. *I'm
going to kill the gray-haired stranger and save my Daddy.* Dean
faced the front door, ready to run through it.

"Daddy?" Dean said. "Are you in there, Daddy?"

Help me, son. Help me.

He growled as he heard his father's voice calling to him. His
hands formed fists as he swung into the metal surface of the
front door. Giant welts decorated the surface as his power
pushed the door back. Saliva frothed from the edge of Dean's lips,
boiling foam ran down his chin, creating splats onto the porch.
Dean centered his right fist into the front door which caused it to
retreat an inch. The frame cracked, barely holding.

"I love you, Daddy," Dean said. "I love you."

Another shot from his fist caused the door to explode off its
hinges, blowing out large splinters that floated in the foyer air as
the door was thrown back onto the staircase. The anger did not
stabilize or weaken, it grew. *I love my Daddy with all my heart.*
Dean stepped through the broken threshold, eyes searching for
Daddy. *What has the stranger done to my father?* The house was
foreign to him as he had never stepped foot in Daddy's house

before. Every conversation had remained on the front porch, in the gym. *The gray-haired stranger has taken my Daddy from me, made this house his own.*

Dean noticed the photograph frames decorating the foyer walls, examining them close. His eyes captured many photos of young children, along with the gray-haired stranger and another woman. No photos showed Dean as a child, teenager or now. *No photos of my mother are here. The gray-haired stranger won't allow that.* Dean's eyes spread across the parade of photographs. Pictures of the stranger with other people he had not met. There were celebratory photos of Daddy holding large trophies, displaying a fish with a group of men that Dean had never been introduced to. *The gray-haired stranger has erased me from my father's life.*

No photographs were displayed of Dean's time in boot camp, nor photos of his weight lifting competitions over the last two years. *The gray-haired stranger doesn't believe I'm good enough for my father.* Dean's eyes centered on a large block of photographs mounted at the end of the foyer wall showing Ulysses Turner. Each photo showed the champion posing in stride, accepting awards, standing with the gray-haired stranger. *This is the son that my father always wanted.*

Dean saw his reflection in the glass picture frames. He leaned in, eying his raw face with deep grooves. His brow jutted out, cheeks sunken as were his eye sockets. *I am my father's Frankenstein. Built to perfection to show how imperfect I truly am to him.* Dean smashed the picture frame, erasing his reflection as the glass imploded into shards that fell around his feet. Dean flung the frames as disks across the hall, letting them crash into the kitchen at the end. His eyes shot up to the ceiling, hearing footsteps. *That's where he's holding my Daddy hostage.* Dean eyed the staircase, moving to it. His feet went heavy on each wooden step traversing the climb.

"Daddy, I'm coming for you," Dean said. "I'm coming to get you."

His left fist smashed through the plastic wall next to the staircase causing huge chunks of chalk dust to cake his hand. He clutched the banister, unhinging the wooden frame from its moorings. Dean tossed sections of the rail into the foyer below as he stomped closer to the second floor. Anger white hot, Dean saw the gray-haired stranger exit a bedroom, holding a pistol. The man's grip was tight, but the gun shook. Dean grinned, winking at the stranger.

"I love my Daddy," Dean said. "What have you done with him?"

Dean's mouth curled into a wicked laugh as he charged forward. His hands formed claws, swatting at the gray-haired stranger. The pistol was ripped out of the stranger's hands. It careened into the foyer below, discharging. Dean clutched the stranger's arms, slamming his feet down onto the man's toes to keep him close, looking into his eyes, seeing fear. *No one hurts my Daddy, do you hear me?*

26

His ears caught a sound of thunder in darkness. It sounds like a gunshot. The report ripped by his head, ending quick. No trailing sound whistled.

It can't be a bullet. The curiousness caused Peter Volov to open his lids in an attempt to see. They refused his command, remaining stiff. His nostrils picked up gun powder and The Serg's cigarette smoke. A soft waif of classical music filtered into his ears. He forced his lids free, his pupils attacked by the light twisting, bending as they focused. Peter's mind screamed as he blinked, adjusting to the room.

Oleg stood in front of him, offering a grim look, cigarette burning from the side of his mouth. White smoke puffs shrouded his face until the Russian goon waved them away. Seeping, red wounds laid on his right cheek and above his eyes. *Did I do that to him?* Peter fought grogginess as another thunderclap rolled through his right arm into his head. His lids curtained his view again.

"Wake up, my friend."

Oleg's voice caused Peter's lids to open. Thick strands of saliva tumbled from his mouth as he eyed the room. His naked body was touched by warm summer air. Oleg spoke fast Russian, saying gibberish that Peter soon realized was not to him. His lids closed and popped open again. Oleg displayed a nail gun in his left hand. Peter wanted to scream, but nothing came from his throat. Oleg moved close, putting Peter's left arm against a wall, pressing the nail gun against it, squeezing the trigger. The shot fired off in Peter's ear, the pain rolling through his arm. Peter unleashed a scream, squeezing his lids shut to erase the nightmare.

Peter heard The Serg's voice, saying something in Russian. Oleg's voice saying something back to The Serg as the sound of Stravinsky's *The Rake's Progress* played in the room. Peter felt his cheeks slapped. When this did not raise his lids, he caught the smell of cigarette smoke as the tip burned his cheek. Peter felt his right lid forced open by Oleg's holding his thumb and finger as the goon laughed. Peter's head was turned to witness his right arm nailed to a wall. A thick seven-inch roll of metal had gone through his left palm. The bridge between his finger and pinkie were split.

He screamed, delighting Oleg. They were at the cabin, white and green crates filled the room. Wires attached to his chest ran to an E.K.G. which beeped to ensure he was kept alive. Peter opened both lids to see his right hand pinned against the wall. Another nail had been hammered into his right thigh. Oleg moved, revealing The Serg sitting on some crates at the end of the room next to Doctor Xhang.

The old Russian wore bandages across his face, left shoulder. A glucose bag was hooked into his arm, keeping The Serg's strength up. The Serg sat, laughing as he puffed his hand-rolled cigarettes, giving Peter a wink. *How did they find me out?* Oleg gestured to Xhang to move forward. The Chinese doctor moved emotionless out of the shadows, producing a black sharpie, applying three dots on Peter's arm. *To prevent them from hitting an artery.*

Xhang spoke fast in a Chinese-Russian combination to The Serg, who gestured for Oleg to continue with his work. Oleg removed his large nail belt, fitting smaller ones to the gun. Oleg shot three nails into Peter's torso. Each rocked his body hard, causing Peter to drift into unconsciousness. A mechanic whine churned up in Peter's ears amid The Serg's yelling. An explosion of thunder caused his lids to leap from his eyes. Xhang was in front of him, holding resuscitation pads against his bare chest. The E.K.G. machine beeped on. *They won't let me die.*

Peter begged The Serg to stop, pleading with him. *Why are they doing this to me?* The Serg came off the crates, clutching the glucose bag, moving toward Peter. He stepped toward him, eyeing Peter with faint sympathy.

"You want me to stop?" The Serg said, unsure.

Peter nodded, saying yes, please, god, stop this.

The Serg's face became cold, shaking his head. "It does not stop. Not until you cannot be revived." The Serg slapped Peter across the face, snapping his fingers at Oleg. The Serg winked at Peter. "He enjoys tools. Nail gun suits him." Oleg produced pliers, handing them to The Serg while mumbling Russian that Peter did not catch. The Serg displayed the pliers to Peter. "What you say, is not important," he said. "But you will scream. If you pass out, you will be revived, until there is no life in your body."

Peter saying to The Serg, why are you doing this to me?

The Serg and Oleg shared a laugh, confused. The Serg saying to Oleg, can you believe this guy? Oleg shrugging, saying I've heard many things from dying men, this is not surprising. The Serg nodded, saying this could be true.

The Serg grabbed hold of Peter's face, separating his lips with calloused fingers which held a concrete taste as they navigated his gums. The pliers went in, clamping down on Peter's front tooth, then yanked back, hard. The tooth ripped free with a squelching sound of skin, blood tearing. Peter screamed, passing out as his lids collapsed, letting his world become black. The Serg and Oleg spoke angry in Russian, Xhang talking in Chinese-Russian in garbled words.

Peter's lids were pushed open by The Serg's thumb, his pupils rolling back into his skull to hide from the piercing light. He caught glimpses of Oleg prepping a syringe gun with vials of Pink Cadillac. The Serg yelling in Russian to hurry before it was too late. Doctor Xhang watching the scene with passive interest as Oleg moved to Peter, squeezing off the syringe gun into his neck.

Lightning charged through his body as fuel rode his blood stream. The pain was removed by an electric current that shielded his flesh. Peter screamed, trying to tear out his arm from the wall. The Serg and Oleg stepped back, cautious, while Xhang moved in, giving Peter a shot of blue liquid in the neck. The pain returned. Peter blacked out, his lids caking his eyes. It was then that his memory returned to him.

I stood in the Exit One parking lot late afternoon. I had prepped all week, knowing I had to move fast. The Serg and his boys were planning something big. I was instructed to bring back several white and green crates, with three Kevlar body suits. Gave them to the muscle boys who came through after talking to The Serg and saw their leader, Stew, who said the muscle boys were going to make history.

I had planned ahead, grabbing a few concussion grenades, a MP5 carbine rifle with some extra clips, and a bunch of pink and blue fluid vials for Anthony. After Stew unloaded the crates from the van, grinning at me, saying you've got no idea what's coming, brother, I knew I had to move. After Stew left, I grabbed a burner cell phone, texted FBI agent Sam Brown the coordinates to the cabin, then received one back that said a raid on the cabin would come at dawn. I destroyed the burner cell phone, stomped it into oblivion.

I grabbed the backpack full of grenades and a syringe gun with blue vials, took up the carbine rifle from the van. Went back into the Exit One club and shot up the place. The Serg, Oleg and others were caught by surprise. Tossed all four grenades, let them explode and emptied two of my three clips into it. Heard screams of dancers, guests as I smelled sulfur, everyone pinned down or wounded. I went downstairs to rescue Anthony. I found him asleep inside, put the syringe gun against his neck, squeezing the trigger. I emptied five blue vials into Anthony and when he woke, none of that madness stayed in his eyes.

I had to slap him a few times to get him conscious as he was weak and barely functional. I told him who he was, got the response that he was Anthony. He talked as if he knew he was a DEA agent. Brought him out of the room, hearing him ask what happened to Andrea. I told him that she was waiting for him.

He moved with me, getting out of the room to the rest of the basement. That was when we both got zapped by Oleg's cattle prod. I listened to The Serg's laughter but could not place it. Anthony got shoved back in his room by Oleg who zapped him with the cattle prod to make him scream. I failed him. I'm sorry, Anthony. I'm so, so sorry.

His memory blanked for a moment before his ears caught the whirr of the resuscitation pads. Then a sound of thunder rolled as Peter felt the impact on his chest. He opened his lids, back at the cabin with The Serg, Oleg, and Doctor Xhang. His mouth spilled blood, several of his teeth were scattered on the floor. Xhang loaded a purple liquid vial into the syringe gun, then pressed it against Peter's neck, firing until the contents from the syringe were in his system.

"Give him everything, Xhang," The Serg said. "Leave not a drop. We want him ready for the F.B.I. in a few hours."

Peter faded, his lids closing. *Am I dying or becoming something else?* He listened to The Serg's laughter below in the darkness. *I failed you, Anthony. I'm so sorry. Please forgive me.*

He entered through the back alley into the gym, feeling his skin stained with blood, heart thumping his chest. His mind was calm in a night fallen to rich, black depth. *I'll never be alone in this world again.* He rubbed his face as a headache surfaced, smacking against the sides of his temples. He looked at his palms which bore red stained swatches. *He's turned me into a killer.* His lids fluttered as the tightness in his neck bit his muscles as he moved through the threshold of the gym toward the showers. *I killed a man for my father tonight.* His rags fell off his body, allowing his nude form to enter the shower stream spitting hot water, cleansing his soul. His father sat in the corner shadows, watching him rinse clean.

I'm proud of you, son, Daddy said.

"I know you are, Daddy."

The stream of heat washed against his face as the red ran from his limbs, pooling around the shower's drain. His flesh boiled at the water's touch but he remained until the stream burnt off the last vestiges of his anger. His arms weakened, his legs held him up. Dean brought his hands up to his face in the deluge, examining them. *Whose hands are these?* His muscles quaked possibility, feeling as if he had the power to tear a man apart.

Dean emerged from the shower without turning it off and

looked at his father who stood in the corner shadows, smiling proud. *Look what you made me do for you, Daddy.* He eyed a mirror and went over to it, wiping the steam free to reveal his foreign reflection. Gums expanded, teeth separated by huge gaps of black. *I am growing into something.*

You are the son I always wanted, Daddy said.

Dean pointed at his father. "I was never good enough for you until I changed. But you never had to change for me."

You're still weak after all of this, aren't you? Daddy said.

Daddy shook his head in the corner shadows, disappointed. Dean stalked over to the corner, but Daddy vanished from sight. Dean looked around, confused. *I hate you, Daddy.*

Dean grabbed a gym towel, wrapped himself and entered the main gym. Lynyrd Skynyrd was playing over speakers, talking about that smell. Kyle and Stew were loading up syringes of Fireball, kneeling against a long bench. They took turns giving the other a shot in the ass. The electrifying dose charged them into shouting out primal screams as the syringe's plunger hit the needle's nose, the juice pushing through their system. Dean caught their gaze, nodding. He removed his towel, turned and bent over.

"Do me."

Both men shouted in celebration, Kyle doing the honors on

Dean with the shot of Fireball. He got him with a shot in the right cheek that Dean felt pump through his system, tingling as it bolted up his back, down his legs into his feet. Dean felt alive, ready to lift. He noted Kyle's pupils, dilated as he breathed excitement. Stew bellowed a scream that filled the gym.

The lifter clutched an M-16 carbine off the pile of weapons provide by The Serg, attached the M203 component to launch grenade shells, then cocked back the hammer, screaming again. Kyle beat on his chest, screaming, followed by Dean's inclusion. It formed an ancient ritual, a brotherhood of intensity that continued for an hour until they ran short of breath. Kyle turned to Dean, grinning.

"I got the plans from the Russian."

"Show me," Dean said.

Dean and Kyle exited the gym into Dean's office where a large map was spread on the floor, showing the downtown city district, points marked off with sharpie. Dean's fingers ran along the map. *This could work, it could really go down easy.* He grinned at Kyle as the builder screamed back at him. Then Dean returned a scream of his own.

I have no son, Daddy said.

Dean stopped looking at the map, searching the room, unable to find his father. He eyed the corner shadows but saw nothing.

Pain seared Dean's skull, seeing his father's face covered in blood. *Who did this to him?* Dean held his hand, stumbled backward as pain pulsed his skull. His legs grew weary but Kyle caught him, holding him up. *Daddy blames me for his pain.*

"What's going on, man?" Kyle said.

Dean caught Kyle's gaze, the builder's pupils no longer dilated. "I don't know."

Kyle helped Dean into his chair, letting him rest as he felt the Fireball flush from his system. *It goes so fast. I need to get more.* Dean breathed, calming himself. *Daddy's not hurt, I saved him from the stranger.* He leaned forward, feeling another slice of pain in his head. An image shot through his mind. *I'm standing over my father, beating him to death with my hands.* Dean winced, then heard a tapping sound below him. He looked down, seeing drops of blood hitting the linoleum.

Dean looked at Kyle, who had his attention on the maps, looking at strategy. *I killed my father because he never loved me.* Dean wiped away the blood from his nose, using a forearm, ignoring the drip. *Daddy wished I was never born, so I destroyed him.* His eyes followed Kyle's finger as the builder pointed out various sections on the map.

"Stew met up with the contact, name is Turk," Kyle said. "Pitchfork is three main alleys that lead up with a main one.

Turk's gonna have two guys in an armored truck enter the top fork at nine a.m. They load up the three banks, then go after the jewelry stores. Maybe catch fifteen mil on this."

"If we're not in the bank, what does he need us for?" Dean said.

"Crowd-control," Kyle said. "See, this thing is going to get heavy after the first bank goes down. We make sure they get the rest of the places hit by keeping the doors open and the heat off."

"You sound like you've done this shit before."

"Cash and carry jobs?" Stew said, entering the office. "Kyle and I got sent up for one."

"But you got caught."

Kyle: "No, we got stupid."

"Yeah, we should have plugged the cop rather than do two-a-piece," Stew said. "A lot of cons at *The Sides* talk the same way. They all held back from ending some asshole and keeping their freedom."

"Won't be that way tomorrow," Kyle said. "Tomorrow, we make history."

"Ain't doing another twelve when I can try to spend fifteen mil," Stew said, holding the M-16 at his side. "Any witnesses go down tomorrow, end of story, no debate."

Kyle gave Dean the eye, waiting for protest. "End of story, right?"

Dean wanted to fight the insanity, but the fuel raged through his brain again. He wanted to put someone down. *Make them hurt.* He nodded, grinning. "We waste them." *I don't recognize myself, I'm different around them.* Dean didn't care. *I want the juice, need it to survive. Otherwise I will be weak.* Dean saw his father sitting in the corner shadows, ashamed. *Look at the son you've created, Daddy.*

I have no son anymore, Daddy said.

Dean rose from his desk, spitting in the corner. He left Daddy in his office without offering a retort. *I will show you, Daddy. Tomorrow, I'll make history without you.* Stew and Kyle followed Dean as he headed towards the M-16 carbine rifles. Dean noticed the Kelvar body armor vests, sleeves and leggings. There were riot helmets and about thirty thousand rounds of ammo. His eyes danced over the additional assortment of Beretta pistols, grenades, combat boots, knives and gloves. He focused on the armory, selecting out an Uzi-nine-millimeter which he held, enjoying the feel.

Stew said. "Thought you might want that one."

"We could take a hundred banks if we wanted," Dean said, smiling.

Kyle grinned, gesturing to Stew. "We thought the same thing. Gonna do this thing, maybe a few more in the day."

"I gotta score to settle with a native asshole at that casino that killed Ulysses Turner," Stew said, leaning in to Dean. "You want to do one over for Turner, don't you?"

"Yeah," Dean said, liking the sound of payback. "We could take on the entire Army."

Stew to Kyle: "Show him the other things."

"You got more?" Dean said.

Kyle produced a rocket-propelled-grenade launcher, petting it. "If any of the city's finest want to make a roadblock, we'll blow them back to creation."

The builders stood soaked in madness. Kyle selected a combat blade, drawing a small cut on his hand. Stew followed, then Dean. They were brothers bound by blood oath. They smacked palms together, forming a triangle of rage. Unafraid of the consequences beset tomorrow, they were of one blood which dripped from their palms, hitting the floor in splats between them. Ten minutes later, their wounds were healed.

The Fireball took over inside Dean. The others felt it too. They stripped clothes, did repetitions throughout the night. *It's the same as the first time when we raged on Pink Cadillac, screaming and hitting the weights as Gods among men*. The burn excelled as the electric current charged through their veins, pushing them faster, harder, meaner. Dean eyed his father in the corner shadows, seeing the old man shaking his head, disappointed. *I don't care anymore, Daddy. You're nothing to me. Tomorrow, I'll show you how much of a man I can be, without you.*

What are you up to, dear brother? Mikhail said, sitting in the corner shadows.

"He has betrayed me with those builders," Tony said.

Mikhail laughed, his facial features blanketed by the darkness. Tony glared at his brother. *Is he real or a ghost who haunts me?* An image seared into Tony's brain, causing him to wince at the quick migraine. *Andrea is lying on the ground, being choked to death.* Tony frowned at the revelation. *Who killed my Andrea?* Tony beat at his head while Mikhail mocked him with more laughter.

Your life is in these walls, Mikhail said.

"Shut up," Tony said. "I am D.E.A."

Do you even know what that means? Mikhail said. *If so, tell me.*

Tony could not remember. Things had fogged since he had been zapped with the cattle prod and placed back in his cage. *Peter Volov took me from this place, telling me about Andrea.* Tony shook his head to revive his memory with little success. Another image hit him hard. *Peter is choking my Andrea, killing her.* Tony screamed, pounding on the walls. *Peter has betrayed me.*

You cannot trust what your mind tells you, dear brother, Mikhail said. *Your thoughts have cracked.*

"I am not weak," Tony said, screaming. "I am a God."

Tony looked down at the floor of his room, seeing a syringe gun by Mikhail's feet. He grabbed it, examining the weapon. His eyes caught the five vials sitting in there. Two blue, one pink, another purple. Tony placed it against his neck as Mikhail shook his head. *My brother wishes to keep me a caged animal, weak.* Tony injected himself with all of the vials, squeezing the trigger until all of the vials were empty. The rush was a confused one. Tony had moments of weakness course his veins, then a charging rush, and then something deeper, something more.

Now you have done it, dear brother, Mikhail said. *Now you can never escape.*

A pounding sensation hit Tony's skull. He screamed as blood came from his nose. An image hit his mind. *Dean is choking my Andrea, killing her, feasting on her flesh, devouring her eyes.* Tony squeezed his fists, swearing vengeance on Dean. *He killed her. He destroyed my Andrea.*

"Quiet, you animal," Fedor said, screaming.

Tony looked up at Fedor, who banged a cattle prod against the slot. His beautiful eyes were searching the room to find evidence of someone other than Tony and Mikhail. Tony licked his lips at Fedor's pupils, considering them a delicacy. Another image attacked Tony. *Dean has kidnapped my Andrea.*

"The Serg does not want you worked up before a match," Fedor said.

Listen to him, dear brother, Mikhail said.

Tony pointed at Fedor. "Come stop me, you son of a Georgian whore."

The door's dead bolt turned, unlatching. Tony waited as the door opened, Fedor entering, pressing the trigger of the cattle prod, zapping it with excitement. *I will kill you, then my brother.* Tony waited, saliva foaming on his lips.

"Respect the order of things, Mikhail," Fedor said.

Tony's rage grew. "I am D.E.A."

Fedor stopped, laughed at the comment. "And I will punish you for it."

You've made him angry, dear brother, Mikhail said.

Tony pointed at Mikhail as Fedor approached. "Stay out of this."

Fedor grinned, zapping the prod at Tony. "The Serg's pet is a lunatic."

Tony screamed, pounding his chest, charging forward onto Fedor. He latched his claws into the Russian goon's shoulders, chest, letting his teeth carve into Fedor's face. Tony bit deep, chewing out a gigantic chunk of flesh that he spat at Mikhail's feet. Fedor howled at the assault, releasing the prod which Tony caught as it dropped. Tony zapped the man into oblivion, smelling charred skin. He beat Fedor until he heard the soft whistling of oxygen expend a final time from the Russian goon's lungs.

The Serg will not be pleased with this, Mikhail said.

Tony's eyes went to the door. *I will destroy Dean for hurting my Andrea.* He didn't understand who Andrea was, but felt protective of her. Tony turned toward Mikhail, who vanished from the corner shadows. Tony's eyes searched the area, unable to find him. "You cannot hide from me, Mikhail. I will kill you."

Tony ran out of his room into the basement, listening to the muffled thump of music upstairs. He ran across the room, around the sand pit, toward a map of the city. Showing the Pitchfork alleyway marked. *Dean will be there tomorrow, and I will avenge my Andrea.* Tony smiled, seeing an old petroleum heater rocking in the far corner of the basement. *I will destroy The Serg for giving Dean all of my fuel.* Tony grabbed at the metal brace, letting the heat singe his hand as he ripped it away. Air curled as gas belched from the hissing cord. Tony stumbled back from a blast of fumes in his face, but the grogginess thinned and he was able to head upstairs as the basement filled with gas.

Tony entered the upstairs letting the bass wash him, seeing a sex club of naked women on poles, men floating currency while songs played in endless rotation. The lights were dim causing him to squint. Tony eyed the bar as he passed, seeing a person glaring back at him. *I will kill you, Mikhail.* Then Tony realized he was staring at his nude form reflected in the mirrors.

"What you doing out of your cage?"

Tony turned to face a Russian goon. He struck the man in the face, then twice in the throat in rapid succession. The goon felt back onto the stage, toppling a naked dancer who broke her arm in the fall. The entire club stopped its commerce, staring at Tony as he moved through the shroud of music and sex. Tony exited the club, basking in the warmth of a summer night. Behind him, a goon screamed at Tony, threatening him if he did not return. Tony ran on, smiling as the club exploded in flames, becoming a funeral pyre.

He saw a semi truck idling by the side of the road. Tony ran up to the cab, opening the door, and yanking out a sleeping driver behind the wheel. The man broke his nose, shattered teeth in the face first asphalt fall. Tony drove the semi truck away, toward the city. *I will kill you for what you have done to me, Dean.* The rage burned through him fierce.

29 F.B.I. Agent Sam Brown laid across the ground on his belly amid the edge of trees which ran down into a valley surrounding a dilapidated cabin in the center of a field of overgrown grass. He eyed the cabin suspicious. None of the windows offered views inside, covered by drapes. The cabin was dark, black which meant nothing in terms of occupants. The dawn brought a cold sun over the east which was cresting the hubris of hilltops toward the valley below. Sam turned to the F.B.I. tactical leader, Vernon Jones, who was next to him. Both watched the cabin with binoculars, Jones assisted by a small parabolic dish aimed at the cabin, earbud hooked into his left canal.

"Anything?" Sam said.

Jones shook him off. "Strange music. Classical? Low enough, maybe left on by accident. Nothing else I can get from what's inside."

Sam: "My intel is reliable."

"So was Custer's," Jones said. "Has your contact checked in again?"

Sam shook his head. "No."

Peter Volov had gone dark for twelve hours since his last text to Sam, giving the F.B.I. coordinates of the cabin. The text had arrived from a burner cell. No way to trace or to contact Peter in case plans had changed. *We have to trust he sent us the right stuff.* Sam didn't feel good about the decision, but knew that there was no other way.

Jones: "We take four front, four back, two on the sides for support. Any objections?"

Sam shook his head. "I'll buy a round afterwards."

"Shit, at this rate, you'll be buying a few."

Jones patted Sam's shoulders, then left to brief the other tactical unit members. Sam joined the crew of ten F.B.I. agents, dressed in Kelvar vests with M4 carbines, ready to move. They headed down slow as the sun broke over the hills, signaling morning. The unit slid past Sam, with Jones leading in a slight crouch staying low over the three foot-high lawn surrounding the cabin. A white fog hovered light stretches across the grass tops for additional cover.

Jones signaled each group to advance ten paces then halt to avoid detection. The sick suction of soil belched from each member's boots below the grass. Sam slipped but caught himself, getting his left knee touching the ground, soaked wet. He swiped it off, smelling a faint stench of fuel. He reasoned that the marsh collected it from the off-gassed pipes feeding the cabin's heating system. *Place probably has run on propane for fifty years.*

The frontal assault unit crept to the cabin's front. Jones

signaled for a small battering ram. One swing from the team member collapsed the door into a heap of rotting wood. The remainder of the unit charged inside, M4 carbines shining red beams into the dark. Sam heard the team members screaming at someone inside. He rushed the cabin, his ears catching a little electronic whine that faded as he breached the cabin's threshold.

Sam's eyes caught Peter in the living room with several team members aiming their carbines, little red beams focused on his face and chest. The man was naked, bloody, up against the far wall. Sam thought Peter had extended his arms to prevent being shot. Then, he noted the wounds, seeing the nails laid into Peter's flesh. Sam looked into Peter's eyes, seeing a rage, a madness milked over the pupils. Peter shook, screaming, attempting to rip his limbs free from the wall. *He wants to kill us.* The tactical team members stepped back, M4 carbines trained on Peter, ready to fire.

"Get out," Peter said, with a mouth full of blood.

Peter unleashed a primal scream which pierced Sam's ears. All eyes focused on Peter's chest, Jones pointing at the word written in black ink which said "*BOOM.*" Sam turned to the front door, spotting an electric tripwire device. The electric whine grew louder as Sam's eyes ran from the tripwire to a large brick of C4 mounted on the wall. *Oh, shit.* The tripwire's light went dead, and the cabin exploded into a ball of flames.

30 Morning emerged as Dean sat inside the darkness of a white cargo van. He eyed a bullet hole in the van's wall that was ancient, then duct-taped his body armor leggings in a mummified fashion. Kyle drove to the Pitchfork while Stew sat across from Dean, loading up the Kevlar vests with additional clips, ready for war. Stew laughed, insane. Dean joined him. Lightning went down his back. About twenty thousand milligrams burnt through their systems. *The dragon is alive in us now, because we need it. There's no going back.*

Dean's heart pounded, ready to burst from his chest. The fuel pulsed through his veins, charging as he unleashed a primal scream at Stew, destroying the silence. Stew grinned, unoffended, and returned seasoned hot acid breath into Dean's face. Kyle offered up his own scream, and the three shouted as the van headed through the underbelly of the city. They were ready for war, the power alive in their bodies, pushing them forward.

The night had been a restless one. *Daddy has abandoned me, left me to die.* Dean had woken up expecting his father to be sitting in the corner. *He doesn't approve of what I am doing or who I am.* Dean closed his eyes, wishing Daddy was here. *He's left me because he never loved me. He thinks I am a coward.* Dean opened his lids, seeing the Fireball milk over Stew's eyes. *Man isn't staring at me, he's staring through me.* Dean grinned, letting saliva expend slow from his mouth.

"We're tanks," Stew said. "Nothing's gonna stop us."

Stew hoisted up his M-16 rifle, cocking it, gnashing his teeth, Fireball raging his veins. A purine sweat smell caked the back of the cargo van. Stew hooked grenades onto his belt, then patted the M61 Vulcan rifle which sat between them. The Vulcan was a Gatling-style six barrel, rotating 20mm shells of death. The Serg had provided six thousand rounds in three belts. *Just in case we run into trouble.* Dean prayed for someone to get out of line. *I want to show Daddy that I'm a man.*

"Had trouble getting it into the van last night, a heavy mother," Stew said. "Now, feels like a feather."

Dean smiled, nodding. *We're different on the juice, it enhances us.* Each could run harder, faster, with one hit. Dean eyed Daddy, who sat in the van's corner shadows. Daddy shook his head, disappointed. Dean spat in the corner of the van, but Daddy had vanished. Dean focused on his body armor, strapping the Kevlar leggings on his calves. He received an Uzi 9mm from Stew, confused as the builder grinned back at him.

"Got a silencer for it," Stew said. "It suits you."

"It does?"

Stew: "Trust me, it's you."

Dean mounted the silencer onto the Uzi 9mm, then loaded in the clip under the handle. He held it out straight, aimed it to the back of Kyle's skull as the builder drove them deeper into the city amid sparse morning traffic. *I could waste him right here, blast him into oblivion.* Dean lowered the Uzi 9mm, gripping it, smiling. He placed the weapon on his lap, then clamped his hands together, squeezing them tight. The fire burned through his system, quaking. Dean eyed Stew, seeing saliva drool from the builder's mouth as he unleashed a hound's growl back at Dean.

"This is it, ain't it?" Dean said.

Stew: "What else is there?"

"Nothing, exactly," he said.

Stew's form bulged out from under his body armor. Arms hanging at forty-five degrees by default anytime the man walked. Coupled with the Fireball, the Kevlar offered them enough protection to face off against anything the heat could endure. The plan was solid; Stew had organized everything. The Serg would be waiting in the valley for the pick-up after the job was done, bringing them more fuel for their efforts. *Then we hit them hard, like we talked about this morning in the gym. We take all of the juice they got and we destroy them for what they've done to us.*

Dean cocked the Uzi 9mm, showing Stew he was ready. The big man relaxed, Kyle slammed his fist into the van's ceiling in celebration. The road bumps went on as the van charged downtown. A moment of clarity struck Dean. *We can do this, get out alive. Because we're no longer men. We're gods.* Dean tightened the grip on the Uzi 9mm handle, hoping to take down anyone who got in his way. *Especially you, Daddy, I can't wait to come to your house after and destroy you for all you've done to me.*

Kyle stopped the van a few blocks from the Pitchfork in an alleyway. He turned to the back, saying this is it, boys. Dean eyed through the windshield, seeing an armored truck pulling in. The boys would be jumping out, idling and waiting for us to take it over. From one of the city streets, an older man broke into their view. He was walking with a limp, had two white wingtips against black hair and a pug nose. An ugly mother if Dean had ever laid eyes on one.

"This your boy, Stew?" Kyle said.

"That's Turk," Stew said. "Act cool, Kyle. Keep him distracted until I do my part."

Kyle rolled down the window, talking to Turk. Man seemed a little nervous as he pointed to the Pitchfork, telling Kyle that they would stay back unless there was trouble. Stew moved to the back of the van, slipping out the back door with Dean. Stew grabbed the Uzi 9mm from Dean as they listened to Turk and Kyle continue to banter.

Kyle saying, okay, but do we get paid if we don't do nothing?

Turk saying, he didn't know and was probably being honest.

Saying he had to call The Serg to check back, that he had rigged a

corvette in the back of the alley to explode in five minutes, to serve

as a distraction so the armored truck could escape with the loot.

Kyle saying that was a good idea. Stew edged around the end of

the van, pointed the Uzi 9mm and shot Turk in the skull. Dean

saw splatters of red and brain blossom. Kyle spitting, wiping at

his face, saying, shit, I got his mess in my mouth.

Dean and Stew moved around, grabbed Turk's arms and

carried him back behind the corvette. They threw him inside

without any trouble. Dean eyed the timer, seeing they had three

and a half minutes to go before the car exploded. He pointed it

out to Stew, who signaled to Kyle, who put on his ski mask. Dean

and Stew followed suit, standing in the back. They took turns

duct-taping their Kevlar chest plates shut.

Dean felt his skin sealed by perspiration, breathing heavy

chugs of air. He listened to long breaths, his lungs expanding,

deflating. The morning was fresh, few cars passed through

downtown as the day began. Dean watched as a jogger passed by

the mouth of the alley, listening to an iPod, unaware of the army

about to be unleashed. The van offered a guarded view of streets

as Kyle slid it into a five-mile-an-hour pace. Stew and Dean hung back in the back of the van, walking with the two doors open to shield people from seeing them until it was too late.

The van crept out of the first alley, crossing the street. Dean noted an open café, where city dwellers were served conversation along with their meals. Daddy sat with them, staring at Dean, seeing the old man shaking his head, disappointed. *The hurt doesn't go away, no matter how much Fireball I take.* Dean tightened his eyes, feeling the shame from his father burn into him. *Daddy never loved me, he's ashamed of who I am.* A rage quaked deep beneath Dean's skin, he turned the Uzi 9mm and its long silencer toward the crowd, squeezing the trigger to kill his father. The barrel emitted a *swat, swat, swat* sound.

The crowd screamed under the attack. The breakfast nook had bodies crash into tables as Dean covered the area, trying to kill his father. He squeezed off another burst of *swat, swat, swat* but did not see his father lying amongst the dead as the caravan passed into the next alley, hiding the nook from view. He turned, seeing Stew smiling in approval.

"That's why I gave you the Uzi-nine, man," Stew said. "Teach them all a lesson."

"Wanna teach one, in particular," Dean said.

They walked as silent troopers through the next alley, their nostrils filled with sour milk and waste. Apartment fire escape ladders hung low enough that Stew had to avoid hitting one with his face. The ladder's bottom edge brushed against his Kevlar, grooving a scratch. Their boots smacked against broken pavement in ritualistic fashion, pounding forgotten puddles of water, oil. The rage excited Dean as he thought of finally destroying Daddy.

His mind was covered in residue from the history with his father. *I was never good enough for him.* Dean remembered his mother, begging him to forgive Daddy after she was forced to sign divorce papers right before her cancer surgery. *I tried to love him again for her because she had always asked so little of me.* Dean remembered kissing her hand after promising that he would continue to try to be a good son to his father. Watching her wheeled into surgery, a woman he loved gone within the hour. *Leaving me alone with my father, a man too scared to stay by her side.*

They passed the second alleyway and Dean glanced to his left, seeing a familiar face. A feeling crept on him as he tried to place the person. *It's not Daddy, he's too young.* Dean didn't raise his Uzi 9mm to greet the person. The man stood in a blue workman's uniform, front was stained, black with dirt. A ball cap hung low, covering his face, as the man pretended to move metal garbage cans. He was thirty feet from the alley, curving around the corner. The man eyed Dean quick, then looked to the ground to conceal his identity.

Dean's eyes caught a tattoo marking the man's face but he could not place where he had witnessed such a nightmare before. The Fireball clouded his memories sometimes. The thought stayed with him until the van crossed into the Pitchfork. He focused on the plan, taking down the bank inside, and the fuel that the builders would share after getting the job done. Dean felt someone watching him, then saw Stew turn back. The van crept forward a little without them.

"Someone's back there," Stew said. "Recognize them."

"You want to go back?"

"Screw him," Stew said. "He comes after us, he needs an army."

Stew and Dean rejoined the van after a slight jog. Ahead the Pitchfork was curved into three prongs. The armored car sat idling, emergency flashers lit. Dean grinned, loading a fresh clip into the Uzi 9mm, cocking it. *No one understands what we're capable of. Not Daddy, not anyone.*

31 He spotted the men from behind the cream colored van, letting the saliva boil from his mouth. Tony Hell eyed them, dropped his gaze as one of them looked back. *They are on the fuel too, they can do as much damage as I can. The fuel is what bonds us together.* He tended to his metal garbage cans, his eyes seeing the van's reflection in a store-front window until they had disappeared into the Pitchfork. They donned black ski masks, a mold of fabric armor, stomping their way through the gaping mouth of the alley. Tony flushed his fear, confident he would murder each of them. *They took my life from me. They made me an animal.*

Tony moved away from the garbage cans, heading toward the alley in a long, focused march. His blue workman's uniform switched between his legs, stolen from the semi truck with a pair of broken black leather Doc Martens with yellow stitching. The rubber grips chewed the street, stomping wet cobblestone into the alley. Tony unleashed a primal scream, yanking at the sides of his uniform, tearing it apart at the seams. The uniform's buttons sprayed, torn from the fabric. Tony's cap left him, the remaining bits of fuel charging through his system. A woman's scream from the street alerted him as he was about to cross into the mouth of the alley after the men who destroyed his life.

Tony eyed her, seeing her face stricken with horror. His features frightened her, the lady backed away, stumbled over the cobblestone as her heel caught on a crack. She fell onto the street, then struggled to move away. Tony's eyes followed her movement, hungry. *I could pounce on her, rip her flesh with my teeth.* He turned his attention back to the armored men, reminding himself of their importance. *I want the fuel to keep going. She can wait.* Tony's pupils dilated with excitement.

Stop this madness, Mikhail said.

Tony eyed up the street, seeing Mikhail standing in a blue workman's uniform, alive. *He's still breathing, to taunt me with his comments.* Tony spat on the ground, then charged at his brother, attempting to tackle him. Tony crashed into the sidewalk cobblestone, feeling pain bite into his shoulder as he picked himself up. *How is he able to allude me so easy?* Tony shook off the pain, then pointed at Mikhail.

"I will devour you, brother," Tony said.

He took a swipe at Mikhail, his hand sliding through his brother. Tony held his left paw up to his face, stunned. *My brother is a specter. He does not exist anymore.* Mikhail's face grinned at Tony as the revelation sat between them.

You are broken, dear brother, Mikhail said. *Your mind has cracked.*

Tony shook off Mikhail's comments, squinting his eyes. He stomped through the ghost of his brother, paying no attention to the spectral plane he crossed while going into the Pitchfork. Mikhail called after him, but Tony ignored what was said. *I have no time for this distraction, especially from him.* He felt his brother's hand on his shoulder, but it carried no weight and drifted away as Tony continued on toward the armored men.

Tony unleashed another primal scream; it filled the alley, bouncing off the concrete mortar. His feet raged into a mad dash, leaving Mikhail behind. The air wrapped the edges of his skin as he charged at full speed. The two men behind the van did not turn to face him, attending to their large rifles as they prepared to ambush an armored car that the van approached. Each step strode closer to the target. Tony gnashed his teeth, spreading his arms wide.

He leapt into the air, smashing down on top of the man who had called him animal. *The one named Dean.* Tony brought his hands forward, letting his fingers slip into Dean's fabric armor, clawing the man as he became aware of the attack. Dean howled in pain, squeezing the trigger of the Uzi he held, firing off twenty silent rounds. The shots caked the inside of the van, slicing through the windshield, killing the armored car driver sitting outside his truck, smoking a cigarette.

"Get him off me," Dean said.

Tony's heart raced as his eyes shot to the other armored man who stood pointing a large gun at Tony's face. They watched each other for brief seconds, Tony licking his lips at the beautiful marbles which hung in the armored man's eyes. He leapt off of Dean, catching three rounds to the chest. Tony howled as he dropped in mid-air, the world collapsing into a fiery siege of madness. A sound of thunder covered his ears as his lids dropped into black. His face hit the ground, teeth smashed and he slid into unconsciousness, waiting to die.

32

Dean picked himself up off the ground, aiming the Uzi 9mm into the maniac's back, ready to fire. Three blocks behind them, a car exploded. The blast carried a soft wind to Dean, who turned, eyeing the destruction. Sirens descended down the alley, car alarms blared. The entire Pitchfork alley security system went into an automatic lockdown around them as the car bomb was detected. Large metal gates crashed down over the mouths of the entrances. It sealed the bank, six jewelry stores, trapping customers inside. Bullet-proof shields lowered over the glass display windows behind the gates, protecting the guests from errant shots.

"Shit," Stew said. "Wasn't supposed to happen like this."

"You mean this quick?" Dean said. He pointed at Tony. "Or this asshole."

"Both."

Dean edged around the van and went to the armored truck. Kyle was attending to the armored truck driver, seeing that the man had been shot up with several rounds from Dean's Uzi. The second armored guard called out for help. Dean and Kyle eyed the second guard, seeing that the second gate had smashed down on his back and had locked. He twitched as blood pooled from underneath his body. Kyle withdrew a Glock from his Kevlar vest, squeezing off two rounds into the man's head to end his misery.

"We gotta move this shit fast, get out of here," Kyle said and went to the armored truck, jumping behind the wheel. He moved it forward, past the back of the van. He got out and pointed to the van. "Let's load this stuff up, that way we got more protection."

Dean moved to the mouth of the Pitchfork, edging his eyes around the corner to watch the open city streets. The bank alarms hammered on as more store front gates closed, smashing down metal shields which locked into place. The citizenry fled the streets in panic. Police sirens blared, Dean listened to patrol cars speeding through the city streets, hitting the brakes and turning their sides to create a barricade around the Pitchfork. Dean eyed Stew and Kyle, who were loading the Vulcan and other ammo into the back of the armored truck while it idled.

"We got company, boys," Dean said.

Stew and Kyle lifted the maniac up, tossing him into the back of the armored truck along with the weapons. Kyle headed up to Dean, getting his own look. *Seeing the same thing I do, street cops holding little more than a pistol and a prayer, shielded by a cherry top patrol car.* The entire financial district around the Pitchfork had descended into lockdown. Streets were swept into vacancy. More police officers rushed out of their precinct three blocks away to cars, carrying small arms. Dean eying Kyle, witnessing that madness milked over the builder's eyes. He felt it too. *A surging anger to do something, make them get what's coming to them.*

"Road blocks at both ends," Dean said. "How are we breaking though that?"

Kyle smirked, saying that was easy.

Dean eyed Stew, who was dragging the maniac's body by his left arm. Stew picked up the maniac, tossing him into the back of the armored truck with the ammo. "Why are you taking him?"

Stew stopped, smiling. "He's The Serg's pet. Man was gonna double-cross us, jumped too early."

Kyle: "We drop The Serg when we bring him back his pet, get us enough Fireball to never need a re-up."

Dean's attention was taken away by a helicopter. Its blades flapped overtop as he felt the air swirl inside the Pitchfork, causing garbage to float. Dean turned to Kyle, seeing hot saliva push through his clenched teeth. "We need cash for The Serg to meet us."

Kyle grabbed Dean by the throat, pulling him close. "Don't you think I know that?"

"Hey," Stew said, drawing their attention. "I got that covered with the casino."

Kyle released Dean, smiling, nodding at the idea. "It works for me."

"Yeah," Dean said, ready to go. Kyle's pupils were fully dilated; big black orbs reflecting Dean's image. *Same as in my eyes, I'm sure.* They were consumed by the madness. Dean pointed at the flock of television helicopters which hung above the police barricade. "What do we do about them?"

"I got something special for that," Stew said. He drew out a rocket-propelled grenade from the black duffle bag in the back of the armored car. "Remember what they say about the news. If it bleeds, it leads."

Stew loaded the R.P.G. with a shell, bent around the corner and fired off the Roman candle. The shot hissed out a small black trail of smoke which weaved through the air. The rocket head cut away from the helicopter's body, veering into the rear rotating blades. The infusion exploded the helicopter, veering it off to its right. The helicopter crashed into a nearby office building. Stew hooted, pounding his chest as gunfire from the police barricade came forth.

Stew was calm, handing off the spent RPG rifle to Kyle. He grabbed an M-16 from Dean, who held his Uzi 9mm ready to go. "Now, we show them the hard stuff."

Stew and Dean stomped out of the Pitchfork's mouth toward

the police barricade, squeezing off bursts. Several of the officers were caught off-guard, turning their attention to the burning helicopter wedged into the office building. The roar of gunfire blossomed from the silent summer morning streets, erupting a chaos that consumed the financial district. Dean imagined himself as a part of a nightmare, marching in symmetry with Stew as the two emptied clips at ten second intervals.

The rounds chewed the barricade. Several sliced through the metal plates, finding home in officers hiding on the other side. Little red splats blew up in powdery form as each round hit a torso or skull. Officers that attempted to return fire left futile small rounds slapping off of the cobblestone streets or flying past Dean's head, whistling without a thought the damage they were unable to do.

A round ate into Dean's protected shoulder. He hesitated, comforted by the lack of pain by the body armor fortification. Smiling, Dean unpacked another clip that he loaded into his Uzi 9mm, sauntering on with Stew. The two squeezed off another clip of rounds into the barricade. Tires blew, the heat melted windshields, and uniformed cops were lying dead on the other side. Several attempted escape in a low crouch but Stew opened up, picking off each defenseless as they went by.

The pair turned, offering up the same punishment to the

opposite barricade. The street cops had escaped from that line after witnessing the brutality expended on their blue brothers. A police tactical helicopter sped in from the north, catching Dean's attention. He opened up with the Uzi 9mm, causing the tail to smoke black. The ghetto bird collided with a skybridge two blocks away. Dean followed it, but his attention was drawn to three uniform cops brave enough to rush him. He brought forth the Uzi 9mm, squeezing off the remaining clip, rounds tearing the unprotected men apart in rapid succession.

Stew unlatched three hand grenades hooked onto the back of his body armor. He clamped his teeth on the pin for each, yanking them out, then softball tossing them over the barricade. Each blew patrol cars into a fiery rage. The police line separated into flames while the blue brothers screamed, some escaping with their lives. Some were caught by the ensuing flames, burning to death. The cake smelt of burnt flesh hung in Dean's nostrils as he moved toward the wreckage. *And I like it.*

"I love this shit," Stew said.

They focused on the armored car, Kyle behind the wheel. He had it idling, nose sticking out of the Pitchfork's mouth. Dean and Stew ran toward the car as the police gathered their dead. More explosions rocked the streets, fire meeting gas tanks from the patrol cars. The wounded screamed for help. Dean grinned at the sound of madness, enjoying it. He went to the armored truck's rear, feeling something slap the side of his armor. Dean looked down, seeing his armor held several rounds. He eyed the back end of the Pitchfork alley. The Serg and his men stood around three black SUVs, firing M-16 rounds at Dean and Stew.

"Told you he double-crossed us before we could do it to him," Stew said.

Stew opened up with a burst on the SUV caravan as The Serg and his men got free. The first SUV was caked with rounds, the windshield belched broken glass. The tires blew from pressure, the engine hissing as the radiator's water hit it, creating a cloud of steam pouring out from underneath the hood. The Serg's goons regrouped behind the second SUV, though one thug took twenty shots from Stew's M-16 and did not make it. Dean was about to join Stew when he noted rounds flying past his head, in the opposite direction. Dean turned, seeing a tactical police force rushing from the opposite alley toward the mouth of the Pitchfork.

"Kyle, we need your help," Dean said.

Kyle left the armored car, M-16 ready. He joined Dean as they moved out of the Pitchfork's mouth toward a black tactical operations team of five trained men heading in formation toward them. The members slid into small areas around the alley, hiding behind a dumpster or doorway, eliminating open shots by Dean or Kyle. They brandished M4 carbine rifles, riot helmets and body armor. *They are as protected as we are.* Instead of scaring Kyle or Dean, it reinforced their efforts to fight harder.

Kyle pointed to the skybridge connecting above the alley. Dean and Kyle opened up on it, causing the skybridge's glass to blow out. The rounds sliced into three gawkers stupid enough not to run for safety, instead desiring to watch the entire madness from above the street. Two of the gawkers were thrown out of the skybridge, onto the street below, landing in front of the tactical team. Kyle softball tossed two grenades, Dean did the same with tear gas canisters which spewed out a green cloud trail. The grenades amplified their explosions by hitting a gas main underneath the street, rolling down through the city in several small mushroom clouds of flame.

The entire street block rocked when the gas main blew. Dean and Kyle managed to keep their footing, watching the tactical team thrown onto their backs, buried in rubble as the buildings on each side had their wall collapse into the alley. Several store fronts had their protective security shields blown out as the gas explosion continued. Bodies littered the streets on fire. Kyle pointed to a tactical van ten blocks away heading toward them.

"They wanted in the game," Kyle said, then turned to Stew.

"You're up, Hoss."

"Right," Stew said, coming up behind them.

Dean eyed the tactical van. It wielded a sharp metal nose and plowed through barricades of rubble, crashing toward them. The van knocked away cars in a nightmare caravan while steam fire explosions shot up from the street's manhole covers. Kyle and Dean opened up their guns on the van but had their rounds careen off the bullet-proof exterior. Stew grabbed the loaded RPG rifle, aiming it at the van. The rocket hissed a smoke trail two feet from the ground.

The rocket met the van's undercarriage, imploding tires into melted rubber, causing the van's cage to slide forward through the street. The van skidded onto its side and collided into the local Apple storefront, breaching its security shield and ran deep inside the building. Stew reloaded the RPG, squeezing off his last shell into the store, causing the hole in the building to ignite, belching out a ball of flame. The tactical van's armament supply cooked off, shooting rounds that snapped off into the city asphalt.

Dean focused on an abandoned city bus sitting a block out. He squeezed off a clip into the windows, puncturing the sides for good measure, screaming while reloading. The shells spat out the side of his weapon, ricocheting off the cobblestone street. The

Uzi nine was accompanied by Kyle's M-16 for support, holding tight on the trigger while the hammer came down on the bus. Police sirens stayed distant, removed in other city blocks. The street was ashen, smoke and the stench of death hung deep. Wounded cops stirred on their backs. Others attempted rescues of fallen brothers but were gunned down by Kyle. Both men reloaded in the warzone, charged by the bondages of rage.

"God, that was fun," Kyle said.

They turned back to the Pitchfork. Stew focused on the alley, lobbing two hand grenades at the dumpster thirty yards down. The explosions sent the bin up three feet in the air. SUV shells burned, screams heard behind them from The Serg's goons. The bin came down on one man, pancaking him. Kyle slapped Stew on the shoulder, congratulating him.

"Now, let's go play our luck at the casino," Stew said.

33 Lance Caron headed to the Rivers End Casino ready to end both his career and marriage. He had stayed the night at the emergency room.

Looking over Keisha after what happened in the diner. He had gone to the bathroom, returned to find that she had taken a steak knife and tried to slice her wrist. It was bad enough that she had been taken to the emergency room and admitted for observation. *I sat there knowing I'm a slave to her. If I try to leave, this is what she does to herself.* He doubted it was any different than his relationship with Scott Tsosie, vowing to change both before the day was through.

While Keisha was sleeping, Lance went to the hospital's business center, typing and printing his resignation letter on one of the computers. He slept an hour or two near Keisha in her room, then left before eight in the morning while she was sleeping. Lance left his cell phone off to avoid the texts or calls from Keisha. *I can't do it anymore.* Lance cried for the first time since his mother had passed as he drove to the Rivers End, wondering if he was a failure. *Why couldn't I make this work? I did so well for a while.*

He entered the hotel lobby and waited near the elevator, noting how the security team eyed him. *As if I am no longer part of the group.* It felt strange to enter the building knowing that he was leaving the casino business. *I made this important, as much as Scott did. But he couldn't do it anymore. Couldn't live with the lies of Scott and Keisha. Couldn't live with the knowing of what they were doing with each other, betraying me as much as they could, while trying to be my friend.* Scott could have Keisha now. *I'm going back to New York, play the piano in some dingy bar if I have to, in order to live the way I've always wanted but never tried.*

The elevator doors opened and Lance saw Col. Civil-Fielder standing inside. The Englishman smiled, which did not feel as warm as it may have been intended. He has a way of making anyone squirm even when he is being nice. Civil-Fielder gestured for Lance to enter the elevator, his hand near the bulge in his suit. *He's going to make me come with him, regardless if I want to or not.* He wondered if Scott had put Civil-Fielder up to this, in order to make Lance pay for leaving Keisha, revealing what he knew.

"Mister Tsosie would like a word, sir."

Lance started saying how he was going to his office, packing his things. Showed Civil-Fielder the resignation letter, which did nothing to impress the Englishman. The chief of Tsosie's security eyed the letter in his hand, then gave it back to Lance. "Discuss it with him personally, sir. In his suite."

Two of Tsosie's private security came behind Lance, blocking his chance to leave. Lance moved forward into the elevator, the

Englishman smiling. Lance's eyes fell to the bulge sticking out from underneath Civil-Fielder's suit, seeing the manifold strap crease that ran up the Englishman's left shoulder and around. *He's carrying heavy artillery today, showing me how rough he can get if I decide to resist.*

The two guards stayed in the lobby. Civil-Fielder did not turn to Lance, instead pushing the button up on the elevator. They stood next to each other, listening to breathing as the Englishman put his key in the control panel, activating the lift up to Tsosie's suite. The elevator jolted up, enough for Lance to brace his balance. He eyed the Englishman, who refrained from losing footing.

"I've never gotten used to that," Lance said, admitting.

"Quite sure of it, sir," Civil-Fielder said.

The doors slid at the end of the elevator ride at Tsosie's private suite floor. Lance moved around Civil-Fielder, exiting into a long hallway running ten feet beyond the lift. He eyed the suite with its door open. The Englishman pushed him forward, moving Lance past several spent bottles of wine and champagne, dead soldiers lying on the carpet. Lance resisted urges to grab, swig one down as he prepared to see Tsosie inside, out of control. *What can he say to me at this point but to kill me to keep me from talking about what I know?* Lance was pushed into the suite and his eyes caught Tsosie on the sofa, hair disheveled, suit ruined, tie a hanging noose.

"Where the hell have you been?" Tsosie said.

Richard Yazzie stood near the fireplace mantel, holding a pistol and offered disappointment at Tsosie. "That's no way to treat a guest, Scott."

Next to Tsosie on the sofa was Brian Locklear, who wore a blood-stained Hawaiian shirt, holding a cloth to his split lip. Yazzie gestured for Lance to move closer to the sofa. Civil-Fielder pushed him from behind to guide him. Behind Yazzie stood one of Civil-Fielder's security men, holding an AK-47 while smoking hand-rolled cigarettes. He flicked the ashes in a glass tray on the mantel, glaring at Lance as he approached.

"What's going on here, Richard," Lance said, unsure.

Yazzie gestured to a stack of papers on the coffee table with his pistol. "House cleaning, I suppose. We've been waiting on you since last night, that important meeting we were having. You didn't show so we waited until everyone was here."

"Lucky me," Lance said.

Yazzie gestured to the sofa with his pistol. "Have a seat."

"Why are you doing all of this to your own people?" Tsosie said.

Yazzie shrugged. "I've never been good enough for the Yamenhi people. What's the point of being an elder if you never get to make the decisions?"

"That's what this is about?" Tsosie said. "You want Brian's job?"

"Maybe at one time, but now I'm interested in dollar signs," Yazzie said, gesturing to Civil-Fielder. "And I'm not the only one."

Tsosie focused on Civil-Fielder. "And you... I fired you... You don't come in here, holding me down cause this guy writes you a bigger check... You're supposed to be loyal."

"Define loyalty, sir," Civil-Fielder said. "I've always worked for Mister Yazzie."

"I'm not sitting through this," Tsosie said, rising up from the sofa. "How dare you talk to me this way?"

Yazzie gestured at Tsosie as the general manager moved toward him. Civil-Fielder withdrew his sidearm, squeezing off a round into Tsosie's hip. It caused the general manager to scream, drop to the ground, blood forming on the carpet around him. Brian Locklear went off the sofa, shielding Tsosie as he lay crumbled.

Yazzie: "Out of the way, Brian."

"This is madness," Locklear said. "You're destroying everything we've worked for."

Yazzie said, "I'm destroying your vision for us. Make my own adventure on some island in the South Pacific, with two women who know how to treat a man."

"I'm in charge of this tribe, not you," Locklear said. "You have no authority."

Yazzie aimed his pistol at Locklear's head, squeezing off a round that created a red plume blossoming out of the back of his skull. Locklear collapsed, dead while Lance stood horrified. Yazzie and Civil-Fielder turned their attention to Tsosie, who was spat on twice. Lance caught the suite's bathroom door in the corner of his eye. *They're cleaning house in here, all that's left is Tsosie and I.*

"You're a fool, Scott," Yazzie said. "Another plastic Indian."

Tsosie grunted, shaking his head despite the pain. "You're a disgrace."

Yazzie tossed the sheath of papers on the table at Tsosie, which floated around him. Lance edged closer to the bathroom, watching Civil-Fielder focused on Tsosie. *I can make it into the bathroom, get in before he can shoot me too.* Yazzie slapped Tsosie across the face, crouched in front of him.

"It's not your money," Yazzie said. "I'm finally getting what I deserve out of this. Waiting by the wayside as long as I did."

"All you are building is a jail cell," Tsosie said.

Civil-Fielder aimed at Tsosie's back, squeezing off three rounds that collapsed the general manager's lungs. Lance stood silent, two steps from the bathroom door. He froze, seeing the eyes of

Yazzie and Civil-Fielder focus on him as Tsosie died.

"Well?" Yazzie said to Lance. "It's pretty evident where you come in."

Civil-Fielder moved his sidearm toward Lance. There was too much distance to go through the bathroom door. Lance thought of the weapons inside the bathroom. *How are you going to fend him off with a can of hairspray and a lighter?* Lance readied to have Civil-Fielder put two in his chest. Then the suite's front door opened, and Keisha came inside drunk, mascara running, and a small revolver in her hand. One of her heels had snapped off long before she entered, but she kept moving in the crooked shoe.

"Keisha," Lance said, surprised.

"You can't leave me," Keisha said, crying. "I won't let you."

Civil-Fielder and Yazzie focused on Keisha, who appeared shocked as they shot her once each. Lance turned to the bathroom and dove inside, hearing gunfire light up the suite. Rounds punctured through the bathroom door, chewing it up. Lance scrambled into the bathtub, curling in as the tile cracked over his head. The onslaught felt as if it lasted for hours, but was less than ten seconds. He could hear Keisha moaning, then another blast from Yazzie's pistol brought silence to her.

The iPod began a loud riff of *She Sells Sanctuary* while the armored truck mounted the Interstate ramp at a clip of seventy-five before cresting at ninety-two reaching three lanes of sparse traffic. Dean Shockley eyed the area and was unsure why the traffic was dead until Stew pointed out state work crews ahead of them. *They shut down the Interstate quicker than I would have imagined.* Kyle hugged the truck's wheel and maneuvered around several cars determined to beat the armored truck to the east of the city. The truck bumped a few vehicles, knocking some into the Interstate barrier.

Dean yanked off his ski mask, shifting body gear and allowed cool air to touch his skin. The smoldering perspiration underneath the armor slacked. Dean eyed Stew, the man huffing big gulps of air himself while eying the truck's back window. A caravan of police cars were giving chase and trailed the truck with their sirens blaring. The Rivers End Casino was less than ten miles away. *We go in, make this withdrawal, and suppress whatever resistance we encounter.*

Stew did up another syringe full of Fireball. Dean licked his lips, feeling the need take him over. He ripped off his right sleeve of armor, enough to get the needle into his skin. He awaited the burn, eyes excited, looked at Stew, impatient.

34

"Give me a taste," Dean said.

Stew appeared reluctant but passed the juice to Dean with chaos deepening around them. It evaporated as the needle sunk through Dean's flesh, brushing back thoughts. His eyes rolled back into the far reaches of his skull, forgetting about the growing track marks on his forearms at the bend. *I'm a mainline junkie for the stuff.* Dean grinned at the destructive path of hell-bent fury unleashed on the world. *I had to prove to them how much of a man I could be. So Daddy could finally see me.*

The plunger hammered down to the base of the syringe and Dean felt weak. The plunger head wiggled underneath the force of his thumb. *I feel... normal again.* Dean listened to his heart supercharge as it pounded away in his chest while he closed his lids and felt the colored images of panoramic hues skyrocket in misshapen forms against the black curtains of his mind. *Nothing else matters but this moment.*

"Good shit," Dean said.

"Yeah, good shit," Stew said, repeating.

Dean felt something smack his head. He opened his lids, ready to unleash his rage. Kyle had swung his arm to hit Dean while driving with his eyes focused on the side mirrors, eying the traffic ahead of them.

"We got a parade behind us," Kyle said. "Get us some distance before we hit the casino."

Stew laughed. "Gonna show them the heat."

Dean unlatched the truck's back doors and caught wind as it picked up. White asphalt marks blurred behind the truck as it sped down the interstate. Stew offered some grenades from the duffle bag, yanking the pin and dropping them onto the road. The first bulb exploded underneath a tailing patrol car which toppled over and took out two police cars nearby. Cars blew end over front as two more grenades went off. The cherry tops swerved to miss some of the grenades and ended up flying off the barricades down onto the city street below the interstate lift.

"Check this shit out," Kyle said, pointing out the windshield.

Dean and Stew eyed the state crew moving a mega-load beyond the armored truck. They were going about thirty-five up the Broadway interchange which ran sixty-five feet off the ground as I-90 turned into Spokane Valley. Stew laughed and got behind the trigger of the Vulcan while Kyle sped up, moving the armored truck around the mega-load. The semi was hauling a three-ton piece of equipment, a large circular concrete barrel strapped to the trailer. Stew aimed the Vulcan at the trailer, squeezing off two hundred rounds. The semi swerved, folded and the trailer buckled. The mega-load barrel snapped off the trailer and started rolling off onto the interstate back down the interchange toward the cherry tops giving pursuit.

There was a moment of contentment while *Paradise City* charged through the IPod. The three men silent, focused rode in the armored truck as Kyle moved to crest the interchange. The weight of the rolling mega-load hitting the interstate caused the columns holding it off the ground to crumble. The entire interstate started to collapse as the mega-load rolled down into the embankment, smashing and obliterating police cars. Kyle rode the truck off the interchange right as the road underneath it started to tear away into oblivion.

Stew opened up the Vulcan at a black helicopter giving pursuit. He squeezed off a couple hundred rounds but the copter managed to elude the onslaught. Dean kept his eyes on the interchange which had fallen onto the ground, sending up gigantic dust clouds which rolled on. *We set off an atomic bomb.* Stew yelled at Dean to move out of the way as the copter returned chase. Stew laughed as the copter's blades twisted up in suspended telephone wires, veering off and crashing into the street below.

The Vulcan focused on office buildings surrounding the interstate. Stew squeezed off rounds, blowing out windows in a charged scream of celebration. The barrel smoked when the Vulcan ran empty at six thousand rounds. Stew released the

Vulcan, watching the destruction in the distance. The dust cloud rose miles high. Stew eyed the body of The Serg's pet fighter who laid near the front of the truck and spat on the body, offering Dean a grin.

"We're making history, bro," Stew said.

Dean returned the smile while enjoying the notion that they were going to be talked about forever. *End of Daddy and his pain, all of those ways he laughed at me when I took it. He can watch the news like everyone else and see what his little boy is up to.* Dean eyed his chest plate and noted the quartz splotches melted into his Kevlar. *My life was meant for something, even if it's this.* He was no longer a person who entered life anonymous as his destiny suggested he exit it. *I'm somebody now, Daddy. Even you have to see that.*

"Exit is coming up, get ready," Kyle said.

Dean took a spare M-16 rifle, loaded and cocked it, eying Stew as he adjusted his body armor. I'm a man buried alive. "Kids in school are gonna talk about this day forever, bro."

"School's out," Stew said, gesturing to his chest plate where splotches of quartz had been stopped by his armor as well. Stew spat on The Serg's maniac again. "This asshole wishes he had done as much as us."

Dean and Stew locked at the forearm, pulling close, offering smiles. Dean: "But he ain't us."

"No way in hell," Stew said. "We survive this story."

Kyle eyed their reflections in the rearview. "Cool it. We're about five blocks out."

"Let's pay this Tsosie man back for his misdeeds," Stew said.

"You got a history with him?" Dean said.

"Not after we're done with him."

The armored truck went off the interstate onto the city surface streets. Stew and Dean prepped their body armor. Dean felt the power of the juice charging through him as he squatted while Stew ran duct tape to seal his armor. It was a moveable tomb but with value. Stew wrapped Dean's leggings and sleeves, then Dean returned the favor to Stew. They donned their ski masks, ready for war. Stew grinned, eyes ignited.

"We get caught, we blame it on Xbox."

"You ever play Xbox?" Dean said.

Stew shrugged. "Who cares?"

"Hold onto something tight," Kyle said.

Dean and Stew braced themselves against the truck by gripping metal latches welded to the roof while eying the casino fast approaching through the windshield. The area was devoid of buildings except for the large hotel that the armored truck aimed for, growing massive in view. Lights flashed from large

L.E.D. screens advertising musician appearances or buffet deals. Kyle jammed his boot onto the pedal, revving the engine which burned hot as the truck shot toward the casino at top speed. The truck cut through the parking lot unmolested to the Rivers End entrance.

Something came out of The Serg's pet on the truck floor. Dean's eyes dropped to the body, wondering if he had heard the dead man moan. *That's can't be possible, he was shot three times in the back*. The sound was short, blubbery, but enough that it caught Dean's ears. He eyed the maniac, seeing the bullet holes which riddled his flesh. Dean's hand went lax on the metal latch until he eyed the Rivers End's glass foyer in the windshield. Dean gripped the latch tight as the armored truck breached the entrance.

The truck punctured the glass entrance at eighty-five and hammered onto the playing floor. Large sheets of glass dropped twenty feet down into the entrance behind the truck and shred casino staff members. One security guard was quartered at the shoulder. The truck shot through the floor and surprised patrons in its path. Elderly were knocked free of their slot machines. Oxygen tanks punctured, exploding. The truck clipped a ten-foot high slot machine display, cracking it in half.

Kyle lost control of the wheel as the truck slammed into the horse betting station and chewed the concrete façade which did

332 | TROY KIRBY

not give way upon impact. The Serg's pet fighter was thrown out of the back of the truck and landed three feet behind it onto the casino floor. Dean and Stew held on to the metal latches, Dean felt his feet lift slightly before returning to the truck's floor. The truck's engine block burst apart in a cloud of steam as it hit the concrete and was pushed back into the cab, thrust into the driver's seat, crushing Kyle with hot metal. He screamed as the heat caked his torso, melting through his flesh.

Stew and Dean unlatched and leapt out of the truck with their M-16 rifles, aiming the barrels at the patrons, unleashing quick bursts. The elderly dropped instantly in the wake of gunfire, some old war veterans who had served over there long enough to understand ordinance. Stew fired on an old lady who refused to leave her slot machine and attempted to play amid chaos. Her oxygen tank near her knees caught two rounds and sent the woman flying into a ball of flame.

Dean went to the truck's driver's door, opening it to find Kyle dead with the engine block on his chest, sizzling hot. He moved to the opposite side of the armored vehicle and noticed three casino security guards rushing down the main floor, holding walkie talkies. Stew edged around the truck, gesturing at the security guards.

"Make your way to the cage," Stew said. "We'll hit the vault in the back."

They moved off the truck, heading to the cashier cage. Dean squeezed off a burst from his M-16 which dropped the casino staff as they approached. Stew aimed above their heads, cutting down a gigantic chandelier that dropped on top of them. A casino guest huddled at the end of the slot machine row was chewed up by Stew's M-16 rounds for no other reason than it felt good to do so. Dean felt more sinister now, and he liked it.

They stopped at the cashier's cage, aiming both barrels at a native woman behind the counter. She quivered, unable to drop underneath the counter. Stew pointed the M-16 at her forehead, ready to end her as she closed her eyes tight. Dean grabbed the cage's door handle, yanking on it. The barrier was unwilling to move and was thick enough that M-16 rounds wouldn't cut it open. Behind the cage was the casino's large vault, the door closed, several handles waiting in circular rotation.

"It won't go," Dean said.

Stew said, "She opens it, or we end her."

Dean eyed the woman behind the cage, her lids opening. "You heard the man, open it."

The woman had tears in her eyes, she leaned as if to open the door, then stopped. Her legs fell out from under her and she ducked underneath the counter for protection. Dean leaned over the counter, trying to spot her.

"Shit," Dean said.

Stew said, "I got an idea. Move."

Dean dropped back a few feet, then saw a contingent of casino security running down the escalator from the hotel into the casino. They held tasers and sidearms. Dean squeezed off a large burst which chewed them up. Several of them were caught on the escalator, clustering in a heap at the bottom. Dean turned back to Stew, seeing the builder unlatch a grenade from his armor, pulling the pin. Stew heaved it through the cage, dropped back. The woman screamed, getting onto her feet and ran for the door. She opened it as the explosion tossed her forward by five feet. The blast severed her hand, holding tight to the door handle.

"I have my moments," Stew said.

Dean and Stew breached the cage, confronted by a large metallic vault door that gleamed steel magnificence while offering the dulled reflections of a black mass of human brutality in the surface. *It's not going to open with a grenade.* Dean felt sweat cake between the armor and his skin. Stew exited the cage, stomped over to the woman cashier. She was lying crumpled, a mess with her back seared in black, hair melted to her head. Stew grabbed her by the neck, brought her up to look him in his eyes.

"Now, what's the combination?"

Richard Yazzie stood in the wake of a warzone. The luxury suite held carnage. Bodies of dead lying around him but Richard had avoided injury. Civil-Fielder stood upright without being hit by a bullet. *Only those who deserve it die today.* The black woman who had entered the suite with a revolver was lying on the ground, three bullets in her from Richard's pistol. Civil-Fielder aimed his sidearm into the black woman's head, ending her life. Richard eyed the bodies of Scott Tsosie and Brian Locklear. Two Yamenhi men slumped together, a shame to their people. Tsosie with only a shot in his side to put him down. *Let him bleed out, slow.* Richard's focus went to the bathroom, where Lance Caron hid. It's all going according to plan.

The radio chatter from casino security took Richard's attention. *The casino floor has been breached?* Richard heard gunfire pop in his earpiece. Richard moved to the suite's bay window, eying the casino floor. Smoke tumbled up as bullets fired through the ceiling. Richard moved away from the window as high-caliber rounds bit into the glass. They sawed large gaping holes. Richard turned to Civil-Fielder.

"Colonel, I need you to seal off the casino floor," Richard said. "We have visitors."

Civil-Fielder gestured toward the bathroom. "What about him?"

35

Richard shrugged. "I'm in charge now. We have him on camera coming up here, and we can act as witnesses to what he did to Locklear and Tsosie."

"Very good, sir."

Richard smiled. "My plan had been to leave the place and take everything I could get out of it. But plans change, don't they?"

"All of the time, sir."

The pair exited the suite, leaving Lance behind in the bathroom. Richard started evolving a plan to have the casino surveillance footage of Lance entering the Rivers End as evidence of his intention to murder Locklear, Tsosie and Richard. *I can tell the news crews that I managed to escape.* Richard smiled, knowing that without the influences of Locklear or Tsosie, the Yamenhi tribe would turn to Richard for guidance. *The one thing I've always wanted.*

Inside the elevator as it descended, Civil-Fielder radioed his security force to meet him in the operations center on the second floor of the hotel. The Englishman appeared delighted at the prospect of war, reloading his sidearm while removing his suit coat, dumping it on the elevator floor. Held by a strap around his shoulders was a small M4 carbine that Civil-Fielder prepped with a fresh clip. Gunfire chatter bounced off the elevator's exterior.

"M-16 rounds," Civil-Fielder said to Richard. "I listened to them nightly while in the Falklands."

The elevator halted at the operations center. The doors unsealed to reveal a full complement of private security soldiers, waiting for Civil-Fielder's command. Richard exited, then the men crammed inside, ready to be lead by the Englishman. Richard eyed the black and white security screens which showed two large, armed men robbing the casino's main vault. Richard turned to Civil-Fielder, glaring.

"Take them down," Richard said. "Neither gets out alive now that I'm in charge."

Civil-Fielder nodded. "Very good, sir."

The elevator doors sealed together as the security force headed down to greet the two armed men. Richard headed into the operations center, watching staff run everywhere. People manned phones, others tracked the two armed thugs on surveillance cameras. One of the men had blown the cashier's cage open with a grenade. Richard saw Phil Quentin standing in the far corner of the room, on a telephone. Quentin looked at Richard, using his hand to cover the mouthpiece.

"Mister Yazzie, the F.B.I. is about ten minutes out," Quentin said. "These guys tore apart the city."

"Who called the F.B.I.?" Yazzie said, angry. "Did you call them?"

Quentin became pathetic. "Sir, we have a war zone on our

casino floor. I can't reach Mister Locklear or Mister Tsosie to alert them to what's going on."

Richard grabbed the phone from Quentin, hanging it up. "Locklear and Tsosie are dead. Lance Caron came in shooting. I escaped, barely."

"Lance doesn't seem like the type," Quentin said, confused.

"No one is the type," Richard said, then lied. "He and Tsosie were the ones who demoted you without reason. You remember our talk yesterday. Something's going on between them."

"This doesn't make any sense."

Richard: "War never does."

Richard input a code into the command center panel. A security closet door slid open, revealing an armament of M4 carbines, Kevlar vests, and combat shotguns. Only Richard and Civil-Fielder had access to the closet. *Tsosie didn't even know it existed.* Richard pointed at Quentin, angry. "We can fight them and win, Phil. No question in my mind that if they want a war, we'll give them one."

"What are you talking about?" Quentin said. "I see only two men on the casino floor."

"Two white men," Richard said. "Another half-white asshole just shot Brian and Scott. And you're trying to bring in the F.B.I.

as if they've never helped overrun a native stronghold by force before."

"What's gotten into you?"

"I've told you before that you're not a plastic Indian. Others see you as another white man, but I know you have native blood in you. I can see it." Richard grabbed Quentin by the nape of the neck, pulled him in tight. The young man had appeared to Richard to need a place in his life. *He doesn't know where he belongs, so I'll give it to him, for now.* "Listen to me, Phil. We're going to end this our way."

He released Quentin, handing him an M4 carbine rifle. Within five minutes, thirty-four security members were outfitted, ready for war. Quentin found his spirit while standing there, getting his focus together. *Man never fired a bullet in his life but now he's ready to fight in my army.* Richard eyed them, smiling proud, then leaned into Quentin.

"We handle our problems at the Rivers End, Phil," Richard said. "Go down there, take back our land."

"Yes, sir," Quentin said, as Richard noticed a fire ignite in the young man's eyes. *He believes in the cause now.*

36

Wake up, brother.

Tony's lids fluttered, light piercing his pupils, causing him to wince. His ears captured a drowning sound which descended upon him. The chatter of gunfire, chaos and explosions surrounded him as his vision stretched. Everything was narrow, deep. Tony moved, feeling his muscles ache, head pulse. He was weak, afraid, wishing he was dead. Gone was his only avenue of excitement that the fuel was lost forever. He felt residue in his arms flush his system.

I told you to wake up, Mikhail said.

Groggy, Tony raised his head, static searing his brain. He lay across spent shells on a carpeted floor. He smelled diesel fumes, burned flesh and gunpowder. Tony's sight curled, blurring, twisted. His eyes went to the back of the armored truck which sat a few feet away. Mikhail hid in the shadows, mocking Tony. *I have no fight left in me to destroy him.* Tony's head collapsed, lids closed, saliva drooling off his cheeks as his fat tongue clogged his throat. Gunfire caught his ears, along with a man screaming in pain.

"I have nothing," Tony said. "Let the vultures take from me what they can."

I have fuel for you, brother, Mikhail said.

Tony's lids came alive, his head up, his focus on the armored truck. Mikhail pointed to a vial lying next to a black duffle bag on the floor, along with a spent needle. Tony turned, lunged into the back of the armored truck, and latched onto the vial and syringe, joining them. The needle sucked in the vial's contents, then was stabbed into Tony's heart, releasing the nectar. A surge of rage burrowed deep in his chest, charging through his eyes, fueling an electrical system shock that made Tony grit his teeth. His muscles roared as he sat up, the needle remained stabbed in his chest.

Tony eyed his brother, deciding his fate. *I should murder him and be done with it.* Tony gripped the syringe, plucking it free from his chest, then snatched another vial from the bag. He dosed himself again, in the buttocks, feeling the energy hit quick, wanting to scream. His throat was dry, coarse and would not allow it. Tony ignored Mikhail, pushing himself free of the armored truck, fire burning in his belly. His chest pounded with delight as excitement raged on inside. Tony eyed his brother sitting in the back of the shadows.

"I will kill you later," Tony said.

I look forward to it, Mikhail said.

Tony stretched his body, mind swimming as he stood with blood rushing out of his head. The wounds dressing his back felt ancient. He moved quick on his Doc Martens, tearing away from remnants of blood-soaked blue uniform sleeves, leaving the lower torso intact. His eyes surveyed the area, seeing chaos and gunfire spread through casino tops filled with destroyed gaming tables and bullet-riddled slot machines. Tony's eyes went to his left, where two armored men were breaching a large vault inside a cashier cage. He grinned, licking his lips as the fuel churned in his abdomen. *I will kill you, Dean.*

His attention was drawn from the vault by a black SUV which rammed through the destroyed front opening of the casino. It charged into a large broken slot machine and stopped. Tony glared through the SUV's windshield, seeing it contain The Serg and three Russian men. They spilled out with M-16 carbines, firing wild at him before he dived between two rows of slot machines. The large rounds ricocheted off the electric squares, causing one of the machines to spill coins out its mouth hitting a jackpot. Tony crawled away from the machines, escaping The Serg's assault.

The end of the slot machine row exposed Tony to gunfire as it lead up to a ramp before heading to an escalator. Tony screamed and charged to the escalator, seeing a pile of dead bodies lying on the bottom, locking the electronic stairs in place. Tony leapt up the escalator, climbing the stairs with three Russian goons firing their M-16 carbines at him. The bullet heat ripped above and below him. The gunfire ceased as Tony crested the top of the escalator.

Surprised, Tony glanced below to see Oleg coming forward, armed with an RPG. Oleg slipped on a pool of blood, squeezing the trigger. The RPG's round nose shot out of the canister, rocketing past Tony's head by an inch, throwing itself down the long hallway in a twisted hiss toward the hotel lobby. Tony chased after the rocket, seeing the shell find home in one of the hotel's foundation columns. The explosion knocked Tony off of his feet as the entire building quaked. Tony grinned as he rose in the chaos, heading deeper into the hotel as flames and wreckage seeped into the lobby.

The lobby had a palladium of glass which cracked along with crumbling the façade that smashed open an entrance to an atrium. The cages housing the animals inside the atrium broke apart, freeing the wild beasts who roared to life, charging through the smashed entrance into the hotel lobby. Tony was clipped by three large cranes who shot out over his head. He rose as the Russian posse came forward, closing in on him. They leapt back as twin gray Rhinos rammed through the entrance, knocking the men off of their feet with thrusts of their heads. The Rhinos broke out of the hotel lobby by charging the large bay windows to the parking lot.

Oleg screamed at Tony while running down the lobby, squeezing off a burst from his M-16 carbine that decorated the ceiling with a myriad of bullet holes. Tony latched onto a chair, tossing it into Oleg's chest, knocking him onto his back. Oleg squeezed the trigger, offering twenty rounds that spat into a zebra running through the entrance. Tony avoided a kangaroo speeding by and escaped into a restaurant filled with Japanese esthetics.

Tony slid under a row of clothed tables in the Japanese restaurant, eying Mikhail who stood at the kitchen entrance, watching him. *I am stalked by a hunter and my brother enjoys every moment.* Tony edged his face above the table, spotting Oleg entering, brandishing his M-16 carbine, ready to destroy Tony. Soothing waterfall sounds tumbled on the wall behind them in tranquil bliss but could not cover the constant eruption of explosions that came from the hotel and atrium.

Oleg spoke in Russian: "Come out, friend. I kill you and end this for good."

Tony's blood surged, pumping, wondering if Mikhail would sell him out to Oleg. Mikhail sat in the kitchen entrance, waiting to be found by Oleg. His brother did not attempt to move from the twin doors with the glass oval, peering out to let Oleg find him. Tony frothed saliva which bubbled from his mouth, a growling hound.

Mikhail is a traitor who deserves to die. I will rip out his eyes and devour them.

Oleg unleashed a burst from his M-16 carbine, playfully lancing shots against the walls. The ceiling crumbled off bits of plaster as the entire hotel quaked. Oleg giggled, firing another round of shots at the waterfall on the back wall, destroying the plaster rock formations, spilling water on the carpet. Tony felt his work uniform pants dampen as water made contact. Oleg had emptied his clip, screamed in a rage, then tossed it over a table, angry that Tony remained hidden. The Russian goon moved away from Tony's table and toward the kitchen.

"Time is up," Oleg said.

Tony rose quiet, slow behind Oleg, focused on the back of his head. His eyes caught twin Katana swords mounted against each other on the restaurant wall and he smiled. Tony moved quick, latching onto a Katana handle while Oleg's focus remained on the kitchen doors. Oleg reloaded the M-16 carbine with a fresh clip. Tony removed the Katana, easing it off the wall slow. He gripped the Katana handle with both hands, stalking Oleg from behind while the Russian goon edged toward the kitchen doors.

"Face me as man," Oleg said. "Traitor."

Oleg charged the kitchen, pouncing inside and emptied his M-16 carbine while unleashing a scream. A parade of chaos filled stainless steel objects as rounds bounced off the exteriors. Oleg laughed as the clip was finished, pulling it out to prep for a fresh one. Tony edged behind Oleg with his Katana raised high, but his foot came down on a shattered porcelain plate. The crunch caused Oleg to turn as Tony brought down the sword, slicing a deep groove into Oleg's right shoulder which ran down his left hip, and out. Oleg's scream was cut short by his lungs filling with blood. His eyes wide open as Tony pulled the Kantana back, marveling at Oleg holding fast to his feet, locking eyes with Tony. Oleg shook, in shock, eyes dropping down to his severed hand gripping the M-16 carbine on the floor. Tony leaned in, spat on the Russian goon's face.

"You should have focused on me, not my brother," Tony said, in Russian.

Oleg's odd expression confused Tony as the Russian goon's features calmed while he collapsed. Blood pooled around his corpse, mixing into the water-soaked carpet. Tony edged from Oleg to the lobby. Mikhail stood there, silent as Tony prepared to strike with his Katana. His energy waned as he moved, causing blurred vision as he stumbled. Tony's grip on the sword weakened, and he had to avoid impaling himself on it as it dropped onto the ground. His head throbbed, the mass of lightning flushing his system. His eyes searched for Mikhail at the entrance, unable to find his brother.

"I will kill you later, brother," Tony said.

The building rocked with multiple eruptions, the atrium shattering into small glass shards that sliced through drywall. Tony fell onto his knees, his muscles ached, fat and heavy. His mouth drooled blood-mixed saliva as his head impacted a giant rug marred with black char, glass and mud. One of his ribs cracked from the fall. Tony's eyes went to the lobby bar as he heard a beast roar. A Sumatran tiger sat across a couch in the bar, watching him. Tony's focus laid on the tiger's black and orange tail whipping back and forth on the couch's end. The animal's large paws extended as it descended off the furniture to devour its weakened prey.

"You look tired, Mikhail."

Tony turned his head to the left, seeing The Serg stand a few feet away with his back to the lobby bar with two of his men, Maxim and Leonid. Each held an AK-47 rifle aimed at Tony's head. The Sumatran tiger approached in a slow crawl off the couch and remained undetected by The Serg and his men. The Serg knelt to Tony, offering a grin.

"I should have killed you before when you double-crossed me," The Serg said. "Oleg thought you would be better as a pet, as a reminder to others not to spy on my business."

"You betrayed me, Andrei," Tony said, weak.

The Serg kicked Tony with his square boot, loosening teeth. Fragments came from Tony's mouth as he laid there, The Serg looming, pointing at him. The Sumatran tiger moved careful watching The Serg, unnoticed by anyone. "I trusted you before, Anthony Batelini. All of this, you have done against me."

"I would never betray you," Tony said, gurgling blood.

The Serg and his men shared dumbfounded looks, laughing at Tony. The tiger bent back ten feet from the group, stretching its legs to pounce. The Serg mocked Tony. "Your mind has cracked. You remember nothing?"

"Andrea," Tony said.

The Serg laughed with his men. "Leonid took care of her." The Serg made a slicing motion with his thumb and forefinger across his neck. "This is what happens to traitors, and their families."

"I will kill you."

"Yes, I am sure," he said.

The Sumatran tiger launched from the ground, its tail mesmerized Tony as it catapulted into the backs of the men. Maxim took the brunt of the tiger's girth and collapsed. Leonid turned to his partner in time to receive a giant slap from the tiger's left paw, its nails slicing through Leonid's face clean. The Serg screamed, scrambling to escape as the tiger took Maxim into its mouth, tossing him back into the restaurant before leaping onto Leonid, bit down deep on his throat as the Russian attempted a scream. Tony's right hand slid over to the Katana, fighting for enough strength to grip the handle. The tiger turned its focus onto Tony, stretching itself back to launch at him.

Tony clutched the Katana as the tiger roared and catapulted toward him. He mustered the power to bring up the Katana's tip and aimed it into the tiger's throat. The blade's edge sliced through until the tip poked out the back of the beast's massive head. The weight of the tiger slammed Tony into the floor, pinning him. He laid listening to the tiger's heart grow faint until it ceased, feeling the coat warm and wet with blood. Tony's head throbbed as the menagerie of lightning robbed him of power. His mind dizzy, he released the Katana's grip, managing to slide himself out from underneath the Sumatran's hide.

Another explosion rocked the hotel lobby, emitting a ball of flame that curled through the corridor. Tony rose, staggering as he wore tattered rags sopped in blood. Tony removed his clothes, nude as he stalked the lobby, toward the hotel entrance.

"We need to hurry, Nicholas."

Tony's eyes cut across the smoke and flame, seeing a squat man near the elevator doors. He was helping another man, elegant and thin, out of the lift, attempting escape through the lobby. The elegant man was drunk, eyes fluttering as he attempted to hold consciousness.

"Nicholas Van Meter leaves for no one," he said.

Tony drew close, watching Nicholas' eyes, seeing divine brown orbs, floating in milk. Tony's heart pounded, blood charged. He flexed his muscles, feeling his arms bent, poised. He unleashed a primal scream which echoed the lobby above the explosions, alerting the squat man and Nicholas to his presence. Tony stalked forward with his prey caught in a look of horror.

"Oh, my holy God."

Tony rushed the elevator. The squat man attempted to close the doors, pressing the control panel, frantic. Tony slammed his arms between the doors, preventing them from shutting. He shoved them apart, glared at the squat man, unleashing another roar which would have made the Sumatran tiger jealous. Tony punched the squat man in the face and he crumbled. Tony entered the elevator, hovering over Nicholas Van Meter. He licked his lips, ready to devour those delicious eyes.

"Who are you?" Nicholas said.

The elevator doors sealed behind Tony, the lift shooting up a higher hotel floor as he knelt, touching Nicholas' face as a lover. The drunk man's pupils offered Tony's reflection; a human nightmare staring back at him. Tony plunged index finger and thumb into Nicholas' socket, sliding them around the bulb. He tightened his grip, yanked out the jewel amid clear fish slime. Nicholas screamed as his left eye suctioned out into Tony's fist, the meaty cord snapped quick. Tony consumed the eye, roared while pounding his chest.

Tony's focus went to the ceiling of the elevator. He was a god. *I've discovered my own source of lightning.* Nicholas' instant sobriety offered him the clarity to cover his vacant socket with his hand, staring at Tony with his free hand. A momentary lapse of reason for Nicholas occurred as Tony gouged out the right eye, consuming it for the energy inside.

37

Ten minutes after the armored truck had charged through the front entrance of the Rivers End casino floor, the security monitors focused on the parking lots. A contingent of police cars surrounded the exterior of the building. Richard Yazzie eyed the monitors from the operations center, feeling a minor quake as an explosion from the casino floor shook the building. The monitors showed the hotel entrance where a team of armed FBI agents were moving forward. *So, this is how it begins, huh?* Richard led Phil Quentin and sixteen security casino staff dressed in Kevlar vests and M4 carbines down a stairwell to the hotel lobby.

"This was their plan all along," Richard said.

"Sir?" Quentin said, confused.

Richard stopped, turned to Quentin and the other security staff. "A siege is about to take place. The FBI are here to claim our land again."

Richard led the posse out of the stairwell as it rocked, shaking. They entered the hotel lobby. None of the men had served under Col. Civil-Fielder's command, but they knew how to handle a weapon. Each stayed silent, witnessing the destruction in the lobby. Oxygen fumes created a thickness of air where the heat had blown out gas. Several hotel columns were charred black from fire. Ceiling hydrants sprayed short mists of water to quell the flame's spread.

The atrium entrance destroyed, along with the lobby bar and hallway back to the casino. Several lay dead on the lobby floor, including a giant orange and black tiger with a sword shoved up through its skull. Richard's focus went toward the hotel entrance, holding his footing as another explosion rocked the foundation. A team of F.B.I. agents were marching up the path toward the hotel entrance, wearing blue windbreakers with yellow lettering across the back, holding submachine guns. Richard turned to Quentin, putting his hands on the young man's shoulders. *I'm guiding him, looking into his eyes.*

"No one understands how valuable you are to this place but me," Richard said, lying to Quentin. "Keep the F.B.I. out of here. This is our home, we'll handle this on our own terms."

Richard patted Quentin's cheek, watching the man look down. "Yes, sir."

"I told you that you would have to find your place in the world," Richard said. "This is it. Right here, standing side by side with me."

Richard went with his security team to the entrance. The F.B.I. crossed through the automatic doors which had remained standing, left unharmed. The fresh air attacked Richard's nostrils, rivaling with the gas odor pluming out from the lobby. Richard eyed the F.B.I. supervisor's submachine gun. *They wanted us out of here, take over operations all along.* Richard figured the two armed men down there were scapegoats for the F.B.I.'s invasion. Richard put his hands up to stop the F.B.I. from entering the lobby.

"The situation is being handled," Richard said.

The F.B.I. supervisor appeared stunned. "You call this shit under control?"

"We are taking care of the two armed men downstairs."

The F.B.I. supervisor shook his head. "This has gone on far enough. We need to assist you in securing the area and evacuating everyone left inside."

"It's under control," Richard said. "You have no rights here. This is our land."

"I don't think you understand."

Richard: "Oh, I understand perfectly. Sovereign is sovereign. It's a tribal matter."

"Where's Locklear?"

"He's dealing with the situation," Richard said. "He'll get back to you when it's over."

One of the other F.B.I. agents in the group spoke up. "Listen up, Chief."

Richard and the F.B.I. supervisor both eyed the agent when he spoke. The white, bald man wearing sunglasses received disgust from both parties. *Betcha they wish the asshole hadn't said it, but that's what they were thinking.* Richard shook his head, blood boiling, he knew he had to get down to the casino floor to help Civil-Fielder handle the situation. Richard turned to Quentin.

"Shoot anyone who comes inside. This is our land, our rules."

The casino security team each raised their M4 carbines, aiming them at the F.B.I. group. None of the staff had any love for the F.B.I. Most were Yamenhi men and women who had generations suffer under reservation control. Richard smiled, noticing his error. *I abandoned my tribe because I thought they didn't have fight in them. How wrong I have been.* Richard left the entrance, heading toward the casino while leaving the F.B.I. facing several barrels. A fireball ignited about twenty feet behind Richard as another atrium tank exploded. He ignored the heat, moving forward, ready to see what was left of the casino before it went up in flames.

38 Lance Caron's head pounded, groggy as he woke in a deluxe bathtub. It took him moments to realize he was alive. Head pulsing, blood dripping down his face, a sharp, piercing noise whined in his inner ear. Chaos reverberated from the floors below. An explosion outside the bathroom offered attention a few hundred feet below, rocking the foundations. Lance exited the tub, stumbling to the bathroom mirror. His reflection revealed a superficial gash where he had smacked his head against the tub surface, knocking him out cold.

He exited the bathroom, the door breaking off its hinges in his hand. The smell of death and gunpowder attacked his nostrils. Lance's eyes caught a shotgun lying on the floor which he picked up. Corpses littered the suite. Lance stumbled, seeing Locklear dead in front of the couch. His eyes went to the fireplace mantel. Tsosie had survived a head shot, his left temple ripped off but he functioned. He had pulled himself up against the wall, holding Keisha's lifeless body in his arms. Tsosie brushed the hair back on her head, crying. *He loved her as much as I wanted to.* Lance and Tsosie shared a gaze, which lasted as another explosion rocked the hotel, the ground quaked. Tsosie gestured with Keisha's revolver for Lance to leave the suite, then brought the revolver's barrel to his head. Lance refused to look back at his friend and crossed the threshold into the hallway, holding onto his shotgun.

In the hallway, Lance heard a single gunshot from back inside the suite. He shuddered at the sound. The elevator doors slid apart at the end of the hallway and caught Lance's attention. He listened to a sick sound of fluids and edged close, witnessing a man dressed in tattoos with his back to the hallway, hunched over as he worked at something in front of him, digging deep, hard. The sickening sound increased. Lance eyed the man's back, seeing fresh bullet wounds holding pieces of metal and blue fabric. A crude tattoo of a mangled black cat moved across the man's spine. Lance's view increased, seeing two men lying inside. One had no eyes, sockets pouring blood with meaty cut cords dangling off his cheeks.

"Jesus," Lance said.

The naked man ceased work, turning around. He stood straight, broad shoulders expanding out with a décor of scars and tattoos and offered a facial mask of a flaming skull. His chest held ornaments of the Kremlin with sixteen steeples. He stepped free of the elevator, screaming at Lance while pounding his chest, then charged. Lance aimed the shotgun barrel, squeezing the trigger. He blasted a shot into the man's chest, throwing him from his feet. The naked man fell into the hallway, dying.

"Mikhail," the naked man said, in disgust.

Air deflated from the naked man's lungs. Lance moved past the man, quick into the elevator, feeling the lift's floor rock as another explosion shook the building. The cabling echoed twisting sounds of steel in the elevator shaft. Lance pressed the control panel to go to the lobby, feeling another explosion reverb through the shaft. His eyes went to the naked man, who clawed at the carpet, attempting to come after the elevator doors as they closed slow. Lance aimed the shotgun, squeezing off a shot that kicked him into the back of the lift. The doors sealed without Lance discovering if the naked man had been hit.

Lance rode the elevator down to the lobby. He listened to the doors unseal, the chime, then stumbled to his feet. His focus fell upon the hotel entrance, seeing two groups of men aiming guns at each other in a stand-off. One was casino security, the other were F.B.I. Each prepared to fire. The elevator closed behind him and returned to the top suite.

"You are in violation of U.S. Federal Law, Mister Quentin. Stand down."

The man leading the F.B.I. group spoke with grave authority. But the casino security refused to budge, holding fast with guns, aimed at the group, willing to fire. Lance eyed Richard Yazzie heading down the lobby toward the casino floor, defiant. Shouts from the F.B.I. and casino security escalated, then both opening fire. Bullets flew everywhere, one hitting Lance in the chest. He laid on his back, breathing careful as he heard his heart beat in his ears, watching the ceiling, dying. Minutes passed but he was unsure about anything, as life rolled out of him. The elevator doors unsealed with a chime. Out stepped the naked man, half his face torn off. He towered over Lance, smiling, then reached down and touched his eyes.

39

"This is easier than it should be."

Dean Shockley looked at Stew, nodding. "Yeah."

The large builders stood at the mouth of the vault, doors open on hinges. Charred remains of the cashier staffer lay near. Dean's focus sat elsewhere, nostrils filled with Kyle's singed remains. The burnt flesh odor plumed from the armored truck's front, blanketing the area. His eyes went to the slot machines, busted and destroyed. Machine circuit boards snapped electricity, buzzing. The entire casino floor remained silent. Dean looked at the casino's music system which pumped out a band playing *Kickstart My Heart*. Stew aimed his M16 to take out the speakers but Dean turned down the barrel, shaking his head.

"Let it play," Dean said. "The song moves."

Stew nodded, the song pumping through their bodies in a cerebral dose of Fireball. Stew headed to the armored truck, standing there, confused. "Shit."

"What?"

"The Serg's pet," Stew said, pointing to the back of the armored truck. "He's gone."

"Maybe he fell out."

"When?"

Dean shrugged. "Who knows?"

Stew reached inside the truck, removing several empty black duffle bags. He returned to the vault and was devoured by the vault's immense mouth. Stew tossed the bags inside, going thirty feet deep where large bundles of plastic wrapped cash sat on a table. Each stack was a foot thick per brick. Stew ripped off his armored sleeves and chest plate to move quickly. The massive beast grabbed arm loads of cash, stuffing them into the black duffle bags. Each would hold a million-five in twenties and tens.

Movement by the ramp leading to the hotel caught Dean's attention. A contingent of men dressed in suits, carrying M4 carbines headed down. They rushed in formation past the escalator, toward the slot machines. *I knew it was easier than it should be.*

"We got company," Dean said.

Stew said, "More assholes?"

"I'll take care of it," Dean said. "You handle the cash."

Dean cocked his M16 carbine, opening up a burst aimed at the ramp. Two hundred rounds emptied on the linoleum flooring, chewing it up. The shots did not catch anyone but everyone hid behind corners and walls for protection. The opposition appeared to know advanced technical training. *Kinda stuff I was learning in marine boot camp.* Dean squeezed off a short burst and watched the men find cover, but stay in formation. *They're a unit like we are.* The men managed to sneak behind a row of slot machines, serving it up as a machine gun nest as they fired back shots amid cover.

The men offered up three hundred rounds of return fire. Not one of the shots were random. Each had focus, hitting within inches of Dean. About fifteen rounds embedded themselves in his Kevlar chest plate. The weight of squished rounds would have dropped other men. *Weaker men than me.* Dean held himself up, resisting the notion to remove any of his armor. He unleashed a primal scream, reloading his M16 carbine with a fresh clip, then spat at the men as he squeezed the trigger.

Dean unlatched a grenade from the back of his body armor, yanking the pin with his teeth. He softball tossed the hot potato across the room, onto the ramp. He unloaded the rest of his M16 clip to keep the group pinned down. The grenade exploded, catching at least two of the men. The M16 shots he laid down offered up more damage as no one on that end could hide from both the grenade and bullet fire. Dean laughed, feeling a surge of fuel rage through his veins. Stew exited the vault, carrying duffle bags stuffed with cash by the straps with his exposed limbs.

"Let's roll," Stew said.

Dean grabbed at one of the bags but drew back when the slot machine gun nest opened up a burst of fire. Shots zipped past Dean and Stew, creating a chasm. *Reminds me of summer lightning bugs in the fields when I was a child*. Stew and Dean had no time to react to the shots which zipped by out of the nest. One round found home in Stew's exposed right forearm. The shot severed his limb at the elbow. Dean's eyes caught the duffle bag landing next to Stew's feet, held tight by his abandoned arm. Stew stood stunned, muted by his lost appendage.

Stew's pupils ignited, enlarging. His body shook into a fit of rage, undefeated by injury. He released the bag in his left hand and swung the M16 strapped mounted on his shoulder around, aiming the barrel at the nest. Stew fired short bursts while ignoring his severed stump. Dean took up the second duffle bag, following Stew, aiming his M16 at the nest. The builders marched, stomping forward and blasted movement. Stew's right stump thinned out its bleeding, the injury clotted quick from Stew's Fireball intake.

"Come out, fight me," Stew said, screaming.

Stew spread his M16 barrel into a wave. A security guard was clipped in the right shoulder as he hid, but stood as a reaction to the wound and received ten rounds in the chest for his mistake. Stew released the M16 which hung by a strap around his shoulder. He reached back, grabbing his five remaining grenades, and bit down on the pin of each, yanking them out, tossing them into the nest in quick succession while Dean offered cover fire. Blasts sent bodies flying. Five spread blasts were finished by silence. Stew turned to Dean, offering him a wink.

"This is how we do it," he said.

Dean: "They didn't know who they were messing with."

Stew's face dropped. "I don't feel so good."

The big man swayed in his boots, eyes into his skull. He had lost three pints of blood which covered the casino floor. He stumbled, the M16 carbine fell off its strap and discharged a small burst into an empty off-track betting area where broken monitors displayed horses racing at Aqueduct. Dean moved to help Stew but stopped as he saw a shadow grow behind him. Drew turned, seeing a mustached man with blood soaking his face come forward with a combat blade.

"You... cunt..." the man said, screamed in an English accent.

The man sliced through the air with his blade. The tip caught the side of Dean's neck, superficial. Dean released the duffle bag and M16 carbine to resist the man as much as he could. The man's white mustache was stained pink with blood. His crazy eyes danced as he charged with the knife, spreading it across sweeping moves that whipped in front of Dean's chest.

"I fought the Grone at Two Sisters," the man said. "I'm not afraid of a cunt like you."

The man stabbed forward with his blade, deep into Dean's chest plate. The blade burrowed hard into the plate. The tip ran hard enough through the Kevlar to bite into Dean's skin on the other side of the armor. The man shoved closer. Dean ripped off the chest plate, letting the armor's weight topple the man. He had to release the knife's handle as he fell backward onto the ground. Dean reached down, grabbing his M16 carbine to eliminate the Englishman.

"This is my casino now."

Dean's eyes shot to the top of the escalator leading back to the hotel. Daddy wore a suit and tie, pointing, yelling at his son. His father held a M4 carbine, firing off a round at Dean that zipped past his head, missing by an inch. *Daddy never loved me.* Another round zapped out from Daddy's rifle, lodging into Dean's right Kevlar pants leg. *He hates me.* Dean stomped forward and left Stew behind, focusing on his father. *I'm a man now, Daddy.* He brought up the M16 barrel, aimed off a shot and fired a short burst. The rounds riddled the top of the escalator and ceiling, Daddy dropped from sight. Dean went to the escalator's base, stepping over the bodies of casino security who had opposed him.

Stew screamed, gaining Dean's attention. He turned to see the mustached man stabbing Stew in the throat with his combat blade. Dean opened up a burst from his M16, shooting both the man and Stew. The man took a round in the left side, falling off of Stew who died from his wounds. Dean reloaded with his last clip, slapping it in with the palm of his hand, turning to the mustached man. The man had vanished into the chaos of the casino floor.

Dean refocused on the top of the escalator, remembering that Daddy was up there, somewhere. *I'm going to show him I'm a man. That I'm somebody now.* Dean ripped free his Kelvar leggings, sleeves. He felt a cool whip of air hitting his skin, standing in competition trunks and combat boots. *The money means nothing to me. I want Daddy to see me, understand who I am.* Dean cocked his M16 and headed up the escalator. *I'm going to show him how tough I am.*

A small trail of blood was at the top of the escalator. It led into the hallway toward the hotel. Dean felt a surge of anger overtake him. The Fireball was raging now, heart pounding electric rage charging through his system. He stomped through the hall, turning the corner, ignoring a plume of black smoke which jetted out from a hallway deli. Daddy was on his belly across the hall floor. He was crawling, bullet lodged in his right leg. *He's a coward.* Dean's eyes filled with tears as he tailed Daddy, bringing up the barrel of the M16 aimed at his father's waist.

"Look what you did to me, Daddy," Dean said. "Look what you

did to your little boy."

Daddy said nothing in return, continuing to crawl toward the lobby. Dean squeezed off a round that missed his father, embedding into the floor next to his belly. *He's been a coward his entire life.* He never had the strength to watch Dean's mother fight cancer. *He never hugged me, went to my games.* The man was weak inside but held Dean to impossible standards. Dean aimed the rifle, squeezing off another round that went into the floor near Daddy's head.

"You can't hide from me, Daddy."

Dean squeezed off fifty rounds which went into Daddy's back. The brunt of force chewed up Daddy until all of the air had left his system. Dean stood silent amid the chaos, eying his massive pecs, those curves extended out. *I spent my entire life impressing a man who refused to look at me.* Dean used his foot to turn Daddy over, and discovered at it was an old native, not his father, who was lying dead on the floor. *Why can't I get rid of you, Daddy?*

"I'm not done with you, cunt."

A combat blade was shoved into Dean's back. It deepened. Dean turned, seeing the mustached man behind him. The man removed the blade from Dean's side and then jammed it forward to stab again. Dean brought up the M16 carbine, squeezing off the rest of his clip. The man's chest bloomed with shots to the chest, throwing him backward. The man turned, falling onto his chest, impaling himself on his own combat blade.

Dean choked on fumes as his hands numbed, back throbbing. He dropped the M16 carbine, stumbling toward the lobby. Huge chunks of concrete façade cracked, fell around him. His feet carried him past a restaurant with two dead men and a large tiger lying dead. He eyed the entrance, seeing bodies of men who held carbines but were dead in a stand-off. Dean closed his lids, collapsing onto the cool floor. He listened to his heart beat soft, slow. Another explosion rocked down the hall as the fuel flushed in his system, his veins draining.

"I found another one."

Dean felt hands touch him, opened his lids, seeing his father attending to his wounds. Daddy wore firefighter gear, showing his face smiling at Dean behind a clear vision. "Daddy?"

Daddy looked down, loving, touching Dean's face, which felt foreign. "Say, buddy, looks like you're bleeding."

Dean smiled, delirious. "Am I going to die?"

"Not today," Daddy said. He talked to someone beyond the hotel entrance. "Hey, Jerry, need a gurney. This place is going up fast."

Daddy looked away from Dean toward the lobby, face horrified. "What in the hell?"

Dean turned slightly, seeing The Serg's pet in the lobby bar, sitting on the couch. Half of the man's face had been blown off. Tony stood, stumbling over to them, speaking fast Russian. Dean turned to the corpses from the stand-off near him, seeing an M4 carbine. He grabbed it, yanking it free from its strap. Tony reached out, grabbing the firefighter by the collar and tossing him across the lobby. Dean cocked the M4 carbine, then turned over and saw Tony looking down at him, anger milking his remaining eye.

"Mikhail," Tony said to Dean, accusingly.

Dean aimed the M4 carbine and unloaded on Tony. He shot off the other side of Tony's face, throwing the man back into oblivion. A piece of façade fell free of the ceiling and obliterated Tony's existence. Dean released the gun, closing his lids. He opened them again as he felt hands from two firefighters pulling him out of the wreckage.

Dean looked back in the lobby as he was wheeled away into the parking lot, seeing Daddy stay behind to rescue other survivors. *That's my father, courageous and great, willing to ensure that everyone is protected.* Dean wanted to be like his father. *My Daddy's a great man who loves me.* Dean was wheeled into a triage tent set-up in the parking lot. His lids dropped again, listening to his heart pound. *I love you, Daddy.* He slipped out of consciousness for moments, hours and dreamt of his father.

"So, we meet again, my friend."

Dean opened his lids, hearing that familiar Russian voice of The Serg. He saw the old Russian gangster lying on the bed next to his. The Serg had a bullet wound in his arm. Dean felt the lightning flush from his system. His voice was weak as words dropped out. "I guess we do."

"You fade now, huh?" The Serg said. "Got to have more stuff."

"Yeah," Dean said, lids half-open.

"Maybe, we come to... arrangement."

He devoured the fury of the syringe as it punctured his flesh and was a god again. The shot sent a lightning bolt through his veins. His lids opened involuntarily. The light attacked his pupils, but he refuted attempts of muscle memory to shut them. Dean eyed the room, standing in a warm meat locker. Lev and Vadim, two new men from the old country, stood as his guards while injecting him with the needle. They pumped him full of fuel amid a body covered in scars from the battles he had waged since coming into The Serg's care.

Are you ready, son? Daddy said.

Dean's focus went to the corner shadows of the meat locker where Daddy sat, watching him. *He's always been there for me, proud of me.* Dean smiled at the revelation. *He knows I am a powerful man.* The burn surged through his heart as the Fireball took hold. *I love you, Daddy. I love you.*

I love you too, Daddy said.

"I'm ready," Dean said, to Daddy.

I'm proud of you, son, Daddy said.

Dean fought back tears when he heard his father call him "son." *I've waited a lifetime to hear that from him.* He hid away his tears, unwilling to offer weakness to the old man. *Daddy is here with me, that's what matters.* His father loved his little boy.

40

The meat locker door opened. Dean's eyes fell upon it as The Serg entered. The old Russian smoked cheap rolled cigarettes, wearing wrinkles and gray. He offered up a photograph of the man that Dean would fight tonight. *The man I will destroy.* A rage churned inside Dean. *I'll devour his strength when I consume his eyes.* He licked his lips at the prospect, putting his hand over the facial tattoo of a flame that The Serg had given him.

"Make fight good before you end," The Serg said. "So crowd love you."

Listen to him, son, Daddy said. *The man knows what's best for you.*

His smile widened as he thought of the opposing fighter's pupils. How he loved the taste of another man's irises. He looked at Daddy, seeing the man nod to him. *He accepts me as a man. Loves me for who I am.* The rage burned deep inside the pit of his stomach, pulsating through his arms, legs as he moved past The Serg, exiting the meat locker for a makeshift pit where a weak opponent faced certain death. *I see his eyes, those beautiful blue orbs, and I hunger for them.*

Inside the meat locker, Daddy sat in the corner shadows and watched, proud. *He's the father I've always wanted.* Dean admired his father, turning to his opponent, ready to destroy him. *I'm the son my father's always wanted too.* He listened to Daddy in the corner, applauding his son into certain victory. It caused Dean's heart to skip a beat.

About The Author

Troy Kirby has worked extensively as a professional writer for over 20 years. In his career, he's written feature stories for two daily newspapers, several weeklies, served as a sports communication professional at two athletic departments, has been a contributed for SEAT Magazine, managing editor of Ticketing Today and founder of the Tao of Sports website - which has provided business news to sports industry professionals since 2012. Kirby has earned degrees from Seattle University, Eastern Washington University and Centralia College. He is originally from Lacey, Washington and has lived in various places throughout the West Coast.

E-mail: Troy@chaoswords.com

TROY KIRBY

ASH WEDNESDAY

Early release has a heavy price

Also written by Troy Kirby:
ASH WEDNESDAY
www.chaoswords.com
6 x 9
338 pages

Library of Congress
Control Number: 2017910900

ISBN 0-9835184-0-8
ISBN 978-0-9835184-0-2

Available in paperbook and ebook/
Kindle Format on Amazon

GETTING OUT WAS THE EASY PART...

Frank's returning early to the city, whether people are ready or not.

He's been given a chance to pick up a stash of stolen diamonds, as well as get payback by settling old scores during his time out.

What no one told Frank about is the sadistic crime boss who runs a local syndicate aiming at taking the diamonds for himself, and that he's willing to do whatever it takes to own a slice of the score.

Frank's inside man also failed to mention that he's been double-crossed by a few ex-partners, who are hunting for the ice themselves. Along with some of the city's finest, who are willing to work off-the-clock for a chance at the score.

It's not going to be the easy pick-up that he was promised as Frank tries to protect himself and his woman in a fight for both of their lives.

www.ingramcontent.com/pod-product-compliance
Lightning Source LLC
Chambersburg PA
CBHW030548180626
46816CB00005B/1463